L J MORRIS

Desperate Ground

(Ali Sinclair #1)

First published by Crow's Foot Books 2019

Copyright © 2019 by L J Morris

Second edition

ISBN: 978-1-9162498-1-3

Editing by Jo Craven
Cover art by Nick Castle

This book was professionally typeset on Reedsy.
Find out more at reedsy.com

To Ruth, whose love and support got me here.

Ground on which we can only be saved from destruction by fighting without delay, is desperate ground.

– *SUN TZU, THE ART OF WAR*

Prologue

The wipers juddered and squealed on Owen Evans' ageing hatchback as they struggled to cope with the torrential rain that was hammering down. Evans took the handkerchief from his top pocket and wiped away the condensation that had formed on the inside of the windscreen. Five minutes had passed since he'd pressed the buzzer on the entrance's sandstone gatepost, but there was still no sign of movement. He began to think he was in the wrong place. He tried to focus on the manor house that he knew was on the other side of the gates, but, although his eyes were becoming accustomed to the dark, he couldn't see anything through the downpour. Maybe he should get out and push the button again?

The sudden flash of lightning and loud crack of thunder made him jump and lit up the imposing house like a haunted mansion from an old horror film. It was a hell of a night to be making a house call, but this could be his chance to get noticed. It could mean a promotion. None of the other analysts had been invited to the house before, but none of them had spotted the security flaw. Evans was glad he'd sent his report directly to the boss.

With a metallic clunk, the estate's wrought-iron gates came

to life and swung open. Evans put the car in gear and crept along the track towards the house, tyres crunching on the gravel. An external light on the porch came on and the front door opened, flooding the driveway with light as the car pulled up. The young analyst climbed out of the car and, holding his briefcase above his head, ran to the entrance and ducked inside.

He stood in the grand hallway; water dripped from his coat and formed puddles on the marble floor. The boss threw him a towel. 'Dry yourself off, Evans.' The older man's voice was polished, educated, upper-class – everything you'd expect from someone who owned a house like this. 'Please, come through.'

'Yes, sir.' Evans followed him into the study. Display cases of antiques and paintings, which Evans was sure were originals, lined the walls.

'Have a seat, Owen. Can I call you Owen?'

'Yes, sir, thank you.' Evans took off his coat and sat in a small leather seat, a few feet in front of the large, antique desk that the boss now sat behind.

'I've read your report, Owen. It makes for worrying reading. Are you sure about this?'

Evans nodded. 'Yes, sir, this has the potential to be a big problem.'

'And the scenario you've put together, could that actually happen?'

Evans sat forwards in his chair, sensing that this was his chance to shine. 'As I explain in section two of the report, sir, in the right circumstances, it could be done. The consequences could be catastrophic. I'm surprised no one has ever noticed the potential weakness before.'

2

'You did the right thing highlighting this, Owen. Have you briefed anyone else?'

'No, sir, I came straight here from the office. I know when to keep things quiet.' Evans sat back in his chair, a little smug.

The bullet struck him in the centre of his chest, he watched as blood seeped out of the wound and spread across his shirt. He started to slide off his seat; his vision began to blur. He looked up; the boss was standing over him, holding a semi-automatic pistol in his hand. 'I'm sorry, Owen. You were just in the wrong place at the wrong time.' The pistol fired a second time and silenced Evans permanently.

The older man put the weapon back in his drawer and sat down. The secure laptop on his desk displayed Evans' report, marked at the top and bottom in red with: TOP SECRET – UK EYES ONLY. Evans hadn't put it through the proper channels, no one else had or would see it. He closed the laptop's lid, poured himself another scotch, and relaxed back in his chair, smiling to himself.

Chapter 1

Ali Sinclair bent her knees and rolled as she landed, but the impact still knocked the breath from her. The ground was more rocks than sand, and was a lot harder than it had looked from the top of the fence. Lying flat, sucking air back into her lungs, she looked and listened for any sign that she'd been spotted. There was no movement on the other side of the fence, no alarms, no shouts, no sound of running boots. If she were lucky, it would be three hours before anyone missed her. She rolled away from the reach of the floodlights, into the darkness, and, after one last check for any pursuers, stood up.

Her hands were bloodied and pain stabbed at her left ankle, but she didn't have time to worry about that now, she had to follow the plan. She wiped some of the dirt and sweat from her face with her shirt, turned away from the lights, and limped into the desert that surrounded the prison.

The new moon didn't provide any light and navigation by the stars wasn't her strong point. Keeping the lights of the prison behind her she was able to travel roughly northeast towards the road that led to the outskirts of Juarez and the Mexico-USA border. Many of her fellow inmates came from Juarez or the surrounding area. The city had a history of bloody violence and brutal murder was still an everyday occurrence, especially of women. The cartels battled each other, and the police, over control of the billion-dollar drugs trade. The cartel's initial promise of easy money and status sucked in innocent youngsters, destroying their lives, destroying their families. For those who were locked up there was no respite. The prisons were run by the cartels and gang membership became a survival strategy.

Juarez wasn't somewhere Sinclair was keen to visit, but it would be easier to disappear in the anonymity of the overcrowded city. The plan was to hide out there for a short time before making a night-time crossing into the US; that was her only chance of avoiding a quick return to prison.

She travelled as fast as she dared. Her eyes adjusted to the darkness but it was still difficult to make out any details on her route, let alone see any distance. She had to feel her way with every step, making sure that the ground ahead was firm before transferring her weight. She listened the whole time, but she could hear no noise over the sound of her own breathing, her own footfall.

After fifty minutes of slow, painful progress, the ground under Sinclair's feet changed. She dropped to one knee. The surface was hard-packed sand and gravel; it was the road to Juarez. From here she was supposed to travel parallel with it and stay out of sight, but it had taken her too long to get to this point. Travelling on the relatively flat, hard surface would be risky but it was the best way to put maximum distance between her and the prison.

She took a few steps away from the road and sat down to check her injured ankle. It didn't feel broken but travelling over the rough, uneven terrain hadn't helped it. Her boot was giving the joint some support so she tightened her laces as much as she could and got to her feet. She couldn't sit and rest; the sun would be up soon and she had to be under cover by then. Water and a place to hide were her priorities now.

She knelt at the sound of a vehicle approaching, and watched as a white pickup trundled past. Its tail lights flickered as it bumped along the road and disappeared over the horizon. Sinclair stood up, checked both ways, and set off.

She walked the first few steps, testing her ankle, then picked up her speed into a jog. The lights of Juarez were now visible in the distance and she gritted her teeth against the pain, concentrating on each step, left, right, left, right. She stopped. Up ahead was a noise; something that didn't fit with her surroundings, something man-made. She crouched, and listened as it grew louder, it was an engine. Headlights appeared over the brow of a hill fifty yards from her. She dived off the road, rolled ten yards and lay still. The white pickup was back again. Sinclair tried to melt into the landscape; murmuring quietly, 'Drive past ... drive past.'

The truck travelled a few hundred yards along the road then turned and headed back towards her. Had the driver seen her? She didn't think so, not in this light, but whoever this guy was, he was searching for something. He wasn't police, so probably not looking for her; it was too soon for the alarm to have been raised anyway. Maybe he was a drug runner or people smuggler. Whatever he was, there was no way Sinclair could travel quickly with him driving up and down the road like that. She had to do something. If she could get the driver out of the truck and steal it, she might even get to Juarez before the sun came up.

She waited until the pickup was only a few yards away, then

stood up and launched a fist-sized rock at the windscreen. The impact of the rock cracked the glass and the driver slammed on the brakes, the truck's wheels ploughed up the road as they skidded to a halt.

Sinclair dropped back on her haunches and held her breath as the driver climbed out of the cab and walked round to her side. The flashlight in his hand created long shadows as he moved it left and right. Sinclair rocked on to the balls of her feet and waited until the light panned away from her, then sprang forwards and closed the gap between her and the driver. He swung the flashlight towards her but she ducked underneath it and drove her shoulder into his gut. They both slammed into the side of the truck and slid to the ground as the driver lost his balance. Her ankle was screaming but it would have to wait. Whoever this guy was, he was strong and hard to get hold of. She straddled his chest and swung a punch at his head, but he was too fast. He blocked the strike and grabbed the front of her shirt. Pulling her down towards him, he shone the light of the torch in his own face.

'Ali, it's me.'

Sinclair stopped her attack and stared into his eyes. This was a face she knew well, a man with whom she had lots of history. Frank McGill, a man she trusted with her life.

'Shit, Frank. What the fuck are you doing here?'

'Change of plan. If you get off me, I'll explain as we go.'

Sinclair rolled off McGill and sat in the dust staring at him.

McGill stood up. 'We need to get you away from here. The Mexicans will be expecting you to be on foot.' He helped her to her feet. 'It's good to see you, Ali.'

Sinclair was glad to see McGill. When he'd visited her in prison and given her the escape plan she hadn't been surprised.

7

He'd always promised he'd get her home and it wasn't the first time he'd put himself in harm's way for her. She reached out and gave him a hug. 'It's good to see you too, Frank.'

They climbed into the truck and McGill turned it east, away from Juarez.

The inside of the truck was a mess. She didn't ask where it had come from but, judging by the dust and the smell, she imagined there was a Mexican farmer somewhere who would be waking up with no transport.

McGill fished a bag from behind the seat. 'There's some water in there, you look like you could do with a drink.'

Sinclair took a bottle and poured half of the contents into her mouth, coughing and spluttering as she tried to swallow it all. Her skin was streaked with dirt, sweat and blood from the escape. Her clothes were ragged, and her normally athletic build looked a little too thin. Two years in hell had aged her.

She poured some of the water on the cuts on her hands. 'This sand gets everywhere.'

McGill noticed the tremble in her voice. 'You okay? I've got a first-aid kit and some clothes at a motel a few miles from the border. I booked in as Mr Smith.'

'Did they buy that?'

'I paid for a week in advance, I don't think they gave a shit.'

Sinclair laughed – her first in a long time. 'I don't know how you managed to pull this off, Frank, but I'm glad you did.'

'Getting you out of the prison wasn't difficult, Ali, I just paid enough in bribes for the guards to leave some doors open and look the other way.'

'But your message said to head for a safe house in Juarez.'

McGill nodded. 'That's right. The guards couldn't guarantee which night you would escape. If I'd hung around here waiting

8

for you for days, someone would've noticed.'

'So why the change of plan?'

'I've been watching the safe house for the last two nights, didn't trust the fuckers.'

'What happened?'

'The police arrived about an hour ago, must've been just after you'd escaped. Someone's tipped them off.'

Sinclair frowned. 'Why didn't they just come after me?'

'Easier to let you come to them, I suppose. Saves them searching a wide area. I got in the truck and came straight here, I was hoping I'd find you in time.'

'All these bribes and safe houses can't have been cheap. Where'd you get the money for all this?'

'I called in some favours. Annoyed some people till they paid me to go away. Basically, made a nuisance of myself.'

'I always said you were a pain in the arse, Frank.'

McGill took a sharp intake of breath in mock hurt. 'I could drop you off right here. You can walk the rest of the way.'

Sinclair gave him a slap on the shoulder. 'Just drive, I'm in desperate need of a shower.'

'Well, I wasn't going to say anything but …' He sniffed the air.

She gave him her sternest stare but couldn't hold it and they both cracked up. It was as if they'd never been apart. Chatting and trading joke insults, the bond between them as strong as ever as they drove towards the motel.

After an hour, McGill pointed ahead. 'It's just up here on the left, keep your head down.'

Sinclair slid down into the footwell of the passenger seat as the truck pulled off the road. The motel was a long, low, single-storey building with an office at one end and doors to the rooms along the front. Its once bright coat of paint faded by the sun, and the walls and windows now pitted with sand that had been kicked up by the wind.

McGill parked outside room twelve and looked around for anyone watching, but there was no sign of any of the other rooms' occupants. The motel's surveillance system consisted of one cheap camera, which he had already turned so only eleven rooms could be seen on the monitor in reception. He opened the room's creaking wooden door then stepped back and knocked on the side of the truck. Sinclair climbed out and hobbled into the room. McGill followed her in and closed the door behind them.

* * *

It took Sinclair half an hour, under the lukewarm water of the motel shower, to scrub all the grime from her body. Towelled dry, her myriad of cuts and scrapes now stung from the antiseptic cream Frank had given her to rub in, and her old clothes had been replaced with a fresh clean set. He'd thought of everything, even got the sizes right, almost. It was the first time in two years that she'd been able to have a shower without the guards leering at her. The first time she'd been alone without the noise and stench of the prison. Tears welled in her eyes as the built-up feelings of fear and the unbearable loneliness of her ordeal combined with her utter relief at being free. She placed her head in her hands and wept.

Back in the room, McGill stood at the bathroom door. He could hear Sinclair sobbing, thought about knocking to ask if she was okay but decided against it. She would tell him about her ordeal when she was ready, when she needed to. Until then, all he could do was let her know he was there for her.

When Sinclair came out of the bathroom she sat on the edge of the bed while McGill strapped her ankle and dressed the deepest cuts on her hands.

'Thanks, Frank.' She stood up and tested his handiwork. With her boots on she should be able to move about without too much pain. She moved to the other end of the room and sat at the small table that was fastened to the wall under the room's only window. 'So, what's the plan from here?'

McGill re-packed the first-aid kit into his bag and pulled out a map. Laying it on the table, he pointed at the various marks he had made to show their intended route. 'We follow the border south, it'll be easier to cross there. I'll drop you on this side of the river and you'll make your way across. I'll be waiting on the other side to pick you up.'

'Getting back home won't be as easy. I can't just jump on a plane.'

McGill shook his head. 'No, we need to get across the border and keep our heads down till we figure a way out of the US.'

'That's not going to be your problem. I'm the one who has to go on the run, you've risked enough.'

'I'm not just abandoning you like they did.'

'You won't be, I'll be okay. As long as I'm not locked up, I can handle anything. I'm gonna need you fighting my case back home.'

'I promise I won't give up on you, Ali. I'll do whatever it takes.'

Sinclair reached out and took his hand. 'Thanks for coming to get me, Frank. You're the only man I trust.'

McGill squeezed her hand. 'Get some sleep. We'll move again once it gets dark.'

* * *

Shortly after sunset, McGill pulled off the road and on to the forecourt of a small gas station. A single fuel pump sat in front of a dilapidated shack that served as both a pay booth and a shop. Sinclair got out and went in the shop while McGill drove around to the large, corrugated steel workshop at the back of the plot. The workshop's roller door opened and McGill drove in. Inside the building there was a vehicle covered with an old, paint spattered tarpaulin. As McGill pulled up and got out of the pickup, a young Mexican man removed the tarpaulin to reveal a brand-new truck with US licence plates – the vehicle McGill had hired to travel to Mexico.

McGill handed over a roll of hundred-dollar bills in return for the keys. 'Muchas gracias. Five thousand, as promised.'

'Thank you, señor.' The young man slipped the roll of notes into the pocket of his overalls and threw the tarpaulin in the back of the old truck. McGill started the engine of his rental and reversed out of the workshop as the young man lowered the door.

McGill returned to the front of the gas station and picked up Sinclair, who was standing next to the fuel pump with a fresh supply of water in plastic bottles. He pulled off the forecourt and drove southeast, parallel with the border.

The frontier between the US and Mexico is not, as some people think, a large fence with guards and dogs patrolling along it. For most of its length, the border relies on natural barriers: mountains, deserts and rivers. Many people die every year trying to cross over but, with only a few patrols to cover a vast area, large parts of the border are completely open and haemorrhage immigrants into the US.

In the area Sinclair and McGill were heading for, the only obstacle was the Rio Grande. Thousands of people made the crossing successfully, but it was still a risk. Many were apprehended and returned to Mexico while others drowned in the fast-flowing water, weighed down by their possessions. Sinclair would have to take the chance that she could make it across the river without being seen. McGill would cross legally and pick her up on the other side. Simple. At least, that was the plan.

They stopped at a spot two miles from the river. 'I don't like this, Ali. Too much could go wrong before you even get your feet wet.'

'It's the only way, Frank. If we take the truck closer, we could be seen. I stand a better chance going cross-country on my own.'

'But if something goes wrong and you have to turn back, I'll already be on the other side waiting for you. What happens then? If I cross back again it'll look suspicious.'

'I'm not turning back for anything, Frank. There's no way in hell I'm going back to that prison. Either I make the crossing or I get killed in the process.'

'I'm not risking that, Ali. I'll make the crossing with you. We can get another truck.'

'No, Frank, both of us getting caught or killed helps no one. This is a risk I have to take on my own. You can't be everywhere.'

McGill's head dropped and he stared at his hands as he desperately tried to think of another plan. After a few minutes he gave up. He knew Sinclair was right but it didn't make him any happier about it. 'Okay. If you make it as far as the river, and don't drown or get picked up by the feds, I'll see you on the other side.'

'Relax. It'll be a piece of cake.'

McGill handed her a map, a small torch and a compass. He pointed at his own map. 'We're here, and I'll meet you here. I'll drive this stretch of road every hour, on the hour. Stay hidden till you know it's me.'

Sinclair placed her hand on McGill's forearm. 'I'll see you in a few hours.' She opened the truck's door and he watched her disappear into the darkness.

Following the luminous dial of the compass, northeast from the road, she kept up a steady pace, stopping every few hundred yards, looking and listening around her to make sure she was still alone. It took just over an hour to cover the two miles and she now lay beside a boulder overlooking the border.

Fifty feet in front of her, on the bank of the river, was a small group of around ten men, women and children. A Mexican family, getting ready to cross over to a better life. There was no sign of any red and blue lights on the other side, but, just as the family picked up their belongings and moved down the bank, a border patrol inflatable boat cruised into view. Its floodlight swept across the surface of the water as a deterrent to anyone entering the river. The family stopped; then walked back up the bank away from the lights. Maybe they'd decided to try another night, or perhaps it was a ruse to fool the patrol. Either way, Sinclair hoped it would keep the Americans busy while she sneaked across unnoticed.

Just as she stood up to make her move, a four-wheel drive roared out of the desert and slid to a halt in a cloud of sand in front of the Mexicans. Two men armed with pump-action shotguns jumped out, shouting and pointing with their

14

weapons. Sinclair ducked behind the rock. These guys didn't look friendly and they definitely weren't happy.

They forced the family to kneel in the arc of light that was being thrown out by the vehicle's multiple headlights. One of the young men stood up and argued with the pair but a shotgun blast silenced his complaints. The other members of the group screamed and the children began to cry. These men weren't local police or federales, she knew exactly who they were.

The last two years of her life had been made hell by the drug cartels that ran the prison. They were ruthless and had the money and resources to bribe or kill anyone they came up against. They also made big money from people smuggling. Coyotes – the smugglers who made a profit from every illegal migrant coming up from South America – paid tax to the cartels to ensure safe passage across their territory. This small group weren't using Coyotes and hadn't paid tax. If they were allowed to get away with it, a lot of money would be lost. An example had to be made.

Sinclair had to get across the border and couldn't afford to hang around, but, at the same time, she felt for this family. She didn't want to walk away and leave them in the hands of these bastards. It was time for a little payback.

Without making a sound, she worked her way behind the four-wheel drive. The two men were standing in front of it with their backs to the light. Dropping on to her stomach, she crawled the last few yards then stood up and peered through the back window. Two nine-millimetre semi-automatics sat on the dashboard within easy reach through the side window.

The two cartel men were preoccupied, shouting at the family, taking any money, or jewellery they had. She approached the open, driver's window, took one of the weapons and checked it was loaded. As the closest man took aim at a woman in the group, Sinclair stepped out from behind the vehicle and shot him. The man fell forwards into the sand, blood pouring from the wound between his shoulder blades. His accomplice spun round to face their attacker but could only make out a silhouette against the lights. As he levelled his shotgun at the dark shape, Sinclair pumped two rounds into his torso before he could pull the trigger.

The family were rooted to the spot, frozen with fear. Sinclair lowered her weapon and shouted at them, 'Go. GO.' It was like someone had fired a starting pistol. They all stood up and took off into the river. The border patrol now had their hands full trying to catch the terrified group as they poured across the river.

Sinclair threw the weapon in the water and ran downstream – away from the unfolding chaos. While the border patrol radioed for backup and tried to round up the Mexican family, Sinclair slipped into the water, unseen, and crossed over to the US.

Thirty minutes later she was sitting in the cab of the truck with McGill. He handed her a towel and threw a blanket round her. 'Any problems?'

She smiled. 'Nothing I couldn't handle.'

Chapter 2

S imeon Carter stepped out of the hotel's entrance and looked up and down the packed pavement. He hated being in London, especially during rush hour. The sky was darkening; car headlights reflected off the rain-soaked street as people spilled out of offices and shops. Rats, racing away from their corporate lives, rushing past without seeing him or each other. He pulled up the collar of his jacket against the chill wind, descended the stone steps and joined the river of bodies flooding into the tube station. Squeezing his small frame into the carriage with the rest of the cattle, he manoeuvred himself so his back was against the wall. An old habit that meant he could watch the people around him without being approached from behind.

He took an envelope from his coat pocket and read the invitation inside. In ornate, gold lettering on the front of the white card it read:

You are cordially invited to the annual reunion of the Berlin Gentleman's Club.

Carter wasn't interested in reunions and, up until now, hadn't attended one. This invitation, however, was different. On the back of the card was a single handwritten word: Broadsword.

He'd read the word over and over in the last week. It was a word he'd never wanted to see again, a code word used between him and the intelligence officers he had controlled during the Cold War. It meant something big was happening, something that couldn't be dealt with using normal procedures. It signified a need for extra security. A black op.

Most of the operatives he'd ran in those days were dead now. Picked up and killed by the Stasi in East Berlin or, more likely, they had finally given in to the effects of stress. The suicide rate was high amongst former operatives. In those days, anyone suffering from psychological trauma was likely to be told to pull themselves together. Maintain the stiff upper lip. Others fell to liver damage, lung cancer or heart attacks. Years of heavy drinking and smoking ushering them into an early grave. Only one was left. He, unlike Carter, had stayed in the security services and risen to the upper echelons. Not one of the figure-heads held up for politicians and the press to salivate over and criticise, Edward Lancaster was one of the faceless, grey men who ran the sharp end of the operation. He dealt with men and women who put themselves in harm's way, on a daily basis, for little reward.

The reunion was taking place in the Wellington. A private members club, close to Whitehall, that was frequented by ex-civil servants. The front of the building was typically Georgian with three floors of symmetrical windows around an ornate porch. The entrance was framed by marble columns and four steps led from the street up to two etched glass and mahogany doors with brass fittings. Carter walked through the doors and into the grand entrance hall. A small, discreet reception desk, manned by a uniformed security guard, occupied one corner of the entrance, with a sweeping staircase opposite. At the bottom of the stairs was a gold-framed message board on an easel. The stick-on letters read:

Berlin Gentlemen's Club. First Floor.

Carter climbed the stairs and followed the noise of drunken laughter along the elaborately decorated hallway to the Waterloo Suite. The room was full of grey-suited men who looked like they'd been drinking since lunchtime. Most of the faces were unfamiliar to him, not many genuine Cold War veterans bothered to attend these organised reunions. They preferred quiet reminiscence and a small toast to absent friends. Events like this had been hijacked by fantasists who swapped stories about operations behind the iron curtain, but had, in reality, never been outside Whitehall. Some of them didn't even look old enough to remember the height of the Cold War, never mind to have played a part in it.

Edward Lancaster stood at the other side of the room; Carter made eye contact and set off through the crowd. After a couple of handshakes, a backslapping, and a drunken 'who the hell are you?' he made it to the bar on the opposite side.

The two men shook hands, just old colleagues reminiscing about their shared past. They looked no different to anyone else in the Waterloo Suite that night. 'It's good to see you again, Simeon, it's been a long time.'

Carter gave a sideways glance towards a large man standing next to them. 'I got your invitation, thought it would be good to catch up.'

Still holding Carter's right hand, Lancaster motioned towards a door beside the bar with his left. 'Why don't we go somewhere a little more private?'

Lancaster's bodyguard reached over and opened the door for them. Carter nodded his thanks to the man and walked through into the anteroom. Lancaster paused at the entrance and whispered to his bodyguard, 'No one comes in.'

The bodyguard nodded and closed the door behind them.

The inside of the smaller room was every bit as traditional and establishment as the rest of the building. Wood panelling covered three walls, with a floor to ceiling bookcase along the length of the fourth. In front of the bookcase was a large mahogany desk with a green leather sofa against the opposite wall.

The two men sat on the sofa and Lancaster placed a brown cardboard folder between them. 'I'll get straight to the point, Simeon. I've a job I need you for.'

As soon as Carter had received the invitation with Broadsword written on it, he'd known that Lancaster would have something unorthodox in mind. He looked down at the folder but didn't attempt to open it. 'I'm retired, Edward. You know that. Just living the quiet life.'

'I know you. You miss the thrill of the chase.'

Carter shook his head. 'I don't miss the bullshit that comes with working for politicians.'

Lancaster smiled. 'You never were one for diplomacy and rules.'

'I got the job done. When it comes down to it, that's all the hierarchy were really interested in.'

'That's all I want for this job, Simeon.'

Whatever Lancaster had in mind, it must be big. 'You've got access to all the resources the security services have to offer. Why do you need me?'

'You can guarantee secrecy. We can't afford any leaks or hacked computer files on this one. We don't want anyone to know, least of all the Americans. This needs to happen off the books.'

Carter knew what 'off the books' meant, it meant deniable. 'Whose high-profile arse are we trying to save?'

'No one's yet. Only a handful of people are aware of this, and no one knows that I've come to you with it.'

'So, what's the problem?'

'In four weeks, phase two of a nuclear missile system will begin deploying in the seabed around the UK. It's being funded by NATO. Its existence won't be made public. It'll be passed off as oil exploration.'

'Surely, the whole point of a nuclear deterrent is that people know we have it.'

'It's not, strictly speaking, a deterrent. The missiles are tactical, low yield. They'll be used to target local areas that may have been compromised by domestic events.'

'Domestic events?' Carter hoped this wasn't what he thought it was.

Lancaster nodded. 'In the event of war, there may be European governments who become hostile to the objectives of NATO. There may be a terrorist takeover or the election of a far-left government. Phase one deployed missiles around the US coast to do the same job in Central and North America.'

'You mean nuke our allies? Who the hell thought of that? Who decides when it's used?'

'The exact details aren't important right now, Simeon. Let's just say they are "need to know".'

Carter had never known the underlying reasons for many of his operations; he'd just got on with his mission. 'Okay, what do I need to know?'

'The company supplying the system is QRL Global Defence. Three weeks ago, Liam Quinn, the husband of their CEO, disappeared, along with their two young sons, while out fishing in the Gulf of Mexico.'

'Tragic, but why would that create so much concern?'

'His wife, Josephine Quinn, was on a business trip in London at the time and the Americans contacted us to track her down. While the police were looking for her, they stumbled across an MI5 surveillance operation that had photographed her with this man.' Lancaster placed a black and white photograph on the table in front of them.

Carter sat forwards and studied it. It showed a man and a woman sitting outside a coffee shop, engaged in deep conversation. 'Doesn't look anything out of the ordinary. Who's the man?'

'We know him as Viktor Bazarov. Although we don't know if that's his real name. He's an arms dealer, drug runner, terrorist for hire, anything he can get paid for.'

Carter tapped the photo with his index finger. 'I've heard that name before, back in the nineties, in Bosnia.'

'The first record we have of him is after the Soviets pulled out of Afghanistan in '89. He's ex-Spetsnaz, hiring himself out as private military muscle. He's been a player in every area of conflict and unrest for the last two decades.'

Carter picked up the photo and studied it. 'No one's come close to catching him before. He changes his location and appearance so often, he's impossible to track.'

Lancaster took the photo and put it back in the file. 'Just after that picture was taken, he disappeared. We don't know where he is now. Getting something to help bring him down would be a bonus, but our priority is Quinn.'

'You want to know if she's clean before the missiles are deployed.'

Lancaster nodded. 'Does she know who Bazarov is? What was she doing with him and what are they planning? We don't want the details of our new defence system sold to the highest bidder. The political fallout would be monumental.'

'And you don't want the Americans to know that we're investigating one of theirs.'

'Once we deal with our problem, we'll let them in on anything we find. If everything checks out, they don't need to know.' Lancaster pointed to the cardboard file. 'That contains the info we have on Quinn, Bazarov, and your team.'

Carter's brow furrowed. 'What team?'

'Two people who can help you, if you can find them and talk them into it. They both have questionable backgrounds but are the best people for the job. I don't want to know any of the operational details, just the outcome.'

Carter laughed, 'And if it all goes wrong you can deny any knowledge.'

'Like I said, Simeon. Off the books.'

'What makes you think I can convince them to help?'

'You convinced me to go into East Berlin, didn't you? If anyone can talk them into it, it's you.'

Carter picked up the folder. 'I can't promise anything, but I'll look over it for you.'

The two men stood and shook hands. 'It's been good to see you again, Simeon. Let me know how you get on, and remember, this is just between us.'

Carter patted his old protégé on the shoulder and smiled. 'Take care, Edward.'

Lancaster opened the door and they re-entered the main room. The bodyguard ushered Lancaster towards a fire escape and the staircase down to the club's rear exit.

Carter retraced his steps back through the drunken crowd, down the sweeping staircase and out through the main entrance to the street.

* * *

Carter sat in his hotel room and looked through the files of his potential team. Ali Sinclair and Frank McGill, at first glance, didn't look anything special. She was a convicted drug smuggler on the run from a seven-year sentence in a Mexican prison. He was a recluse, a suspect in several murders a few years back but never charged with anything. It was only after further reading that their skills became evident.

He looked through their military records. Sinclair, Alison, thirty-one, captain, Intelligence Corps, Special Reconnaissance Regiment, MI6. She was a talented undercover operative who also had frontline tours of duty in Iraq and Afghanistan.

McGill, Frank, forty-five, colour sergeant, Royal Marines Commando retired. A highly decorated career marine with multiple operational tours in Northern Ireland, Bosnia, Iraq and Afghanistan. He definitely wasn't a man that you wanted to piss off.

Sinclair's location was unknown, thought to be somewhere in the US but unconfirmed. She had the skills and the motivation to stay hidden and survive. She had no family to worry about and no one that would give her away. The only way Carter was going to find her quickly was through McGill. He and Sinclair were close, as good as family. They had been serving together in Afghanistan when a roadside bomb had killed her elder brother. If anyone knew where she was, it was McGill; and at least there was an address for him.

Chapter 3

Rock Cottage had been in the McGill family for generations. Sitting on the Cumbrian fells, in the heart of the Lake District, it was surrounded by poetic scenery and enjoyed oil painting views in every direction. Some of the original land had been sold off over the years but it still sat in one hundred acres of rugged hillside. McGill had been approached with several offers from developers but he liked living there. It was quiet, isolated and nobody bothered him. He moved in full-time after the murder of his wife and spent his time trying to renovate the neglected buildings. He rented out some of the land to his neighbours for grazing sheep and used some to try and grow his own vegetables. His next plan was to get a few chickens as he tried to become fully self-sufficient.

Assorted farm buildings were arranged around three sides of a rectangular central yard. The cottage itself was two storeys and was built from local stone with a slate roof. On the left were a low, single-storey barn built with the same stone and, next to it, a smaller, wooden outbuilding. On the right stood a corrugated steel barn that had been built when the original stone building's roof had collapsed. The steel barn hadn't been looked after since McGill's parents died, and the Cumbrian weather had wreaked havoc on its fabric. The walls had surrendered to rust where the paint was faded and flaked. Several large holes had appeared on the most exposed face, and one corner of the roof was covered over with plastic sheeting to try and keep out the rain.

Simeon Carter sat in the passenger seat of his car and looked at the gravel and dirt track, which led up to the farm, as he put on his boots. The sign on the gate said: Private Land, No Parking, No Cold Callers. McGill was a man who valued his privacy and kept his gate locked. Even without the gate, the track would be impassable in winter without four-wheel drive. Carter fastened his coat and turned up his collar, he wasn't looking forward to this. He had a feeling that the buildings weren't the only things at Rock Cottage that were dark and threatening. He picked up his briefcase and set off up the track towards the cottage.

Carter stopped several times to catch his breath as he negotiated the steep, slippery track. He slipped twice and had to put his hand down to stop himself sliding back down to the gate. It was hard going for a man of his age and his hands and knees were covered in mud by the time he reached the buildings.

He stood in the yard and looked around but there was no one to be seen. 'Hello?' There was no reply, no twitching curtains or barking dogs. Maybe the place was as deserted as it looked. He pulled a white handkerchief from his pocket and was attempting to wipe the worst of the mud from his hands when someone appeared from inside the steel barn.

'Can I help you with something?' The man wore waterproof trousers and an old, green combat jacket. The skin below his black beanie hat looked as weathered as the barn and he

27

carried a double-barrelled shotgun in the crook of his left arm.

Carter made sure his hands were in view to show he wasn't armed, he knew McGill's reputation. 'Frank? Frank McGill?'

'Who are you?'

'My name is Simeon Carter.' He held out his hand.

'What do you want?'

Carter withdrew his offered hand. 'I've had a long drive up from London, Frank. Can I trouble you for a glass of water?'

'Leave me alone and get off my property.' McGill turned and walked towards the house.

Carter shouted after him, 'I really need to speak to you, Frank ... It's about Ali Sinclair.'

McGill stopped and looked back over his shoulder at his unwelcome visitor. Carter was an old man and didn't look like a threat, but McGill wasn't taking any chances. He looked down the track and towards the car parked at the gate. There was no sign of anyone else, no driver or backup; the old man was alone. McGill carried on towards the cottage. 'You'd better come in.'

The two men entered the kitchen of the house and Carter placed his briefcase on the table. His handkerchief now had more mud on it than his hands did but what he really needed was soap and water. He looked at the bare brick walls and stone floor. The room only had the basics. Belfast sink, fireplace, table and chairs. 'This'll be a nice place when you've finished it. Reminds me of my own cottage down in—' He froze mid-sentence. His long experience had taught him that there were times when it was best to shut up and do nothing; this was one of those times.

A silenced Glock 17 was levelled at Carter's head. McGill's

voice was calm and quiet. It was obvious that he was in control. 'Lose the jacket, slide the briefcase over here and take a seat.'

Carter did as he was told, hanging his jacket on the back of the chair and sitting down with his hands flat on the table. He wanted to make sure he looked as unthreatening as possible. 'I didn't come all the way up here to harm you, Frank.'

McGill pulled out a chair and sat down opposite, the Glock still pointed at Carter. 'Trust me, if I thought you had you'd be dead already.'

'The information you need is in that briefcase. Take your time, I'm not going anywhere. Though I'd prefer not to do this with a gun in my face.'

'I don't give a fuck what you'd prefer. Tell me what you're doing here or I'll kill you now and feed you to my neighbour's pigs.'

Carter was in no doubt that the veteran marine meant what he said. He had dealt with men like McGill before – hard men, able to kill without hesitation, a valuable tool in certain circumstances. He held up his hands. 'I have a proposition for you, Frank, an opportunity to bring Sinclair back into the fold, to bring her home.'

McGill placed his weapon on the table and took the file out of the briefcase. 'Okay, I'm listening, but this had better be good, and keep your hands where I can see them.'

As McGill picked through the contents of the file, Carter filled in some of the details. 'It's a simple intell gathering job. We want Sinclair to go in, find out the connection between Quinn and Bazarov and pass the data to us.'

'What makes you think Ali will work for you lot again after you abandoned her in that prison?' McGill sounded calm but Carter could sense the underlying menace in his voice.

29

'Six couldn't jump in and get her out, it would have blown her cover from her previous job. If she hadn't pleaded guilty, she'd have been released after a few months when the fuss had died down.'

'She only pleaded guilty to get Quinn released. They were friends and Ali thought you'd get her out.' McGill was becoming more agitated.

Carter shifted in his seat, uneasy at the change in tone. 'Sinclair wasn't working for us when she was arrested. She was supposed to be on holiday with an old university friend. We did what we could.'

McGill slammed his fist on the table, his hand hovered inches from his Glock. 'You did nothing for her. She spent two years in that shit hole.'

Carter held up his hands, he wasn't going to win this argument, but he had to calm it down somehow. 'I wasn't involved in any of that and I wouldn't have left her there. Look, Frank, I wouldn't blame Sinclair if she had nothing to do with us again, but we need her. She's the only one who has an existing relationship with Quinn. They're old friends and spent time together in a Mexican hellhole. Quinn will trust her, and definitely owes her.'

McGill closed the file and threw it back into the briefcase. 'Why don't you get the Yanks to do this? They could pick up Quinn and threaten her with terrorism charges. I'm sure she'd squeal like a pig.'

'It's not that easy. The US Government could cover it up to make sure we buy in to their system and not develop one of our own. We need to do this without American involvement.'

'They won't be happy with us operating on their soil.' That was an understatement. The Americans didn't take kindly to foreign agencies interfering in their business at all, let alone operating in their backyard. There was every possibility that, if caught, he and Sinclair would be thrown into a deep, dark hole for a long time.

Carter was well aware of the risks. If things went wrong, the best Sinclair could hope for was finishing her time in the hell of a Mexican prison. 'Well, it's up to us to make sure they don't find out.'

'But if they do, we can be written off as unofficial and thrown to the wolves?'

'Unfortunately, yes.'

McGill laughed. He thought Carter seemed okay, not one of the usual career-driven arseholes that populated Whitehall these days. They were only interested in enhancing their own reputations on the backs of people like him and Sinclair. Carter was old school from a different generation; it didn't mean McGill trusted him though. 'If you were just coming to me with this job, I'd kick your arse back to London.'

Carter knew McGill thought of Sinclair as family and that he would do anything he could to protect her; that was his way in. 'Of course, if Sinclair does this job for us, we can get her home. She can start a new life without the risk of being picked up and sent back to Mexico. Wouldn't that be good, Frank?'

'All Ali wants is to come home, but she's not the kind of person to betray a friend.'

'That's where you come in. I know that you two are close. I'm hoping you'll be able to convince Sinclair that she'll be helping Quinn and, at the same time, helping herself.'

'I'm not going to convince her to do anything. It's her decision. Whatever she decides, you'll just have to accept

31

it.'

The tense atmosphere inside the cottage had eased and McGill was visibly less agitated. Carter was more relaxed, at least he now felt he would make it out of the room alive. 'That's good enough for me, Frank. I'd appreciate any help you can give me.'

'If Ali does agree to do this, I go in as her backup.'

'I was hoping you'd say that. Do you know where she is?'

McGill stood and walked over to a cork noticeboard that was fixed to the wall next to the door. He unpinned a postcard from amongst various receipts and photographs and passed it over to Carter.

'I know where she was a month ago.'

Chapter 4

Ali Sinclair took a long drink of lukewarm water from a plastic bottle before pouring the remaining contents over her face and head. The water ran down her neck and mixed with the sweat that already soaked her skin and made it glisten under the floodlights. She hated the heat. She missed home, the bite of a cold winter's day on her skin, the smell of fresh cut grass after a rain shower, but home wasn't an option. She was an escaped convict, an illegal immigrant with no documents, no passport and nowhere to go. The last eighteen months on the run had, in some ways, been as bad as prison. The constant fear of being found out and sent back had kept her awake at night. She had no real friends, or anyone to confide in, no one here even knew her real name. She was stuck, pretending to be someone else and hiding amongst people who didn't ask too many questions.

A few times she had risked everything to contact Frank McGill. She needed to hear a friendly voice and he was the closest thing to family that she had. McGill was trying to help her back home but without much success. Every solution involved her going back to prison. She had to earn enough money to move on, start again somewhere else. That's why she was doing this.

She swapped the empty bottle for a towel and dried her face and hands before adjusting her black, padded fingerless gloves. Wearing a tight black vest and baggy black shorts, she bounced on the balls of her feet, as if jumping an invisible skipping rope, and waited for her next challenger.

The announcer whipped up the drunken crowd as a local man climbed into the cage. Sinclair's opponents tended to be one of three types: women who wanted to prove they were tough, fat old men who wanted to grope her, or young rednecks who thought beating her was a way into her bed. None of them had posed a real threat and none of them had won. With her unbeaten record, and the way she dressed, her nickname was obvious. The PA system hissed and the fighters were introduced to the crowd.

'Ladies and gentlemen, on my right, standing five feet eight inches tall and weighing one hundred and forty pounds ... our ... un-de-feat-ed champion ... BLACK ... WIDOW.'

Sinclair threw a flurry of shadow punches that always got a cheer.

'And on my left, the challenger, standing six feet four inches tall and weighing three hundred and fifty pounds ...'

Sinclair zoned out – slowing her breathing, blocking out the noise and focusing on the man in front of her. He was big but it was mostly fat. With him were a younger couple, maybe his son and daughter, both in their twenties. She was blonde, heavily made-up and wearing a tight white vest and cut-off denim shorts. He wore a black 'Don't mess with Texas' T-shirt, jeans and a grubby baseball cap. They cheered the big man on as he walked around the cage with his arms raised in a premature victory salute. He wasn't ready for this at all.

The bell rang and the mountain of flesh opposite her

34

wobbled across the ring with his arms outstretched. Sinclair easily ducked under his grasp and spun round behind him. Two quick kidney punches and a kick to his right leg brought the mountain to his knees. Sinclair backed off, giving him the chance to take the count and walk away from the match with only a damaged ego. Spurred on by his screaming supporters, he decided not to take the opportunity and climbed to his feet. Wiping the sweat from his eyes and moving towards her, he pointed at Sinclair. 'I'm gonna fuck you up.'

He ran the last few feet between them. She sidestepped out of his way, but a hand from outside the ring grabbed her ankle and made her stumble just long enough for a massive fist to land a powerful punch to the side of her head. As she fell on her back, the mountain of flesh bent over and picked her up by the throat. He pushed her back against the side of the cage, brought his face close to hers and licked her cheek. 'I'm gonna enjoy this.'

Sinclair raised her hands and pushed a thumb into each of his eyes, forcing his head back. The pain made him release his grip and Sinclair wriggled free, rolling across the ring away from him.

Rubbing his bloody eyes, he looked across at Sinclair. She took a step towards him and threw a straight left into his solar plexus that bent him over. She followed with a right uppercut to his jaw then, grabbing the back of his head, drove her knee into his face. A stream of blood poured from his shattered nose and two broken teeth fell out onto the canvas as he pitched forwards, unconscious.

The crowd cheered and the announcer prepared to climb into the ring but Sinclair caught a flash of movement out of her left eye. Her opponent's daughter flew across the ring

35

screaming, her hands out in front of her with fingers like claws. With her left hand Sinclair blocked the red painted talons that slashed at her face, and smashed her right elbow into the other woman's face. The daughter held her hands to her split eyebrow and, staggering backwards, tripped over the still unconscious body of her dad. Junior was next up. He jumped into the ring throwing wild, ineffective punches that put him off balance. Sinclair dodged each one and, picking the perfect moment, brought her right foot up in a powerful kick to Junior's groin. With watering eyes and his balls on fire he folded himself into the foetal position, his mouth open as if to scream but with no noise coming out.

Another wild cheer erupted from the crowd, who were still chanting her name, as the man with the microphone held her arm aloft and declared her the winner and still undefeated champion.

* * *

Showered and changed, Sinclair sat on a log with a bottle of beer and stared at the dying embers in the makeshift barbeque pit. She looked up at the sound of a police siren. Was it coming this way? Sooner or later they would be coming for her, but not tonight. The siren faded into the distance and her heartbeat returned to normal. She drained the last mouthful of beer and threw the bottle into the plastic sack with the other empties.

Walking back to her trailer she was blinded by the headlights of a vehicle directly in front of her. She shielded her eyes just as something hit her hard across her back. She tried to focus on her assailant but another blow, this time to her stomach, forced her to the ground. Two kicks to the ribs winded her and punch after punch slammed into her body.

As Sinclair curled up in a ball to protect her head, the punches stopped and Junior and his sister stepped back to admire their handy work. Junior laughed, 'You're not so tough now, are ya?'

His sister shouted over to the van, 'Hey, Pa, you want a piece o' this?' There was no answer. 'Pa?'

The two of them turned round. Pa was on his knees in front of the van, vomit and spit dripping on to his chest as he gagged on the barrel of the pump-action shotgun that was in his mouth. Frank McGill cocked the weapon. 'Get away from her.'

Junior had already had his arse kicked once tonight and wasn't in the mood to back down. 'Who the fuck are you?'

McGill's finger hovered over the trigger. 'Get in your van and leave or I'll blow fat boy's teeth out through the back of his head.'

Pa stared wide-eyed at his son and tried to speak, but it only made him gag more.

Junior held up his hands. 'Okay, we're going.' He grabbed his sister by the arm and climbed into the van.

McGill led Pa round to the door of the vehicle and pushed him in, keeping the shotgun levelled at them as the van drove off.

'You okay, Ali?'

Sinclair was on her knees regaining her breath. 'I've been better.'

McGill took her hands and helped her to her feet. 'We need to get out of here before they come back for more.'

'What are you doing here, Frank? I told you to stay away,

37

you've risked enough.'

'And I told you I would never just abandon you like everyone else. I owe you at least that much.'

Sinclair looked at McGill for a moment. They had a shared past; memories that defined their relationship, experiences that bound them together. She knew he would always be there to back her up. It wasn't simply a matter of mutual respect; they were brother and sister, thrown together in adversity. The ties between them were unbreakable.

'You don't owe me anything, Frank. You helped me as much as I did you.' She gave him a hug. 'It's good to see a friendly face though.'

McGill kissed her on the forehead. 'Grab your things, time to go.'

Sinclair didn't have many possessions, she had to travel light in case she needed to drop everything and run. As McGill kept watch outside her trailer, she threw some clothes and a washbag into a small backpack. The money that she'd managed to save was in an old leather wallet, which she tucked into her back pocket before re-joining McGill outside.

'You got everything?'

Sinclair nodded. 'There's nothing else here I need.'

'Good. Follow me.'

McGill led the way to the back of the trailers where he'd parked his small motorhome. He'd bought the vehicle for cash when he arrived in the US, it was easier than trying to find motel rooms to stay in, more anonymous. Sinclair threw her bag in the back and joined him in the cab. 'So, where to?'

He started the engine and pulled away. 'We're heading east. We've got a meeting.'

After an hour McGill turned off the road and parked up out

of sight. He switched off the headlights and pulled a curtain across the windscreen to cloak the light from the inside. 'Time for a drink.'

Sinclair took the mug of coffee that McGill had made and sat at one side of the small table in the back of the camper, 'So, who's this guy we're meeting?'

'His name's Simeon Carter, ex-MI6, he ran a team of agents in East Berlin during the Cold War. He seems fairly straight, for a spook.'

'He wants me to spy on Jo Quinn?'

'Yeah, gather some intell on her and this Russian guy. See if she can be trusted.'

'I trust her. She's not involved in anything. Not knowingly anyway.'

McGill toyed with his mug. 'I know she's your friend, Ali, but her family are missing. She must be in pieces, it would make her an easy target.'

'Losing family does mess with your head. We both know that.'

They stood up at the sound of a car approaching. McGill picked up the shotgun he had taken from the rednecks and switched off the lights. He opened the door and they both went outside.

The car was parked fifty yards from them. The lone passenger, arms outstretched, was working his way round to approach from the north. Not the obvious direction to come from but the one they had agreed earlier.

Carter stopped in front of them. 'Evening, Frank. Captain Sinclair.' He held out his hand for Sinclair to shake. 'I'm Simeon Carter.'

Sinclair kept her hands in her pockets. 'I'm not a captain any more, Mr Carter.' She turned and walked back to the camper.

There was only room for two to sit at the table, so McGill made them all a coffee then stood in the kitchen while Carter and Sinclair talked.

'Frank tells me you seem okay for a spook.'

Carter smiled. 'Does that mean you'll listen to what I have to say?'

'I might listen for a while but it doesn't mean I'm interested.'

'Well, it's a start.' Carter took a sip of his coffee then leaned forwards as if he was trying to avoid being overheard – a hangover from his Cold War days. 'Okay, here's the deal. You get close to Quinn and find out what's happening, quick, simple and low risk.'

'If it's so easy, you don't need me, why don't you do it?'

'I'm not her friend. You were at university together. Then there's Mexico. Two months together in a Mexican prison will certainly forge a friendship. It would take us too long to get someone else close enough to be effective. There's a time limit on this.'

'Your time limit isn't my problem. I'm not going to help you lock her up.'

'I'm not interested in locking her up, that's not my job.'

'Then what do you want?'

'I just need to know what Quinn's relationship with Bazarov is. Is she actively passing on information to him, or is she being played? Was the meeting in London planned or just a coincidence? I pass the information to Whitehall, job done.'

'And what's in it for me?'

'Whatever you want. Money, new identity, tickets home.'

Sinclair stood up and jabbed her finger at Carter. 'You think I'll screw over a friend for money? You don't know me at all.'

She turned her back on him and stood in the kitchen shaking her head.

Carter looked at McGill but his face didn't give anything away. 'Look, Ali, I know you think of her as a friend.'

Sinclair spun round to face him. 'You don't know anything. We were arrested in Mexico on a made-up charge because someone was trying to get at her family. She had all kinds of fancy lawyers but they weren't getting anywhere.'

'So you took the blame.'

'Yeah, I took the blame. It got her out and I thought that MI6 wouldn't just leave me there. What a fuck-up that was.'

'If we'd jumped in and got you out it would have blown your cover from your previous job.'

'So I got seven years for something I didn't do?'

'The government would've got you out eventually.'

Sinclair picked up a mug and threw it across the kitchen, smashing it against the wall. 'Fuck you. If it weren't for Frank, I'd still be there. The Firm would've left me there to rot. They didn't want the embarrassment of claiming me as one of theirs.'

Carter raised his hands. 'I'm sorry for that, Ali, but I wasn't involved. I'd retired by then. I spent my years in Berlin and I promise you that I never left anyone behind.' He dropped his hands back to the table, took a breath, and let the tension diffuse. 'Look, if you decide you don't want to do this that's your decision, but, look at this way, if Quinn is in trouble, you could be the only person who can help her.'

Sinclair sat back down at the table, her hands trembling. 'I need a real drink.'

McGill took a beer from the fridge and passed it to her. She watched as the condensation ran down the outside of the

41

bottle. 'Okay. I'll go in and see if there is anything I can find out, anything I can help her with, but I'm doing it for her, not you. When it's over, you get me home.'

'It's a deal.' Carter finished his coffee and stood up. 'I'll leave you two to work out the operational details, I don't need to know them.' He opened the camper's door. 'Goodnight, Frank, Miss Sinclair. I'll speak to you soon.'

Carter got back in his car and fired up the engine. He was quite pleased with himself; pleased with the way the meeting had gone. He still had his talent for persuasion. When he turned on the headlights he realised that McGill had followed him to the car and was walking round to his side. Carter lowered the window as McGill approached. 'Did we forget something, Frank?'

McGill bent over so his face was level with the open window, inches from Carter's. 'If I ever find out you've double-crossed Ali in any way, I'll track you down and I'll cut your fucking heart out.'

As Carter drove off, he looked in his mirror. He'd had threats before but never one so cold, so matter of fact. If anything happened to Sinclair, Carter was certain that it would cost him his life.

Chapter 5

C arter arrived back at Heathrow only a few hours later. He picked up his bag from the carousel and headed for the taxi rank. After forty-five minutes he found himself, once again, back in the chaos of central London's early evening traffic. Nothing ever changed. Cars and buses honked their horns and battled for room while cyclists zigzagged between them, risking life and limb just to save a little time. A seemingly endless stream of pedestrians poured into the underground to fight for space aboard already overcrowded trains. Carter couldn't understand anyone wanting to go through this every day. Surely there were better ways to earn a living? At least this time he didn't have to use the underground. Lancaster had arranged a hotel for Carter to stay in as long as was needed. The taxi drove him straight to the front door.

The hotel was small, discrete and within walking distance of Vauxhall Cross, perfect if he needed to meet up with Lancaster in a hurry. Carter checked in and insisted on a room at the far end of the corridor, he didn't want anyone to have a reason to walk past his door. The receptionist obliged and Carter walked over to the lift and pressed the button.

Up in his room he pulled out his mobile and sent a text message to a number he knew by heart. There was another member of the team that he needed to recruit, one who Lancaster would know nothing about.

One of Carter's operatives in Berlin was Bobby Kinsella, a man who Carter considered to be a real friend. They'd been working together for a decade and had completed more successful operations than they could remember. Not just in East and West Berlin, but all over the Eastern Block. It was the late eighties, not long before the wall came down, things had eased off by then and it wasn't as tense as it had been during the height of the Cold War. He and Bobby had been given a seemingly simple mission to pick up a Soviet Army colonel who wanted to defect to the West. It was something they'd done before, and it had become routine. Looking back, Carter would say they had become too complacent, too cocky.

There hadn't been much of a plan, no need to pick up the defector from East Berlin and risk a border crossing. Their target was part of the honour guard at the Soviet war memorial in West Berlin's Tiergarten. He would be taking all the risk.

Once Carter had pulled up, in front of the memorial, Kinsella had planned to get out of the car and, using his best American accent, pose as just another tourist. Looking around and taking photos while making sure everything was good to go. Any problems and he'd get back in the car and abort the pick up. When Kinsella was happy, he would give the signal and the colonel would make a run for it. By the time any of the other Soviet guards realised what was happening it would be too late to do anything about it, he and the colonel would be in the back seat of the car and they would be driving away.

The memorial was in the British sector, so a chase was unlikely, and once they were at the safe house they would have nothing to worry about; another successful mission for

Carter and Kinsella.

The mission had begun smoothly enough. They'd picked up the car and set off, chatting as they went. They'd talked about Kinsella's plans for a family holiday during his upcoming leave. His wife and new-born son were waiting for him at home, life was good, and he was living it to the full.

As the two men had approached the memorial, they'd quickly run through the plan for the pick up and what they'd do if it all went wrong, but it wouldn't go wrong, they were feeling relaxed and confident. The one thing Carter and Kinsella hadn't known, what they couldn't have known, was that the KGB had been tipped off about the defection and had put one of their men in the honour guard.

They'd arrived at the memorial and Carter had stopped the car, checking for any signs that they had been compromised. He'd made sure their backup team was in place, but they wouldn't be needed. Kinsella had opened the door and stepped out onto the pavement, but something was wrong. The colonel hadn't waited; he'd made a break for it and run towards the car. As soon as he had, the planted KGB officer had taken aim and opened fire.

Carter had screamed at Kinsella, 'Get back in the car, Bobby.' But it was too late. The first bullet had hit Kinsella in the shoulder and he'd fallen against the side of the car. The second and third bullets had taken down the colonel before he'd gone more than twenty yards. Four, five, six shots, Kinsella and a member of the backup team were killed in the hail of bullets. Carter had got out of the car and returned fire but the Soviet agent had stopped shooting and dropped his weapon, content to surrender now that his mission was complete.

The backup team had run past Carter and surrounded all

45

the guards, disarming them. Carter had run to Kinsella but there was nothing he could do. A bullet wound in the side of Bobby's head was the hit that had killed him. He hadn't stood a chance. Carter had lain Kinsella down and covered his body with his coat.

In the aftermath of the botched mission, Carter, his boss, the backup team, everyone was hauled over the coals. For some it was the end of their career, for others, Carter included, it was a black mark on their record that would never go away.

The diplomatic fallout had disappeared amongst the usual background noise of normal Cold War relations. With the Soviets demanding their men back and MI6 keen to hush up their involvement, the whole thing was covered up. Kinsella was listed as being killed in a road traffic accident and his body was shipped home to his family.

Carter had been given a series of shit jobs, so he was under no illusion how badly he'd fucked up. That hadn't bothered him, but he would never get over the guilt he felt. He was supposed to be in charge; he should have looked after his operative, his friend. Carter was godfather to Kinsella's son, Danny. He had been left to grow up without his dad and Carter was determined to do anything he could to look after the family. Not because of his guilt or as an act of atonement, but because he'd always promised Bobby that he would.

* * *

Danny Kinsella was born just as computers were becoming commonplace and he grew up surrounded by them. He had an understanding that went far beyond knowing how to operate the equipment. The technology, devices and networks all made perfect sense to him. He could read computer code as if it were plain text and was writing and selling his own software while he was still at school. Put simply, he was a genius.

After he'd graduated from Cambridge, he followed in his father's footsteps and joined the security services. Not frontline operations like Carter but GCHQ. They'd spotted his potential while he was at university and he'd soon proved to be a valuable asset. He became a rising star of the intelligence community, able to hack his way into any system. The best security software in the world simply wasn't good enough to keep him out. His career was going well and he was on the fast track to the top, until he was caught hacking the wrong people.

Kinsella had never lost the need to get recognition of his father's sacrifice, the fact that he'd died on active service. Carter had told him what he could but Danny wanted evidence, he wanted to know who had killed him.

GCHQ were far from happy when evidence surfaced that Danny had been snooping around MI6 files. Some of the most senior people in the organisation had been involved in the Berlin cover up. They couldn't afford to lose Kinsella but they wanted him warned off. Danny was having none of it, either he got the recognition for his father or he left. The organisation had declined; Danny Kinsella had walked away.

A man with his talents wasn't going to be out of work for long, companies were lining up to offer him work. He'd preferred to stay freelance – creating security software and charging major corporations a fortune for advice on what they needed to keep people like him out of their systems. After he'd hacked in and shown them just how vulnerable they were, of course.

The text message Carter sent to Kinsella had invited him to the hotel bar for a drink and a chat. There was no need for a clandestine meeting, no need to hide; they were family. If anyone did see them, it was easily explained.

When Carter walked out of the lift, Kinsella was just coming through the main door into reception. He was a tall, slim man who always dressed well. A designer suit and expensive watch and shoes helped him fit in with his clients in the City. He strode confidently over to Carter, arms outstretched and a big smile on his face. 'Simeon. It's great to see you.'

The two men embraced warmly. 'Good to see you too, son, how's your mum?'

'She's great. I've moved her into my house in the country. She asks about you a lot.'

'I'm glad to hear she's okay, I'll have to pay her a visit.' Carter pointed towards the bar. 'Shall we?'

Kinsella put his arm around the older man's shoulders as they walked through the door. 'I'll get these, you have a seat.'

Carter picked a booth by the window and sat down. It was far enough away from the other drinkers that they wouldn't be overheard but it wouldn't look like they were trying to be secretive. Kinsella brought two drinks and joined him at the table. 'Haven't seen you for a couple of months, Simeon, where've you been hiding yourself?'

'You know I don't like London, I'm happier out in the sticks.'

Kinsella looked at their surroundings. The bar wasn't anything special. A multicoloured patterned carpet under a scattering of small round tables and wooden chairs, with booths along the far wall and under the window. The window seats had rectangular tables and bench seats with wood and stained glass partitions. Old photographs of the local area

48

hung from just about every inch of wall space, it looked like it hadn't been decorated for some time. 'What brings you here? You could have stayed at my flat. I've got plenty of room.'

'I know that, but this is work.'

'You old bugger, I knew you couldn't stay away from it, retirement my arse. What is it? Anything exciting?'

'It's something big, Danny, something I need your help with, but if we get caught it'll plunge us into a whole world of shit.'

'Sounds like my kind of project. When do I start?'

Carter pulled a brown envelope from his jacket and slid it across the table. 'Right away if you're up to it. I need background info on the people and the company in that envelope. I'll be getting intell from the field and I'll need you to tell me the significance of it, quickly.'

Kinsella picked up the envelope. 'Not a problem. Might mean accessing some government databases.'

'We'll need that anyway. I want you to keep an eye on any mention of this by MI6. It's not that I don't trust Edward Lancaster, I just don't want any bombshells from Vauxhall Cross.'

Kinsella nodded. 'Understood.'

'Lancaster said he picked me for this job because he didn't want an electronic trail leading back to them. They must be covering for someone, see if you can find out who.'

'Will do. I'll set up some disposable email addresses for us to use to communicate, it's not the most secure way but the risks are minimal.'

'Whatever you think is best, Danny, you're the expert.' Carter knew he could rely on Kinsella to get him what he needed. His godson had spent years building up multiple fake, online identities. If one was compromised, he simply walked away from it and used another. He could have the security agencies chasing false trails for years. 'The people I've got in the field could use some fake identities, one each for this job in the States, and another as a fall back. There are pictures and details in the envelope.'

'Okay, I've a friend in the US who can hook them up, no questions asked, and I'll work on something more watertight for the backup.'

'Good, I promised I'd help them out. They've both had a rough time of it.'

'Just like us, eh, Simeon.'

'Yeah, birds of a feather and all that.' He finished his drink and slid the empty glass across the table. 'Now, get the old man another drink and you can fill me in on what you've been up to.'

Chapter 6

McGill pulled into the car park of a small motel in southwest Houston, just south of Route 59. The only other vehicle there was a burned-out wreck in one corner. The building itself was a two-storey, rundown, concrete box, with a row of doors along the front of each floor and a main door to reception. It wasn't the sort of place you brought your family for a holiday.

They walked through the main door and up to the hole in the wall that passed for reception. There was no one about so McGill rang the bell. A young man appeared from a room at the back. 'Yeah?'

'How much for a room?'

'It'll cost you twenty bucks for an hour, on top of what you're payin' the hooker.'

McGill pulled two ten-dollar bills from his wallet and threw them onto the desk. 'A piece of advice, my friend, watch your fuckin' mouth.'

The receptionist handed over a door key and winked at Sinclair. 'See you later.'

They walked back outside and along the front of the motel to their room.

The room was typical for this kind of motel: bed along one

wall, TV on the other. McGill checked the bathroom, water dripped from every appliance and the ripped shower curtain looked like something out of *Bates Motel*. The room had two doors, the one they had used from the car park and another that opened towards reception at the back. The door to the inside was damaged. The lock had been replaced and the frame repaired. It looked like it had been kicked in at least once.

Sinclair sat in the room's only chair and switched on the TV. There were only three channels: sport, music and porn, obviously catering for a specific clientele. She switched it off and looked out across the car park. 'What time is the meet?'

McGill checked his watch. 'Any time now.'

'Whichever direction he comes from, we need to be ready to back out the other way if it goes pear shaped. Okay, Frank?'

He nodded. 'If anything happens I'll keep them busy, you start the van.' The throwaway phone in his hand vibrated and he pressed the button to answer. 'Yep ... room seventeen.' He put the phone in his pocket. 'He's here.'

Sinclair put one eye to the gap in the curtains. A tall black man was approaching their door from across the car park. 'Here he comes.'

McGill opened the internal door to check for anyone trying to come at them from the corridor. He gave the all clear and closed the door but stayed next to it, listening. Sinclair let their visitor into the room and stood at the window, checking for any movement.

The man who entered the room wore jeans and a hoodie. He was just over six feet tall, middle-aged and had a strong, muscular physique. He looked every inch the ex-Marine Corps captain he was. His shaved head glistened with sweat,

52

which he dabbed at with a white handkerchief. 'Okay, I don't know your real names and you don't need to know mine, you can call me Bob.'

McGill nodded to him. 'What have you got for us, Bob?'

Bob put the large holdall he had brought with him on the bed and placed an envelope on top of it. 'In there you'll find UK identity documents for you both, courtesy of your friends in London. They're good enough to fool any local law enforcement and, if anyone checks your details, we've put back-stories in place that'll hold them up for a while. If the feds, or anyone else, look deeper, they won't hold up. It's all we could do at such short notice.'

Sinclair opened the envelope and took out a passport. 'It says here that I'm Alison Sutherland. It'll do I guess. The picture's definitely shit enough to be genuine.'

Bob unzipped the holdall. 'I was sent a shopping list of kit you might want. Night-vision, radio, sat phone, it's all in here. The bottom of the bag unzips, the weapons are in there.' He zipped up the bag and turned to walk out. 'Have fun.'

McGill held out his hand. 'Thanks, Bob, from one ex-marine to another.'

Bob took McGill's hand and gave it a firm shake. 'You take care now.' He opened the door and walked out.

Sinclair closed the door behind him and watched through a crack in the curtains as he got into his car and drove off.

McGill picked up the holdall from the bed. 'Let's get out of here.'

Sinclair was still watching through the curtains. 'Wait. I think we've got company.'

On the other side of the car park, the guy from reception was talking with three young men. They were all gang members from the look of them – same colours, matching tattoos – fucking cockroaches. The reception cockroach pointed towards room seventeen then scuttled back under his rock. Sinclair watched as the remaining three split up, two inside, one outside. 'We've been set up, two coming your way.'

McGill pulled a nine-millimetre Glock from his jacket and screwed on a suppressor. 'We can't negotiate with these pricks. They must be planning to rob us and do god knows what to you. Take them all out, no warning.'

'Looks like number one is head roach, he's coming to the front.' Sinclair took a butterfly knife from her pocket and opened it with a flourish. 'Ready?'

McGill drew back the slide on his Glock. 'Do it.'

Roach number one approached the door while pulling a chromed semi-automatic from his waistband. Sinclair stood behind the door and McGill stepped back into the bathroom. The roach didn't even hesitate. He walked up to the door and, without breaking his stride, brought his foot up against the lock. The doors weren't designed to withstand any kind of onslaught and the wood around the lock splintered. Their attacker strode into the room expecting to catch them with their pants down; he barely had time to register what happened next. Sinclair stepped out from behind the door and thrust the blade of the butterfly knife into the base of his skull. With his spinal cord severed he dropped to the floor like a broken mannequin.

The other door burst open at the same time. McGill, standing in the bathroom, fired two silenced shots. Roach number two took one in the chest and one in the forehead. He fell forwards, dead, onto the carpet. Number three, following close behind, tripped over his gang buddy onto his face.

McGill came out of the bathroom and fired a single shot into the back of the final roach's head.

McGill closed the door while Sinclair stood back beside the window, watching for more attackers. 'There's two more getting out of a car, heading this way.'

McGill grabbed the holdall. 'Let's go.' He opened the inside door and they hurried down the corridor to reception. The reception guy saw McGill coming and knew something had gone wrong. He brought up a weapon from behind the desk but, before he could use it, McGill shot him, knocking him back into his hole.

Once in the car park, they ran for the camper. The two remaining cockroaches came out of room seventeen and gave chase but McGill dropped them both. Sinclair took the holdall and loaded it into the van. She jumped in and turned the ignition. McGill checked for any witnesses, but in this neighbourhood gang shootings were commonplace. No one ever saw anything. He unscrewed the suppressor from the barrel of his Glock and climbed in the van.

Sinclair put the van in gear and they pulled out of the car park. 'We don't need any shit like that. If the cops get involved, I'll be winging my way back to Mexico before you can say illegal immigrant.'

'From here on in we don't need to involve anyone else. We've got all the kit we need and we can sleep in the van.'

'Sounds like the best idea. Which direction do we go from here?'

McGill pulled a road map out of the glove box. 'Route 59 will take us out of Houston. We'll stay away from the interstates, it'll be safer. Quinn's ranch is southwest of here.'

'Okay, let's get there and do this. I need to go home.'

* * *

At the motel in Houston the local police department had cordoned off the car park and emptied the building. There were only four remaining guests and, as usual, they hadn't seen or heard anything. There were no witnesses across the street, or driving past, and no survivors to interview. The Houston Police Department normally marked these shootings down as inter-gang rivalry, but Sergeant Maria Rodriguez had the experience to realise that this was something different. This was no drive-by or normal gang shootout. Whoever had taken out these six men had done it before the gang-bangers could fire a single shot. They'd done it without firing any stray bullets and, in one case, killed an armed man with a knife. This wasn't some local disagreement. She'd have to bring the fed's task force in on this one.

Chapter 7

The Quinn ranch occupied three thousand acres of
South Texas, one hundred miles north of the Mexican
border. The family home, enclosed within a twenty-
acre compound in the southwest corner of the ranch, was
built in the style of a Mexican hacienda. A sprawling, square,
whitewashed building with red, terracotta roof tiles above
simple, square, framed windows that ran along three sides of
the building. Each window was set into a stone archway, with
the windows on the upper floor opening out onto individual
balconies. Several of the balconies had potted plants that
twisted between the surrounding, ornate, iron railings. The
front of the house had the same arrangement of windows
but in the centre, there was a large, arched entrance that led
through to a central courtyard. The floor above the entrance
extended upwards into a clock tower that housed a sundial
on its front face.

Behind the house was a long, single-storey row of wooden
stables and, to the left, a guest bungalow that mirrored
the Mexican design of the main house. A large patio and
rectangular swimming pool, between the two buildings, kept
them separate but connected. One hundred metres beyond the
smaller building, the green painted walls of a large corrugated

steel barn were partly obscured by a row of bushes, rendering it almost invisible from the front of the house.

A gravel driveway, lined with palm trees, cut its way between two manicured lawns from the main entrance to the wrought iron gates that hung between two stone pillars. Either side of the pillars was ten metres of matching stone wall, with the rest of the compound surrounded by eight-feet-high iron railings. Cameras on top of the stone pillars monitored the gates and more cameras, mounted on poles along the fence, covered the whole perimeter. One of the cameras panned around to track the approach of a beaten up pick-up truck that rattled and coughed its way along the road outside.

The vehicle pulled up at the gates and Sinclair climbed out, grabbing a bag from the back. She thanked the driver for the lift and waved to him as he drove off. She walked up to the gates and, after looking through them to check for any sign of the occupants, pressed the button on the intercom box that was mounted on one of the pillars.

A disembodied voice crackled through the speaker. 'Yes?'

'I'd like to see Jo Quinn please.'

'She doesn't want to see anyone, go away.'

'Please tell her I'm here.'

There was no reply. Sinclair pressed the call button again. The crackly voice returned, this time sounding annoyed. 'You can't see her, leave now or we'll call the police.'

Sinclair was pretty sure they weren't going to phone the police. 'Tell her it's an old friend from Mexico, and I'm not going anywhere till she speaks to me.'

The speaker fell silent. There was the whirr of an electric motor as the camera above her head turned and zoomed in to get a closer look. She threw her backpack on the ground and sat down on it; she sensed she was in for a long wait.

Twenty minutes passed, Sinclair took a bottle of water from a side pocket of her bag and took a drink. The heat was stifling, there wasn't a cloud in the sky, and the only sound was the hiss of the sprinklers that kept the lawns well watered and green. A sharp contrast to the sundried, brown vegetation on this side of the wall. She took off her baseball cap and wiped the sweat from her face and neck with a bandanna.

The intercom sparked back into life and a different voice, a woman's, crackled from the speaker. 'Hello, who's there?'

Sinclair stood up and brushed the dust from her jeans. Moving back over to the box she pressed the button, and at the same time looked straight up at the camera. 'Hello, Jo, it's me.'

After a few minutes a golf buggy appeared and made its way down the drive, stopping just in front of the gates, which opened with a metallic clunk. The two men who got out were dressed identically in black trousers and polo shirts. They were armed with handguns, not an unusual sight in this neck of the woods, and both carried radios. They looked just like the thousands of other security guards who patrolled high value properties across the US.

Guard number one pointed at the backpack lying on the floor. 'I'll need to check your bag.'

Sinclair picked it up and threw it to him. 'Help yourself.'

Guard number two was carrying the same type of handheld metal detector used at airports. He motioned towards her. 'Arms out to the side.'

She did as she was told and the guard waved the detector over her whole body. Nothing. He looked over to his colleague. 'All clear.'

Number one closed the flap on the bag and threw it back to Sinclair. 'Okay, get in.' He pointed towards the buggy with his head.

With all three of them now aboard, the buggy made its way back up the drive as the gates closed behind them.

They drove through the archway at the front of the building and onto the paved surface of the central courtyard. A large fountain sprayed cool water into the air and seemed to keep the temperature in this part of the house more bearable. The surrounding architecture matched the style of the outside of the house with one difference; the arches round the windows on both floors connected together to form upper and lower walkways. Sinclair got out of the buggy and scooped some water from the fountain onto her face and neck while her two new friends drove back out to the drive.

On the other side of the fountain was another arch – a grand entrance into the house. There were two solid wooden doors, almost reaching the level of the top floor windows, flanked by palm trees that stood in terracotta pots. One of the doors opened and Jo Quinn stepped out. She rushed across the courtyard and threw her arms around Sinclair. 'Ali, it's so good to see you.'

'You said if I was ever in the area I should look you up.'

Quinn smiled. 'You should have come here sooner. I've been so worried about you.'

'You've got more important things to worry about than me, Jo. How are you doing?'

Quinn's eyes moistened. 'I feel numb. I don't really have anyone I can talk to.'

Sinclair placed her hands on Quinn's shoulders. 'I'm here now, you can talk to me.'

'I've missed you, Ali. Where've you been for the last eighteen months?'

Sinclair could just make out a figure, standing to the right of the door, watching them as they talked. 'It's a long story, let's get out of this heat and I'll tell you all about it.'

The two old friends walked arm in arm towards the house and, as her eyes adjusted to the interior lighting, Sinclair turned back to look at the figure in the shadows. Even with shorter hair and clean-shaven, Bazarov's face was unmistakeable. His light brown hair was now streaked with blonde, but the crescent shaped scar under his right eye was more prominent against his freshly tanned skin. It was him. Whatever was going on between him and Quinn, the meeting in London was no coincidence. Bazarov held her gaze then turned and walked off into the courtyard – he wasn't happy that she was there.

The open-plan room they walked into had a vaulted ceiling with oak beams that rose to the full height of the house. On the left was a spacious kitchen with tiled floor, oak cabinets and professional grade, brushed steel appliances. In the middle, a dining table with room for ten to sit comfortably. The right-hand side was a sitting area where three luxurious, red leather sofas were arranged in a horseshoe round an expensive looking rug and the biggest flat screen TV Sinclair had ever seen. Matching staircases ran up the walls at each end of the room to a balcony that led to the rooms on the upper floor. Various pieces of artwork, paintings and sculptures hung from the walls or sat on podiums under individual spotlights. The whole house left visitors in no doubt that this family had money.

Sinclair stood on the rug, mouth agape. 'Wow, this place is

huge.'

'It's too big for me on my own.'

'I'm sorry, Jo, I didn't mean to …'

Quinn sat down on one of the sofas. 'It's okay, I just … the place is so full of memories.' She shook her head. 'I miss Liam and the boys so much.' Her voice faltered as she fought to hold back her emotions, but it was no use. She held her hands up to her face as the tears began. Sinclair sat on the sofa and held Quinn in her arms, she was genuinely sorry for her friend but at the same time felt a sharp stab of guilt.

For the next hour Sinclair forgot the real reason she was there, and just concentrated on being Quinn's friend, someone she could confide in, pour her heart out to.

* * *

After a shower and a change of clothes, Sinclair made her way from her room back down to the kitchen. Quinn was preparing a meal for them both. She looked much better, although her eyes were still a little red. She smiled at Sinclair and poured two glasses of wine. 'Have a seat, I'll bring the food over.'

Sinclair took their wine and sat at the dining table where Quinn had set two places. 'Mmm, something smells good.'

Quinn picked up two plates of pasta and carried them to the table. 'Nothing fancy, just quick and simple.' She sat down and took a drink. 'Now, enough of my problems, tell me where you've been hiding.'

Sinclair didn't have to invent a backstory for this job – no legend or fake identity. She told the story exactly as it had happened, just leaving out the parts about Frank and MI6.

When she spoke about the hell of the prison her emotion was real. She'd need a long time to get that out of her head.

Quinn reached out and held her hand. 'I'm sorry you had to go through that.'

'It wasn't your fault, Jo, we were both stitched up.'

'But it was my family they were trying to get at. If you hadn't taken the blame, I would've been in there too. I wanted to help you.'

'You did help. Your lawyer visiting every couple of months, bringing me one of your letters and some money, made things a little easier.'

After finishing their meal they moved to the comfort of the sofas and talked and drank late into the night, both trying to forget their recent traumas. Sinclair kept Quinn's wineglass topped up but drank only a little from her own. All the time she was gathering information: the locks on the doors, the alarm system. By the time she went to her bedroom she knew all the security arrangements inside the house and the location of Quinn's home office; that's where she would start.

* * *

Sinclair had the perfect view of the outbuildings as she stood next to the window of her room. There were no lights on in the guest house and no sign of movement; she assumed that was where Bazarov was staying. She couldn't risk searching the bungalow until she knew more about his movements. All of the activity outside was close to the barn. The lights were on and guards were moving in and out of the large double door as they took their turn to patrol the property. It was obviously where they were stationed, and hopefully from where the

63

external cameras were being monitored. The whole property was set up to detect and stop an intruder from outside, not from within.

She knew there was no one else in the house and Quinn's room was on the other side of the building. Her friend had drunk enough wine to knock her out for the rest of the night but Sinclair still had to be cautious. Keeping as quiet as possible, she left her room and made her way down the staircase towards the kitchen.

Two corridors led from the open-plan area and gave access to the rooms on the side of the house. She crept across the kitchen and along the right-hand passageway, keeping her back to the wall. She stopped every few feet to check for telltale sounds or lights, or someone she might have missed. The office was the third room on the right. She turned the handle and pushed, the door wasn't locked. She opened it an inch to check for any noises coming from within but it was empty. Sinclair was relieved there were no creaking floorboards or hinges to give her away as she stepped into the office and closed the door behind her.

She lowered the blind over the room's only window and switched on a small torch. The lens on the torch had been changed so it only gave out red light – it made it less likely to be seen from outside and also preserved her night vision.

She panned the torch left and right. The room was set up as an everyday, small, home office. A simple desk with a phone, computer screen and laptop docking station, faced away from the window. She moved over to the filing cabinet in the corner and checked the first drawer. It wasn't locked. It could be a lucky break, but most of the time it just meant there was nothing in there worth hiding. She was right; the filing cabinet contained nothing more secret than electricity bills and stationery. Wherever Quinn kept her work files, it wasn't here.

From the corner of her eye she picked up the slow pulse of a green LED on the opposite side of the room, where a smaller desk held a stack of paper and a laser printer and copier. She lifted the lid on the copier, a single sheet of paper lay face down on the glass; someone had scanned a document and forgotten to remove the original. She turned the page over and shone her torch on it. It was a hand-drawn sketch of an island, showing a collection of buildings. Several numbered arrows pointed at locations on the map but there were no names to give away its location. This could be important, or it could be Quinn's next holiday destination. She placed it back on the glass and pressed the copy button.

A light came on outside the room; someone was in the kitchen. Sinclair grabbed the copy and switched off her torch. Keeping one eye closed to keep her night vision intact, she opened the door just enough to see along the corridor. Quinn opened the fridge door and took a drink from a bottle of water – washing down two aspirin to counter the effects of too much wine. She didn't suspect anything; she was trying to be quiet so she didn't wake Sinclair. She put the cap back on the bottle and took it with her. She switched off the light and went back upstairs.

Sinclair finished her search of the office but didn't find anything else. One hour after entering the room, Sinclair was standing back at her bedroom window watching the movement outside the barn. There were more guards than she had seen during the day. They were only coming out of the barn at night, disguising how many of them there were. Only some of Bazarov's men were being used as security. Sinclair needed to get a look inside, but not tonight. It was too late and far too risky with so many people about. The guest house was an easier target, but first she had to make contact with Frank.

Chapter 8

McGill's camper was parked away from the road, two miles from the ranch. To any casual observers he was just another tourist, or a wannabe survivalist out prepping for the end of the world. Either way, he wouldn't have any curious visitors poking around. Too many people in this part of the world were armed to the teeth and no one wanted to risk getting shot by someone practising their right to bear arms.

The camper looked like a wreck from the outside. The bodywork was dented and rusted with a variety of paint colours from previous spray jobs showing through the latest flaking topcoat. Underneath though, McGill had made sure the engine was in good condition and had fitted a full set of new tyres. It wouldn't let him down when he needed it. Beneath the floor, a previous owner had installed an extra storage compartment. Maybe it was for smuggling drugs, or just for storing camping equipment; but it was perfect to keep his kit out of sight and hidden from a casual search. If anyone was conducting anything more in-depth, he planned to be far enough away that it wouldn't matter any more.

He knelt down, rolled back a strip of vinyl flooring, and lifted the compartment's lid. Two Glock 17s, a Heckler and

Koch MP5K sub-machine gun, spare magazines for both and boxes of ammunition all fit inside comfortably. He also had a daysack, radios, spare mobile phones, binoculars and night vision goggles; everything he needed to back up Sinclair. He also had a ghillie suit – the camouflaged clothing worn by snipers to blend in with their surroundings – in a canvas bag. McGill spent hours weaving grass, twigs and leaves from the local area into the netting of the suit. Once he was in position, the suit would blow in the wind and react to conditions in the same way as the foliage around it; he'd be almost invisible.

He holstered one of the Glocks and picked up the ghillie suit, binoculars and a backpack water pouch. He switched off the lights in the camper, locked the door and set off into the darkness.

McGill arrived at Quinn's compound just before dawn and settled into a slight depression in the hard, dry ground, six feet from the fence. His camouflage blended in well and, unless someone tripped over him, he wouldn't be spotted. He watched the coming and going of the guards and tried to work out their schedule; there was something going on in that barn – something for him and Ali to check out.

As the sun came up, the temperature rose quickly under his camouflage cover. He knew he was in for a long, hot day but he had to wait for Sinclair to make contact. If she didn't manage it, he would be back every day until she did. He was used to this kind of operation. Acting as backup for undercover ops was long, boring work but it was absolutely necessary. He had to be there whenever Sinclair got the chance to pass him a message.

Sinclair left her room and went down to the kitchen for some breakfast. Quinn was already up, dressed and on her way out of the door. 'Morning, Ali.'

Maybe it was just the effect of the previous night's drinking but Quinn looked rough. Her face was pale and drawn and she had dark rings under her bloodshot eyes. Her hair and clothes were unkempt, by her normally polished standards, and a nervous tick pulled at the muscle of her right cheek. She was on the verge of a breakdown.

'Are you okay, Jo?'

Quinn nodded. 'I'm just a little tired.'

Sinclair knew there was much more to it than that but let it go, for now. 'Where are you off to so early?'

'I've got to go away on business overnight, is that ok?'

'Yeah, sure. Where are you going?'

'Nowhere exciting, just boring business.'

A car stopped outside with Bazarov sitting in the passenger seat. Sinclair gestured towards him. 'Who is that guy? He looks a bit creepy.'

Quinn looked nervous. 'Just a business associate of Liam's, he's helping me out.' She put her hand up to her face as the tick pulled at her cheek again.

Sinclair could see her friend was lying to her. They'd always been open with each other, no matter what was happening. This wasn't like her at all. She wanted to tell Quinn that she was there to help, that people knew something was wrong, but she couldn't risk it. She needed Quinn to carry on as she was. Having her and Bazarov away overnight was the ideal opportunity to continue the search of the ranch.

Quinn grabbed her briefcase and headed for the door. 'There's plenty of food in the house and if you need any clothes just help yourself. I'll see you tomorrow.' She walked out of the door and got in the car.

Outside the compound, McGill watched as the car drove away from the house and out through the gates. It was followed by two four-wheel drives and a van full of guards. He checked the barn, only a couple of men had been left behind. If he could pick out a blind spot in the security, he could get in, grab all the evidence they needed and get Ali out of there, but he'd promised her he'd wait here until she contacted him; he wouldn't let her down.

Sinclair changed into shorts, T-shirt and trainers, grabbed a bottle of water from the fridge and headed out for a run round the perimeter fence. Once she'd passed the map to Frank she'd search the guest house – the guards who were left were staying in the barn so it shouldn't be too difficult. She set off, at an even pace, down the drive and turned right just before the gate. All the cameras were pointing outwards from the property, no one was watching her; they weren't interested in anything she was doing. Ten minutes into her run she stopped by the fence to take on some water and do some stretching. 'You okay, Frank?'

From somewhere under the foliage came the reply, 'I'm sweatin' my arse off under here.'

She tried not to laugh. 'I checked out Quinn's office last night and found a map. It shows an island with some buildings on it, but no location or name.'

'Do you think it's relevant?'

'It only has one word written on it. Kraken.'

'That's the code name for the missile system.'

'Yeah, we need to know the significance of the island.'

'At the bottom of the fence is a rock, that's our dead letter drop. There's a phone in there, I've checked but there's no coverage. Use it to take pictures of anything you find then put it back in there.'

Sinclair bent down, as if to tie her lace, removed the phone from under the rock and replaced it with the map. 'I'm going to search the guest house now. There doesn't seem to be any guards about.'

'I've been watching, there are only two left. I'll create a diversion tonight. As soon as you see the guards leave, you're good to search the barn.'

Sinclair took a drink of water and set off again, McGill kept an eye on her as she looped round the barn and approached the bungalow from the north. There were no cameras watching the pool, this area was kept private and was shielded from the gates and the barn. She took off her trainers and left them beside the pool. The bungalow's glass door was open and she stepped in.

The layout and décor inside was similar to the main house, just smaller. The kitchen and lounge shared a single, open-plan space with a small dining table. There was no desk or home office that might yield some evidence and no drawers or cupboards. She had a feeling that this search would be pointless. The bathroom was no better, just an empty medicine cabinet above the sink. Next to the sink, another door led to a walk-in wardrobe – nothing there either. The other end of the wardrobe opened into the bedroom, where a double bed was positioned below a four-bladed fan that turned slowly in the centre of the ceiling. On the other side of the bed was a bay window with thin curtains that blew in the breeze from the open window. As the curtains parted she saw a figure standing outside.

Sinclair dropped to the floor behind the bed; she didn't know if the guard had seen her or was just on a routine patrol.

Keeping low, she crawled out of the bedroom and into the kitchen, crouching behind the cooker. The guard walked across to the pool and stopped at the patio door, he must have seen her trainers. He came through the door and stood in the lounge. Sinclair needed a weapon; if she was caught now, Bazarov could have her killed. She slid a knife out of a block on the shelf beside her and readied herself for an attack.

The guard went into the bathroom and through to the walk-in wardrobe, this was Sinclair's only chance. She stood up, ran out of the bungalow and slipped into the water. The guard came out only a few seconds behind her. As he stood at the poolside, Sinclair surfaced, shaking water from her hair and wiping it from her face. She looked at him and gasped. 'You scared me.'

The guard had a thick Eastern European accent. 'I see you come here. Want to know what you do.'

'I've been for a run and wanted to cool down, is there a problem?'

He looked back at the barn then shook his head. 'Stay at main house, okay?'

Sinclair nodded. 'Okay, keep your hair on.'

The guard turned and walked back towards the barn. Sinclair puffed out her cheeks and let out a long breath. That was too close, she needed to switch on. She hadn't done anything like this for a long time and it showed. Tonight would be much more difficult, but she knew the barn was more likely to yield results. She climbed out of the pool and went to dry off.

McGill lowered his binoculars and shook his head. He'd seen the guard approach the bungalow but was unable to do anything about it. They'd got away with it this time, next time they might not be so lucky. From now on, he'd make sure he had all his kit with him. If anyone got that close again he'd take them out and get Ali away from there. She was more important to him than any mission MI6 wanted her for.

* * *

By sundown, McGill was back at the compound watching the guards through the green tint of his night vision goggles. The two men he'd seen during the day were now sitting outside the barn smoking, and drinking Tequila. They must have decided, with the boss away, it was time to kick back and relax. It would make searching the barn easier, no need to create a diversion or take the guards out, just wait for them to drink themselves unconscious.

He picked a spot in the fence, away from the cameras, and climbed over. He knew no one was watching, but old habits die hard. He kept low and approached the barn from the rear, out of sight of the guards. As he got closer, he dropped to a crawl and moved until he was within feet of the two men. He could hear them talking, Russian, Polish, it definitely sounded Eastern European, but he wasn't great with languages. Ali would know. She was fluent in a couple – another one of her strong points.

He watched for a short while to make sure the Russians weren't about to go on an impromptu patrol. One of them refreshed his tequila while the other lit up whatever it was they were smoking. It wasn't tobacco; McGill could tell that much from the smell that drifted towards him. They were too close to the barn for Sinclair to just walk in and start searching, but it didn't look like they had any intention of patrolling anything. At least it would be easier to move around the rest of the property without being spotted.

McGill made his way round the back of the barn and over to the main house. The only light was coming from Sinclair's bedroom but he knew she wasn't in there.

Sinclair had moved into position as soon as it was dark. She was crouched behind a trellis attached to the outside of the house. There was no moonlight but the light she'd left on in her room was enough that she could make out the outline of anyone approaching – before they saw her. She was dressed in a black tracksuit, T-shirt and beanie hat. She couldn't be seen with the naked eye but McGill's goggles gave him the edge and he could see her in the shadows. He checked in every direction then used a small torch to flash a signal.

Sinclair saw the light flash three times and realised that McGill had sneaked up without her seeing him, he was good at that, she should have expected it. She moved out of the shadows and quickly joined him next to the bungalow. 'Jesus, Frank, how do you do that?'

'Didn't you know? I'm a ninja.'

Sinclair smiled. 'Owning a pair of black pyjamas doesn't make you a ninja.'

'That's rich coming from someone dressed as Catwoman.'

She looked down at her outfit. 'It was all I could find. Anyway, what's the plan for tonight?'

McGill motioned towards the barn. 'The two Ivans have decided to have a little party out front. With the amount of tequila they've downed, and shit they've smoked, we'll get plenty of warning if they decide to come looking.'

Sinclair nodded. 'What's the best way in?'

'There's a window open at the back. It's small but you'll

get through it. I'll go round the front and keep an eye on the Ivans.' He handed her a small radio with an earpiece attached. 'If they move I'll let you know.'

Sinclair took the radio and slipped it in the top pocket of her shirt. 'Okay, let's get this done and we can go home.'

'Sounds good to me, Ali.' McGill put on his goggles and led the way back to the barn. 'Give me a couple of minutes to get in position. I'll give you one click on the radio when it's clear. Be careful.'

'You too, Frank.'

McGill moved quickly along the side of the barn and lay down next to the front corner. He slid forwards just enough to see where the guards were sitting. They hadn't moved, one was trying to relight his spliff and the other looked asleep. McGill got out his radio and pressed the push-to-talk button once.

Sinclair heard the single click in her ear, time to go. The window was only open a couple of inches but that was enough for her to check for any alarm sensors. She looked from every angle but couldn't see any cables. Windows like this would normally have a contact switch but, as this one was already open, she was pretty sure it didn't have one. She looked into the room for any telltale flashing lights from infrared sensors but couldn't see any of those either. Even if there were any fitted, she doubted the guards would have switched them on. She slid her hand through the opening, unhooked the latch and opened the window all the way.

The room on the other side was some kind of workshop. Various tools hung from the wall, on either side of the window, with a workbench underneath. Two metal racks on the opposite wall held a collection of cardboard boxes alongside containers of detergent and rolls of duct tape. At least she didn't have to worry about being seen while she was halfway through the window. She grabbed hold of the frame and, after one last look outside, climbed in.

Sinclair got down on her knees and looked under the workshop door. She could make out a dim light at the other end of the barn but saw no obvious movement. She checked for cables and sensors in the same way she had for the window and, again, found nothing. She gripped the handle and turned it. The door opened with a quiet click.

The main part of the barn was one big space that looked like a cross between a car mechanic's garage and a groundsman's hut. There were gardening tools and a ride-on lawnmower, a golf buggy in pieces, and two cars covered with tarpaulins. Part of the far end had been cleared and resembled a dormitory. There were two rows of collapsible camp beds, a television and a coffee pot. Sitting between the two rows of camp beds was a table with four chairs. The table had various magazines strewn across it, along with a pack of cards and a chessboard. A small fridge humming away in the corner completed the facilities; it reminded her of some of the army accommodation in Afghanistan.

A portable light had been set up by the main door, and to her right was a steel staircase that led up to a second level that was directly above the workshop. There was light coming through the steel mesh above her, it was dimmer and flickering, it must be where the cameras were monitored. That was the riskiest place to search but, by the look of the rest of the barn, the most likely to hold information. A single click on her radio and the reply from McGill meant the guards were still outside. She climbed the steel stairs and crouched down behind the guardrail.

There were two rooms on the second level: one that housed a row of monitors for the security system, and a second room set up as an office. Keeping below the level of the guard rail, she crawled into the office and closed the glass door behind her.

The desk in the office had three drawers full of the usual office junk: broken pens, stapler, Post-it notes. On top of the desk were a phone, notepad with several pages torn out, and a copy of the map that she had found in the main house. She scanned the rest of the office and found a waste basket with four pages from the notepad screwed up in it. She picked them all out and sealed them in a plastic bag, which she placed in her pocket.

There was even less in the monitoring room: two chairs in front of a bench that held four black and white monitors. No notepads or waste basket to look at and no drawers to search – she'd found everything there was to find, time to leave.

Back on the ground level, she went as close as she dared to the front of the barn but couldn't see anything interesting. It was obvious that Bazarov kept any important information either with him or in his head. She wouldn't find anything more unless she spoke to Jo, but that was dangerous. If Quinn was heavily involved in whatever the Russian was planning, confiding in her would be suicidal.

Sinclair made her way to the workshop and climbed through the window, putting it back on the latch as it had been when she'd got there. She gave two clicks on her radio to signal to McGill that she was clear and within a few minutes he was standing beside her. 'How did you get on?'

'Not much in there, they're using it as accommodation for

Bazarov's army. I don't like the look of it, he's gearing up for something big. These guys are all mercenaries.'

McGill nodded. 'There are too many of them to be just for security. Did you find anything useful?'

'Just these.' She handed him the four pieces of screwed up paper that she had picked up from the waste basket. 'They might have something on them. I didn't get a chance to look.'

'I'll get copies to Carter, he can check them out and decide what happens next. You need to tell Quinn you're leaving. You've done all you can.'

'If I could talk to Jo about it I'd find out what's really going on.'

McGill shook his head. 'Too risky. If she's in on it, you'd be blowing your own cover.'

Sinclair held up her hands. 'I know, I know. Let's just see if there's anything on those scraps of paper first, then I'll start making excuses to leave.' She handed McGill the radio and set off back to the house.

Both guards had slept right through most of Sinclair's incursion into the barn but one of them now stirred from his drink and drug induced stupor and rubbed his eyes. His buddy was still asleep so he took a quick swig from the tequila bottle and walked to the side of the barn to ease the pressure in his bladder.

As the guard was refastening his trousers, he saw someone moving from the barn towards the house. There was no one else here, only the woman who was staying in the house. What was she up to? Walking as steadily as his drunken body would allow, he stumbled after her.

McGill stayed where he was and watched Sinclair heading for the bungalow. He heard a noise off to his right, stood back against the wall and watched as the guard appeared from the corner of the barn and set off in pursuit of Ali.

The night vision goggles gave McGill a perfect view of what was happening. The guard followed Sinclair's path to begin with then veered off through the line of bushes and sped up. His course would intercept hers at the pool. McGill wasn't worried about staying quiet, and sacrificed stealth for speed. Catching up to the guard was more important.

Sinclair rounded the bungalow and drew level with the pool when the Russian voice shouted at her, 'Don't move.'

She froze; she wasn't in a position to do anything else, the guard was at the other side of the pool with a handgun levelled at her head. She couldn't rush him and she didn't have a weapon of her own. All she could do was put her hands on her head and turn to face him.

The guard had one eye closed as he tried to focus on her. 'Turn around and walk backwards over to me.'

Sinclair did as she was told. As she moved she looked to try and find something to help her out of this, but there was nothing. Her only option was to attack as soon as she was in striking distance.

The guard stepped towards her. 'Stop. On your knees.'

He was three metres from her and well outside her range. Even though the guard was drunk he still knew what he was doing.

'Now, lie down, put your hands behind your back and cross your legs.'

Sinclair looked over her shoulder; if she didn't attack now she was as good as dead.

'Do it now.'

The guard barked the order but Sinclair had seen movement

behind the bungalow. A black-clad figure burst out of the shadows; the guard tried to spin round and aim his weapon but McGill had already closed the gap between them. He drove his shoulder hard into the Russian's ribcage and knocked him to the ground. The guard's head slammed into the concrete and their momentum took them both into the pool.

Sinclair looked into the water but could only see a dark outline of the two men against the white tiles, there was no way to tell what was going on. She picked up the handgun the guard had lost when he was hit and dropped to one knee, checking all around her, she had to watch Frank's back.

The guard broke the surface and Sinclair took aim but quickly realised that he was no longer a threat. He wasn't moving, he was floating, face down, with a cloud of blood spreading out from the ragged gash in the back of his head. McGill appeared at the side of the pool, coughing and spitting out some of the water he'd swallowed.

'You okay, Frank?'

'Yeah, he didn't fight me for long. I think the head wound had finished him already.' He climbed out of the pool and looked over at the dead guard. 'We need to get out of here, before this job turns into more of a cluster-fuck than it already is.'

'I'm not leaving Jo on her own to face the shitstorm this'll cause, she needs our help.'

McGill grabbed Sinclair's arm and moved her into the shadow of the bungalow. The last thing they needed was for the other guard to show up and catch them out in the open. 'If we hide the body, they'll know something's wrong and we're fucked. If we leave it here, they'll know something's wrong and we're fucked. You can't stay, this changes everything.'

'Look, Frank, being undercover is what I do best, you know that. I can deny all knowledge and play the dumb blonde. "How terrible, a guard got drunk and fell in the pool, poor man." They'll buy it.'

McGill didn't like it. 'And if they don't?'

'Whatever Bazarov is up to he needs Jo. If he didn't, he wouldn't be here. She's on the verge of a breakdown, killing me would tip her over the edge and mess up his plans.'

'You're taking a hell of a gamble.'

'I can take care of myself. Besides, Carter needs time to analyse any data without Bazarov knowing we're on to him.'

Sinclair was right, as usual, but McGill still wasn't happy about it. 'If there's even a hint that Bazarov knows who you are, get the hell out.'

She squeezed his shoulder. 'I will.'

McGill watched until Sinclair was back in the house, threw the guards weapon into the pool and left.

* * *

Back at the camper McGill checked his watch. The quicker he got the intell to Carter, the quicker they could pull out of there. He opened the plastic bag and emptied the four scraps of paper onto the table. He opened them up and flattened them out as much as he could. The first three showed nothing, just scribbles and doodles – the kind of thing people do absentmindedly while on the phone. There was nothing he could make sense of but he copied them anyway; they might mean something to the analyst back in London.

The fourth scrap was much more interesting. Amongst the random scribbles were three words: Kraken, Apocalypse, and

Lone Star. Kraken was the same word written on the map Ali had found, the codename for the missile system. Apocalypse didn't sound good, could be another codename, the American military did like to use dramatic sounding names for things. The third word, Lone Star, he'd seen written all over the place in Texas – The Lone Star State. It had a six-figure number next to it, which could be anything from a telephone number to a grid reference. He photographed it and sent an anonymous email over his satellite phone to Carter in London. There was a six-hour time difference, Carter could get to work straight away while McGill kept an eye on Sinclair.

Chapter 9

Simeon Carter didn't make it to his bed most nights, preferring to snatch a few hours in front of the hotel's TV. He was always the same when he had operatives in the field, caring too much to sleep well while they were at the sharp end. He was woken by a beep from the phone beside his chair. He picked it up and swiped his finger across its fingerprint scanner. An icon on the screen blinked, he had a message from Frank. He opened up his laptop and clicked on the attachments. They didn't look like much, just scraps, but in the past he'd seen thrown away pieces of paper jeopardise some of the Cold War's biggest operations. Danny needed to see these. He had the background information to decide if the words on the paper were significant or just random scribbles. Carter selected the email and forwarded it to a third anonymous account, writing one word in the subject line: Broadsword.

Danny Kinsella put down his coffee cup next to the keyboard on his desk. He looked at the six screens laid out in front of him that he used to access and monitor multiple networks simultaneously. He didn't have a desktop computer like most people. He had installed a professional grade rack of processors and servers in his flat to allow him to do all his work from there. The equipment was water cooled and the room air-conditioned for optimum temperature. He lived in the penthouse of his block so didn't have to worry about neighbours beside or above him. He had the floor soundproofed to block out anything being heard from the floor below and had the room screened to block out all radio signals. No one could eavesdrop on anything he was doing.

He had several software applications to mask and fake his identity – he routinely routed his traffic through servers in other countries and utilised the Tor network for maximum anonymity. Even government agencies couldn't track him down.

He accessed the disposable email address he'd created and opened the pictures Simeon had sent him. He processed the first three through software that would look for patterns in the seemingly random lines and swirls, but he didn't expect to find anything. He opened the fourth and immediately recognised Kraken as the word on the map. They already knew that was the code name for the missile system.

He'd identified the map as an island that belonged to QRL Global. Leatherback Cay sat in the Caribbean, sixteen miles off the coast of the Yucatán peninsula, where Mexico borders Belize. The Cay had a small harbour and a collection of buildings that QRL used for its research and development. A small workforce was stationed there to keep the facility running, with engineers and scientists either shipped or flown in when needed. Leatherback Cay had been used to test the Kraken but, once the system had been proved and deployed, that equipment was mothballed and the island no longer hosted any weapons.

He ran the other two words through a quick search but they

84

were too common and threw up hundreds of thousands of hits. He set up a search to look for Apocalypse and Lone Star in the same sentence as Kraken, and another search to look for Lone Star in the same sentence as the six-figure number. He set the searches running through normal internet sites, conspiracy theory sites, and UK and US government networks. This was going to take time; all he could do was check back regularly to see if anything had been flagged up. He sent an email back to Carter and arranged a meeting.

Carter left the hotel and set off for the nearby park. They could have met at the hotel, or Kinsella's flat, but it was better to vary the locations. Meeting up too often would be a change in their behaviour, something any watchers would be looking for. They wouldn't be overheard in the park and could see if anyone was watching them. Carter knew it was unlikely but he wasn't willing to risk it.

He walked to the middle of the park and sat on a bench near the boating lake. He took some bread from his jacket and threw it to the ducks, just an old man passing the time. Kinsella arrived and placed a newspaper between them. 'Afternoon, Simeon.'

'Afternoon, Danny. You got anything for me?'

'There's an envelope in the newspaper, all the details are in there. I didn't want to email it, it's got keywords in that could show up in a search. I'm still working on the new stuff.'

Carter picked up the newspaper and tucked it in his pocket. 'Anything we should be worried about?'

'Not yet. The map is a test facility that hasn't been used much recently. I've checked all the government agencies and there's info on Kraken, Quinn and Bazarov but nothing to link them all together. There is mention of Bazarov having a contact within the government, some kind of mole, but no clues to the contacts identity. He just has the code name Vadim, we need to watch for him, other than that, nothing.'

'You need to keep looking, we can't afford to be blindsided by something we've missed. McGill and Sinclair are depending on us to pull them out if it really hits the fan.'

'I'll let you know as soon as I've got something.' Kinsella stood up and shook Carter's hand. 'Take care, Simeon.'

'You too, Danny.' Carter walked off in the opposite direction to Kinsella and back to his hotel.

When he got to his room he took off his coat and opened the envelope Kinsella had given him. It was all pretty mundane, background stuff, nothing that would help Ali and Frank in the field. The talk of a mole within the security services was worrying. He'd had to deal with that kind of thing in the past and it never ended well. He would have to find out who it was just so he knew who might come after them.

All he could do for McGill and Sinclair was tell them what he had and get them to question Quinn about it. It was looking like that would be the only way to get the information Lancaster needed. He opened his laptop and sent an email from his anonymous account. All it said was:

Map is Leatherback Cay off Belize. Used as test facility for K. Approach Q and question.

He settled in his recliner and turned on the TV.

Danny Kinsella got back to his flat and checked the hits his searches had thrown up – there were still thousands. It was going to be a long, long night. He made himself a cup of coffee and sat down to analyse the data.

* * *

In another air-conditioned equipment room, on the other side of the Atlantic, young FBI analyst Robert Tyler sat at his work station and began a search through the picture databases to try and find a match for the photo he'd been given. It wasn't great quality and was from a camera in a shop across the street from a crime scene. It showed a blonde woman getting into a motorhome in the car park of a motel. He had cleaned up the picture as much as he could and was now running it through facial recognition software. If the woman had been photographed by any government agency in the past, he should get a match.

Chapter 10

McGill switched off his satellite phone and put it in his daysack. He wanted to keep it with him in case Carter gave the order to abort the mission. He wasn't happy with the way things were going, they were pushing it too far and taking too many risks. There was no way Sinclair could pump Quinn for information about the island without giving the game away. They would have to gamble on Quinn being involved only under duress or unwilling to see Sinclair get hurt. It was a big gamble.

The previous night's events could blow Ali's cover as it was, without inviting more shit to rain down on them. His plan for today was to get back to the house and keep an eye on things. In fact, that was his plan for the rest of this mission, everything else could take a backseat.

Bazarov and Quinn were due back at the house in a few hours and McGill wanted to be within reach. The body floating in the pool was going to cause an extreme reaction of some sort; there was just no way of knowing what it would be. The arms dealer would go for either Sinclair or his surviving guard. If he went for Ali, McGill had to be in the compound ready to jump in and pull her out. Bringing out Quinn, and taking down Bazarov too, would be a bonus, but not his priority.

If the Russian believed Ali's story that she'd slept through the whole thing and it must have been an accident, then the other guard was going to have a bad day. Hungover and unable to explain how his buddy had ended up face down in the pool, McGill was sure that Bazarov would be an unforgiving boss. Whichever way it went, it wasn't going to be a good day for someone.

McGill gathered his kit together and put it all in his daysack, filled up his water pouch and grabbed the ghillie suit. He had two hours before it got light and he wanted to be in position within the compound by then. Getting in wouldn't be a problem, Ivan number one was dead in the pool and number two was passed out drunk and stoned. Once the rest of the Russian's private army came back however, staying hidden would be a problem.

Sinclair sat in her room, going over her story in her head. She had to be able to repeat it, without any mistakes, under pressure. If Bazarov got violent, she had to force herself not to react like a cage fighter. She had to give the impression that she was frightened, weak and incapable of being involved. The question was, how far did she let it go? At what point did she accept that she was in real danger and protect herself? It would be a tough call but something that she'd had to do in the past. She got into bed and tried her best to get a couple of hours sleep.

McGill arrived at the compound fence and climbed over in the same place as he had the previous night. He found a spot behind the house, where the vegetation matched his ghillie suit, and lay down. He pulled out his binoculars and checked his line of sight. From where he was he could see across the pool to the top of the driveway, and into the kitchen and living areas at the back of the house. He got as comfortable as he could and settled in for a long wait.

As the sun began to shine through the gap in Sinclair's bedroom window, her door was kicked open and Bazarov burst in. 'Get dressed and get downstairs now.'

Sinclair sat up, shocked. She'd been caught unawares. 'What's going on?'

Bazarov put one knee on the bed and brought his face close to hers. 'I said, now.' He stormed out of the room and back down the stairs.

This looked bad. Sinclair considered making a bolt for it. She could climb down from the window and run but her chances of success were slim. She threw on some clothes and went down the stairs, her mind racing, going through her story again.

Quinn was sitting at the dining table, Bazarov stood next to her. He pointed at the table and looked at Sinclair. 'Sit down.'

Sinclair pulled out the chair closest to her. As she sat down, Quinn held her hand. 'Are you okay, Ali?'

'I'm fine. What's going on?'

'One of the guards is dead. In the pool.'

'What?' Sinclair turned round to try and get a view through the side window but couldn't see anything. 'How did it happen?'

Bazarov slammed his hand down on the table, which made both women jump. 'You tell me, you were here.'

'I don't know what happened. I barely left the house yesterday.'

'Tell me exactly what you did.' He sat down at the head of the table.

Sinclair looked at Quinn; her friend was frightened, it showed in her eyes. Sinclair gripped her hand. 'I spent most of the day just hanging in here. I did go for a quick run and a swim in the afternoon but the guards were staring at me. One of them came over and watched me in the pool, he creeped me out. I spent the rest of the day inside.'

Quinn jabbed a finger at Bazarov. 'I told you not to leave Ali here with those pigs.'

'It still doesn't explain how he ended up dead.'

'I told you, I don't know. It sounded like they were having a party when I went to bed.'

Quinn pointed at Bazarov with her head. 'His other goon was passed out when we got back.'

'Well there you go. He must have got drunk and fallen in.'

Bazarov stood up and walked into the kitchen. He opened a drawer and took out a twelve-inch carving knife. 'Okay. I'm only going to ask you one more time then I'm going to start cutting. How did he end up in the pool?'

'I don't know. Really, I don't. Jo, tell him I wouldn't do anything like that.'

'She wouldn't, Viktor, please believe her.'

Bazarov grabbed Sinclair's wrist and pushed her hand flat on the table. He positioned the knife on her little finger and gradually applied pressure. The razor-sharp blade sliced through the first layers of skin and blood began to seep from the wound.

Quinn held on to Sinclair's other hand. 'Please, Viktor, don't.'

Sinclair's eyes were wide with fear, her voice faltered. She pulled her hand out of Quinn's grip. 'I don't know. I've already told you. Please.' If Bazarov didn't back off now Sinclair would strike; he would be dead before he hit the floor.

The Russian pulled the knife away and threw it onto the table. 'Stay inside.' He slowly turned and left the house.

'Are you okay, Ali?'

Sinclair checked her finger. 'I'm fine. Who the hell is that guy, Jo, what have you got yourself into?'

'I can't tell you, it's better for you that way.'

Sinclair had decided that the only way they were going to get the information they needed was from Quinn herself, despite the risks. 'I'm your friend, whatever it is you can tell me, I can help.'

'Not this time, Ali, this is too big even for you.'

Sinclair sensed this was the opportunity she had been waiting for, Quinn was ready to talk. 'Jo, there are things you don't know about me, things you need to know, I can help you.'

Quinn opened a cupboard and took out a small first-aid kit. 'Let's get your finger patched up first.'

Sinclair looked out of the back window and ran her fingers through her hair. McGill saw the signal and let out the deep breath he'd been holding in; she'd pulled it off. He retrained his binoculars on the pool and watched as Bazarov's men pulled the body of the guard out of the water. Bazarov appeared and stopped beside them for a minute, issuing orders. As his men carried the body away, Bazarov walked over to the bungalow and went inside. He wasn't happy, his body language gave that away. McGill knew the only reason someone like Bazarov would let Quinn and Sinclair live is because he needed them. Sinclair wasn't out of the woods yet, Bazarov had plans for her, and McGill wasn't going anywhere until he was sure she was safe.

Quinn and Sinclair sat close to each other at the dining table. They held each other's hands and, even though they were alone in the house, talked in whispers.

'This is going to be hard for you to hear, Jo, but there's no easy way to say it. I was sent here by the British Secret Intelligence Service to find out what you're up to.'

Quinn pulled away from Sinclair and tried to let go of her hands but Sinclair held them tight. Quinn looked around as if she expected someone to be watching. 'What? I thought you were my friend.'

'I am your friend, Jo, that's why I'm here. Not for them or anyone else. I'm here to help you.'

Tears flowed down Quinn's face and dripped from her chin. 'You don't understand what's at stake.'

'Then tell me. I know who Bazarov is and MI6 know you met with him in London. That's why they sent me here.'

'But you escaped from prison, how did they find you?'

'It's a long story but an old friend of mine is here as my backup, he always knew where I was.'

Quinn looked down at the table, sobbing for what seemed like an age, then looked back up at Sinclair. 'It's my kids, he's got my kids.'

'I knew you wouldn't be involved in something like this. I knew you had to be under some kind of threat. What about Liam?'

'Liam's dead. They killed him to warn me that they meant business.'

Quinn was trembling, close to breaking down completely, but Sinclair had to keep pushing. 'I'm so sorry, Jo, I really am. What does Bazarov want from you? Is it to do with Kraken?' '

Quinn looked surprised. 'They know already?'

'It's the thing they're interested in the most.'

'Yes, it's the Kraken system. Bazarov is making me break in to it, to give him control.'

'Jesus, Jo. Are you telling me he's planning to nuke somewhere?'

Quinn could only nod. Sinclair tried to understand what she had just heard. This was much bigger than anyone had thought. MI6 were trying to stop him from selling secrets, not setting off a nuke. 'Look, this can't happen. I have to get a message to Frank. They need to take Bazarov out.'

'No. He'll kill my kids.' Quinn was beginning to panic.

'You're going to have to trust me on this. I can get you out of here and we can get your kids back. Do you know where they are?'

Quinn nodded. 'They're on the Cay. He lets me talk to them sometimes. His men are holding some of my engineers down there. They've been setting up the equipment and systems.'

'Is he ready to go?' Sinclair needed some idea of how much time they had.

'He can't launch anything without the right authorisations. I can't get him past that. I don't know how he plans to foil the security blocks.'

'Where did you go yesterday?'

'My office in Houston. He made me organise transportation for men and equipment he wanted sent to the Cay.'

'What kind of equipment?'

Quinn shook her head and was becoming more agitated. 'I don't know, Ali. He doesn't fill me in on the details. He just said it would be in shipping containers and his men had gone to organise it.' Quinn's voice grew louder as emotion got the better of her. 'I'm not in on his plans.'

Sinclair's voice was quiet and calm, 'I know you're not, Jo. I just need to know as much information as you can give me. Okay?'

'I'm sorry, Ali. It's just ...' Quinn stopped, unable to finish her sentence, not wanting to think of the consequences of what was happening.

'Jo, I need to know if Bazarov is planning to go to the island himself.'

Quinn cleared her throat and blew her nose on a tissue. 'Yes, he wants me there too.'

'That's good, Jo. It'll help us get to the kids. We just need to sit tight.'

'Can you really help me, Ali?'

'I promise I'll do everything I can for you. You'll get your kids back. But you'll have to be strong for a little while longer. Do you trust me?'

A brief hint of a smile crossed Quinn's face. 'Yes. Yes, I do.'

'That's good.' Sinclair past Quinn a fresh tissue. 'Now, you'll have to carry on doing what he wants, it'll take time to put a plan in place.'

Quinn wiped her eyes. 'I'll try.'

* * *

Bazarov sat in his bungalow reading the file on his laptop. He'd spent the day checking up on Sinclair, she was ex-British Army. Served in Afghanistan and Iraq. Imprisoned in Mexico and escaped after two years. Her story checked out with every one of his contacts, but there was something about her, something he wasn't sure about. He knew some of his men were complete fuck-ups at times, but getting drunk and falling in the pool

95

wasn't something they would do.

The sun threw long shadows as it slid down towards the horizon. He shut the lid of the laptop and picked up a glass of whiskey from the table. As he looked out of the window towards the pool he stopped, the glass halfway to his lips. The low, evening sun was shining through the window on the thin layer of dust that coated the bungalow's wooden floor. He put down his glass and got on his hands and knees, his face close to the floor. In the dust, picked out by the sun, were footprints. Not just his booted prints, but smaller imprints of bare feet. Someone had been in the bungalow while he was away.

Chapter 11

Danny Kinsella sat in his flat and stared at his screens. After several searches had yielded nothing, he'd finally come across a file on the US Defence Department's servers titled: Apocalypse Protocol. It made for pretty unbelievable reading. He printed out the main points and sent a text message to arrange another meeting, it was getting late, but Carter would want to see this. Kinsella knew that Carter worried a great deal about the people he had in the field and did everything he could to protect them. The death of Danny's father had affected the old man more than he'd ever admitted. He grabbed his coat and left for the park.

Carter was sitting on the bench next to the boating lake when Kinsella arrived. He quickly looked along the path but there was no one else in sight. He sat down on the bench and handed Carter the cup of coffee he'd bought on his way in. 'Evening, Simeon. Milk and two sugars as usual, keep the cold away.'

'Thanks, Danny.' He took a sip, steam misting up his glasses. 'You find something?'

'I found something that could be big, but hopefully it isn't yet.' He put the pages he'd printed down on the bench. 'I printed out the main points.'

Carter took the printouts. 'I'll have a look at those later. Can you give me a quick rundown?'

'Basically, it seems that the Americans want to keep ultimate control over NATO's new nuclear weapon. They want a little insurance that it won't fall into the wrong hands.'

'What kind of insurance?'

'Using the European based Kraken requires British and American agreement. The Americans wanted to be sure that, if Britain fell or was taken over by insurgents, then the US still had control of the Kraken's missiles.'

Carter had seen this before, during the Cold War. Some in the American military didn't trust anyone, not even allies. 'How were they planning to do that?'

'A little something they call the Apocalypse Protocol. The US executive can take over the European Kraken and re-target it, even against Britain if necessary, from terminals in the US.'

Carter couldn't believe what he was hearing. 'No British government would sign up to that.'

'Maybe that's what MI6 are keen to hide. Maybe we're covering the arse of the person who did sign up to it.'

'Is the agreement mutual? Could Britain take control of the US side of Kraken?'

Kinsella shook his head. 'The Americans would never allow that. The Apocalypse Protocol allows the North American missiles to be launched from Britain, but only by US officials based there. The terminals would be housed in secure American facilities.'

'But what would Bazarov get from that information? It would cause a scandal if it leaked out, but that's it.' Carter couldn't see what Bazarov could hope to gain. 'Could it be used by anyone else? Could someone like you hack in to it?'

'No, that would be impossible. The Kraken isn't connected to the outside world. It has its own secure network of control centres. Even if it was possible for Bazarov to get the launch codes, which it isn't, they would be useless unless he was at one of the control terminals.'

'Would Leatherback Cay have a terminal?'

Kinsella nodded. 'That's where all the testing was done, but the American missiles still couldn't be launched from there without valid codes.'

'What if the Apocalypse Protocol was activated?'

'That could bypass the normal requirement to have the codes, but Bazarov would still need the biometric data of the President, or Vice President to launch. If the protocol was being used, then it's probable that all normal processes had already failed. The US introduced the biometric data as a backup to allow the missiles to be used even if the launch codes were lost.'

There seemed to be plenty of fail-safes in place, but Carter had a feeling in his gut. Bazarov wasn't stupid, there must be something in this for him. 'Can anyone else issue a launch command?'

'The Apocalypse Protocol can be set in motion by two people named on the survivors list. That's the list of who takes over if the top brass gets taken out.'

Carter had heard of the list before. He knew there was always a pecking order of senior military and politicians who took over if the executive fell. 'Can you find out exactly who is on that list?'

'I'll see what I can do. This list exists for all US nuclear weapons, the current executive and senior military are on there, but the Apocalypse Protocol's list will be out of date. It was probably tested using the list that was in place when it was developed a few years back. It won't have been refreshed in the same way when the administration changed. Once phase two goes live, the list will have to be updated with the new executive's details and agreed with the British anyway.'

'We need to be sure, Danny. We need to know if there's a credible threat. Did you have any luck with Lone Star and the number?'

'No, too many hits. Have you any idea how many businesses and places in Texas are called Lone Star something or other? There's even a city called Lone Star. So far, there's nothing I can connect Bazarov to.'

'I'll see if Frank has come up with anything else when I contact him later. Keep looking, Danny. I'm starting to get an uneasy feeling about this one.'

'I'll let you know when I find something.'

The two men stood up and Kinsella patted Carter on the shoulder before walking off across the park. Carter was worried. The Kraken sounded secure enough but there was always something that got missed. He finished his coffee and threw the empty cup into the bin beside the bench.

* * *

Across the Atlantic, FBI analyst Robert Tyler was giving a briefing to his boss, Special Agent in Charge Thomas Johnson. Tyler tapped the touchpad on his laptop and an image from the projector filled the screen that covered one wall of the meeting room. 'This is the still from the one-sided gang shootout at the motel. I've cleaned it up and run it through our facial recognition software to compare it with the image database.'

'And what did you find?'

He tapped the laptop again; an image of Sinclair appeared next to the motel still. 'The system flagged up this woman.'

'Who is she?'

The analyst brought a document up on the screen. 'Alison Sinclair, British national, escaped from a prison in Mexico.' He slid a paper copy of the document across the table.

His boss picked it up and looked through the details. 'She was in for drug smuggling?'

'That's right.'

'That makes this easier. She's smuggling in drugs, the gang didn't like it, and they had a shootout. No mystery there.'

'I don't agree. She, and an unknown male, took out six heavily armed gang members before they could fire a single shot. That takes training.'

'Says here she's ex-military.'

'They'd have to be more than regular military to do what they did.'

'So, what do you suggest?'

'I just need a little more time. I'll run the image through some more databases, see if she pops up anywhere else.'

'Okay, do a bit more digging and see what you can find. Don't spend too long on it though.'

'Right Boss.'

Chapter 12

J o Quinn walked into the kitchen from her office. 'Bazarov wants me over in the bungalow. What am I going to do?'

Sinclair stood up from the table. 'Go. See what he wants. He can't hurt you, you're too valuable to him.'

'But what about you?'

'I'll be fine. If he wanted to hurt me he would have done it this morning. You go, I'll try and contact Frank. When the time comes, he can take care of Bazarov, but MI6 need to come up with a plan to get your kids back.'

Quinn left the kitchen and went outside. She walked round the back of the house and headed for the pool. Once Quinn was out of site, Sinclair went to one of the rear windows and looked out. She knew McGill had planned to be there, but she had no idea if he actually was. She took her small torch from her pocket and pointed it out of the window; two short flashes followed by a longer one, their agreed signal.

McGill was watching as Quinn left the house and crossed the patio. He watched her momentarily before turning his binoculars back to Sinclair's position. The torch signal was clear; Sinclair had something important to pass on to him. He lifted his MP5 and switched on the laser sight. The red dot momentarily appeared on the window next to Sinclair, she knew he had seen her signal and would make his way towards the house as they had planned.

Quinn walked into the bungalow, Bazarov was sitting at the table with a laptop open in front of him. The light from the screen lit up his face and reflected off his glasses. 'Have a seat, Josephine.'

Quinn sat opposite him, fidgeting, her facial tick getting worse. 'What do you want? I've done everything you've asked.'

'That's right, Josephine, you have. I thought you'd like to see your children.' He turned the laptop towards her. On the screen was a video feed showing Quinn's two young boys staring wide-eyed at the camera. Quinn held her hand to her mouth, the image reflecting off the moistness in her eyes. She cleared her throat and tried to appear calm. 'Hello, guys, are you okay?'

The two boys sat close to each other, hand-in-hand, terrified. Tom was the eldest, eight years old, and the spitting image of his dad. Aiden was six and looking to his elder brother for support and protection. Tom's voice was faint, 'When are you coming to get us mom?'

Quinn's chin trembled as she fought to hold back the emotion that threatened to burst through her calm veneer. 'Soon, boys, mommy will be there soon.'

Bazarov took off his glasses and placed them on the table. 'I'm going to ask you a few questions, Josephine. Please don't insult me by trying to lie.'

'Questions? About what?'

'About your friend, Alison Sinclair. I want to know what she's up to.'

'I don't know what you mean. She's escaped from that

hellhole of a prison and just needs a friend. I'm sure you can check up on her.'

'I have checked, but there's something she's hiding, and I think you know what it is.'

Quinn shook her head. 'I ... I don't know anything. I mean, she's not hiding anything.'

'Then tell me this, Josephine, who was it that sneaked into the Bungalow while we were away? Who was here alone when one of my men died?'

'But that was an accident.'

'NO.' Bazarov slammed his fist on the table. 'I don't believe that.' He pointed at the laptop screen. 'Now, tell me everything. Your children's lives depend on it.'

On the screen, Tom and Aiden hugged each other. A man stood over them, a nine-millimetre automatic in his hand.

Quinn stood up, her hands held out towards the screen as if she was trying to grab the boys. To hug them to her chest and protect them. 'No, No, please. I'll tell you. I'll tell you everything.'

* * *

After acknowledging Sinclair's signal, McGill had crawled, a few inches at a time, towards the house. It had taken him over an hour, but he was now crouched underneath the window that Sinclair had stood at earlier. He raised himself up, just enough to see over the bottom of the window, and looked into the house.

Sinclair sat at the dining table, alone, drinking coffee. McGill placed the laser sight's red dot on the back of Sinclair's hand. She brushed at it, as if to wipe it away, and checked behind her. She moved over to the window and opened it a few inches. 'Frank?'

'Who were you expecting, the tooth fairy?' McGill moved into the light. Wearing his ghillie suit, and with his face coated in camo grease, he looked like a talking bush – only his wide grin gave him away. 'You ready to get out of here yet?'

'Not just yet.' Sinclair handed him a folded sheet of paper. 'I've written everything down on there, you need to get it to Carter.'

'He sent us a message. The map you found is Leatherback Cay. It's a private island in the Caribbean, not far from the Mexico Belize border. He wants you to question Quinn about it, but I'm not happy with that.'

'I already have, she came clean about everything. Bazarov is holding Quinn's kids hostage, and he's forcing her to break in to the Kraken system using something she called the Apocalypse Protocol. Bazarov is trying to launch a nuclear strike.'

McGill tucked the paper into his jacket. 'Holy shit, I don't think Carter was expecting anything like that.'

'Not even close. MI6 need to arrange a rescue for the kids, we can deal with Bazarov ourselves.'

'I'll get this straight to Carter, you watch your back, Ali. With this much at stake it could go pear shaped really quick.' He handed her one of the Glocks and a spare magazine. 'Keep this with you. If there's a problem, protect yourself. I'll be near.'

'Who are you, my mother? You worry too much, get out of here, McGill.'

He disappeared into the shadows and Sinclair closed the window. She didn't want to risk keeping the weapon with her all the time, so she went upstairs and hid it under her mattress. She returned to the kitchen just as Quinn arrived in the house. 'Are you okay, Jo? What did he want?'

Quinn was trembling, her face damp and streaked with mascara. 'It was just more questions about the Kraken and Leatherback Cay. He did let me speak to the kids though.'

Sinclair put her arms around Quinn. 'That's good, did they look okay?'

'They were frightened, Ali. I have to protect them. I have to do whatever he wants.'

Sinclair could see that Quinn was close to losing it. It wasn't surprising, husband killed and kids kidnapped, it must be hell. 'It's okay, I understand. We can get out of this. I promise.'

'I don't know what I'd do if something happened to them.'

'When Frank gets the message back to London they'll know what to do. You'll be back with Tom and Aiden in no time.' Sinclair hated herself for telling such a blatant lie. Quinn must know that the chances of getting the boys back were slim. 'Come over and have a seat.' Sinclair guided Quinn over to the sofa and they both sat down.

'Whatever happens, Ali, I need you to know that everything I did was for them. I never meant to hurt anyone.'

'I know that, Jo, and so will everyone else once this is all over.' She had to get Quinn's mind on to something else, even if it was just for an hour or two. 'Why don't you use your magic and rustle us up something to eat? I don't know about you but I'm starving.'

Quinn ran her fingers through her hair. Her hands came to rest on the back of her neck for a few seconds, and then, with a deep breath, she stood up. 'I could use a drink. You go down to the cellar and get us some wine and I'll get started in the kitchen.'

Sinclair felt a little uneasy; Quinn's mood swings weren't a good sign. Hopefully Frank could get some sort of decision from the suits in London and get back here. It was looking more and more likely that they would have to grab Quinn and force her to get out without the boys. She watched her in the kitchen, wandering from fridge to sink to cooker, almost in a daze.

Quinn returned Sinclair's gaze. 'What does a girl have to do to get a drink around here?'

Sinclair got up from the sofa and held up her hands in mock surrender. 'Okay, okay, I'm going. Do you want red or white?'

'Red, I think, unless you prefer something else. Better make it two bottles, the good stuff is at the back.'

Sinclair crossed the kitchen and walked down the corridor to the cellar. She flicked the light switch and opened the door. A set of wooden stairs, with a handrail, led down into the coolness of the cellar. Several rows of wine racks stretched away from the bottom of the stairs. The wine cellar was the biggest Sinclair had ever seen – although, it was only the second one she'd been in. When it came to wine, all she knew was that it came in red and white. Other than the odd glass with a meal, her preference was beer, occasionally a cocktail if she was feeling exotic. After a quick look at the first few racks she went to the back of the room, picked two bottles of red at random and hoped she'd made the right choice.

Back at the top of the wooden steps she kicked the door shut behind her. 'I picked a couple of bottles of red, Jo. I've no idea if they're any good but—' A sudden noise behind her warned her too late. A powerful forearm was already tightening its grip across her throat, cutting off her air. She didn't have long. She had to stop herself from blacking out. She lifted her knee and brought the heel of her boot down hard on the top of her attacker's foot. He gave a pained grunt and the grip around her neck loosened. She moved her head to one side and, twisting her body, smashed the first bottle of wine in his face. He staggered backwards, spitting out blood and teeth.

As Sinclair tried to follow up with a punch, another assailant appeared from behind her spluttering victim. He rushed at her, arms outstretched, aiming for her throat. She swung the remaining bottle in front of her and made contact with the second attacker's head. The bottle shattered and the blow knocked him to the floor, writhing, hands clamped on the gaping wound that the broken glass had left in his skin.

A third attacker hit her with his shoulder in the small of her back, knocking her off balance. As she hit the floor, a fourth and fifth pair of hands held her down. She felt the scratch of the hypodermic pricking her arm, her vision blurred, and noises echoed inside her head. She felt her strength and feeling drain away from her body and then everything was dark.

* * *

Sinclair's eyes flickered open. Her head felt like it was full of cotton wool. The throbbing pain began behind her eyes and seemed to travel down to her neck in waves as her heart pounded. She could make out a dim light but her vision was still blurred, she screwed up her eyes and shook her head to try and clear the fog but it was no use. She realised she had a canvas sack over her head. Her hands were zip-tied behind her back and rope bound her to the chair she was sitting on. She didn't know what had been in the sack before it was placed over her head, but the smell was overpowering. The tape over her mouth meant she could only breathe through her nose and she swallowed hard as she tried to hold back the feelings of nausea. The last thing she needed now was to throw up.

She could hear muffled noises, low murmuring voices, and the sound of feet shuffling. This was about control – fear and control. Bazarov wanted her to know that he was in charge.

Footsteps approached her from behind. Someone hit her hard on the back of the head and shouted in her ear, 'Wake up.'

The sack was pulled off and she took as deep a breath as she could but only succeeded in sucking in dust. With her mouth covered she couldn't take in the air she needed between coughs and began to choke. She couldn't breathe and began to struggle against her bindings in panic.

'Let her breathe.' Quinn pleaded with Bazarov.

The guard behind Sinclair grabbed a handful of her hair and pulled her head back. Bazarov took a step forwards and bent over her, staring into her eyes. Just as she began to lose consciousness again, Bazarov ripped off the tape. Sinclair breathed in hard with a loud rasping sound as her lungs re-inflated, coughing and spluttering as her body tried to clear out the dust she had taken in. When the coughing had subsided, she cleared her throat and spat on the floor. She sat up straight, defiant, as her breathing, still heavy, began to return to normal.

Two portable lights lit up the inside of the barn. Bazarov stood in front of her, his hands in his pockets, his arrogance obvious. Quinn stood behind him, restrained by one of the guards. At least Sinclair knew that Quinn wasn't one of the other two people tied to chairs either side of her. She had to think fast. 'What the fuck is this? Where am I?'

Bazarov stood in front of the light, forcing Sinclair to squint as she looked at him. 'You should recognise the barn, Miss Sinclair. You've been inside here before I think.'

'What? What are you talking about?' Sinclair had to figure out how much Bazarov knew. Maybe she could still get out of this. 'Jo, what's going on? Tell him I haven't done anything.'

Quinn looked down at her feet. 'I'm sorry, Ali. I had to tell him everything. He was going to hurt the boys.'

Bazarov smiled at Sinclair. 'Don't blame your friend too much, Miss Sinclair, you see, I found the footprints in the bungalow. I know you were in there.' He pulled the sack from one of the other captives; it was the guard who had almost caught her. The guard looked frightened. He knew what was going to happen to him. Blood oozed from several deep cuts and ran down his swollen face, mixing with the blood and snot that ran from his nose. Bazarov slapped him. 'This idiot let you search the bungalow while I was away and passed out drunk while you killed one of my men.'

Sinclair pitied the man – it wasn't his fault. 'You can't blame him. He didn't know I was any kind of threat.'

'I pay my men extremely well to be vigilant at all times.' Bazarov held out his hand to one of the other guards. The man cocked a semi-automatic and handed it to him.

The Russian held the weapon to the blood-soaked forehead of the condemned man. 'He failed.'

The man's eyes widened and he tried to plea for his life, but it was in vain. Bazarov pulled the trigger. The sound of the shot echoed off the barn's metal walls. The guard tipped over backwards, onto the concrete floor, blood pooling around his head.

'Bastard.' Sinclair kicked out at Bazarov but he was out of her reach.

Bazarov handed his weapon back. 'Miss Sinclair, you must understand that I have to control my men. There have to be consequences for failure.'

Sinclair slumped in her chair. She just hoped that Frank had managed to send the information back to Carter. Someone had to stop this. She looked at the other hooded figure beside her and feared the worst. If Quinn had told Bazarov everything, she must have told him about Frank.

Bazarov signalled to his two men. 'Take Mrs Quinn back to the house.'

Quinn tried to pull away from them. 'What are you going to do to her?'

'That's none of your concern, Mrs Quinn.'

'If you hurt her then I won't do what you want. I can't do this any more.'

Bazarov turned to Quinn. 'Be under no illusion, Mrs Quinn. I will kill her, you, and your family if you get in my way.' He gave a nod and his men led Quinn out of the barn.

She looked back at Sinclair. 'I'm sorry, Ali.'

'It's okay, Jo, we'll get through this.'

Bazarov laughed. 'I admire your optimism, Miss Sinclair.'

Sinclair looked at Bazarov. 'Okay, Viktor, let's get this shit over with.'

Bazarov walked behind her. 'Don't worry, Miss Sinclair. I have an important job that you are going to carry out for me. Your skills are about to save your life.'

Sinclair tried to look round at him. 'Why the fuck would I do anything for you?'

'Well, I could threaten to kill you if you don't, but I don't think that would work.'

'You would be right there.' If he was going to kill her he would have done it already. Whatever job he wanted her to do, it was important.

'Or, I could threaten to kill your friend and her children.'

Sinclair knew he was bluffing. 'But you wouldn't do that, Viktor, you need her too much. You're going to have to do better than that.'

'That is true, Miss Sinclair. However, I don't need this guy.' He pulled the last sack from the head of the final captive. McGill's face was bloody, but so were his knuckles. He'd taken a beating but Sinclair knew he'd have given just as much back. He was slumped in the chair, his head bowed and his chin resting on his chest. As Sinclair looked at him he winked at her; it was an act. Underestimating Frank was a mistake that no one got away with.

Bazarov placed his hand on top of McGill's head. 'Frank here, is going to be our insurance to make sure you do as you're told. If you don't help me, neither of you is of any value, and I have no qualms about getting rid of people I no longer need.'

Sinclair had to buy enough time for London to put a plan in motion – if they had one. 'If anything happens to him you lose me. I'll do everything I can to fuck you up. I want him cleaned up and his cuts treated before I do anything.'

Bazarov gave orders to his remaining men. 'Lock him in the workshop. There's a sink in there and a first-aid kit. He can clean his own wounds.' He pointed at Sinclair. 'Take her to the house and lock her in the cellar. Watch them both, carefully, they are dangerous.'

Sinclair was untied and frogmarched to the house as McGill

was dragged, still tied to his chair, into the workshop. Bazarov left the barn and returned to the bungalow.

Chapter 13

Carter logged on to his laptop and checked his mail. One message sat in his inbox, a message from Frank. He clicked on it and opened it up. The mail looked incomplete – as if McGill had been interrupted while he was typing it. It contained one sentence: Bazarov using AP to launch.

AP? He must mean Apocalypse Protocol. Launch? Danny had said it was impossible to launch missiles without the biometric data of two people on the list, so it couldn't be that. Frank must mean that Bazarov was planning to launch some kind of security hack. That he was planning to use the protocol in some way to harvest data. Data he could sell on to his clients. But how much more could he find out? If he had Quinn, he already had all the information he needed about the Kraken. The message didn't make sense. Why didn't Frank finish it? That part worried him. If Frank had been compromised, Sinclair must be in trouble too. He'd have to run this past Kinsella to see if he could make sense of it.

Kinsella, as usual, sat in front of his screens. He was monitoring the major news agencies: BBC, Reuters, CNN and TASS. He was looking for any small piece of information that could help him filter his search results, something that would tell him the significance of Lone Star. Lines of data scrolled up two other screens as search results ran through software he'd already created. The software looked for connections between results, cleared out obvious anomalies, and organised the files into groups. On the two screens, directly in front of him, he ran more searches through public, private, and high security networks all over the world. He'd found some interesting connections, possible terror plots, and security leaks. He'd anonymously drop that data to GCHQ as soon as he could. In Texas, he'd found the names of businesses, schools, hotels and communities predominantly located north of Houston but, so far, he hadn't found the obvious or even likely link he was looking for.

His email icon flashed. He opened Carter's message and read it. Simeon was right about one thing. There was no realistic way for Bazarov to launch the missiles with what he had. He was sure that all they were looking at here was an attempt to sell technical information about Kraken on the black market. If he could track down the meaning of Lone Star, he was sure he would find out who the Russian's customer was.

He'd managed to obtain a copy of the launch approval list that was in place when the Kraken tests were carried out and was in the process of tracking down the people on it. Former presidents are protected by the Secret Service so Bazarov wouldn't get close. The other members of the executive who were on the list were still involved in government and had security. That just left the survivors list. Five of them were dead, three were retired, and he was still tracking down the others. Bazarov's chances of getting two of them together, in front of a Kraken console, were none existent.

None of the list members he'd tracked down so far had been

reported missing or kidnapped. If anything were to happen to any of them he'd pick it up on the news wires or from the law enforcement networks he had hacked. He answered Carter's email and set up a meeting at the hotel.

Carter showered, changed, and went down to the hotel bar to meet with Kinsella. They sat in the same spot they had used before. It was early evening and there was no one else in the bar. The hotel was the kind that was full of businessmen during the week but mostly vacant at weekends. The two men had been working round the clock, sleeping when they could, and had lost track of the days. Only now, sitting alone in the bar, did they realise it was Sunday.

'How are we doing, Danny? Anything major to report?'

Kinsella gave Carter a rundown of what he had found, or rather not found, so far. 'Nothing we should worry about. There's no evidence of an imminent threat from Bazarov, the Kraken, or anyone else who might be involved. If this is a conspiracy, it isn't being flagged up on any government databases.'

'So what are we looking at, in your opinion?'

'I've still got some people on the survivors list to track down but I'm convinced this is just old-fashioned espionage. Bazarov is looking for technical intell that he can sell on the black market.'

Carter took a drink and nodded. 'I agree. I think Quinn is being used or threatened to make her provide information. With her family missing she's a soft target.'

'So, where do we go from here?'

'Well, as far as MI6 are concerned, we don't go any further.'

Kinsella gave a slight grin. 'But you don't want to drop it just yet, do you?'

'My first priority is to make sure Sinclair and McGill are okay. I don't want to see them hurt.'

'If I can help with anything there, just say the word.'

'Thanks, Danny.' Carter patted Kinsella's forearm. 'I'll arrange a meeting with Lancaster tomorrow and let him know the Kraken isn't secure. He should advise the UK Government to walk away from this deal.'

'But you want me to keep digging?'

'Yes please. Call it curiosity. I want to know who's involved in this. Find out everything you can about this Vadim, who they are, how high up this goes. If there's a high- level mole in Whitehall, I want to know.'

'I'll get right on to it, Simeon.'

'Get some sleep first. I'll contact Frank and tell him to pull Sinclair out of there. Once they're clear I'll arrange to bring them home.'

'That'll be good, Simeon. I'm looking forward to meeting them both.'

* * *

Robert Tyler was also sitting in front of his screens. He only had to cope with two – the department didn't have the resources, or he the ability, to work with six at once. A mug shot of Ali Sinclair stared out at him from one, as he read the text on the other. He'd used some contacts to get a copy of Sinclair's original Mexican arrest record. It didn't contain a great deal that he didn't know but it did give him a new direction to look in.

He knocked on the door of his SAIC's office and waited. This wasn't big enough to just barge in. He wasn't senior enough to get away with that without a good reason.

'Yes? Come in.'

Tyler opened the door and poked his head round it. 'Am I interrupting, sir?'

'No, no, what is it?'

He stepped into the room. 'I've found something that might be worth following up in the motel shootings.'

'Okay, close the door and take a seat.'

He shut the door behind him and sat down. 'I got a copy of Sinclair's arrest record. It shows that she was picked up at the airport with someone called Josephine Quinn, a US national.' He handed a printout across the desk.

Johnson looked at it for a moment. 'We still don't know that the woman in the motel image is Sinclair. Do we?'

'Not yet, Boss, I'm just working a hunch. I'm looking for anything that will confirm her whereabouts.'

'And what do you think you've found?'

Tyler pointed at the printout. 'This woman, Quinn, she owns a ranch in Texas. I thought, if she lives in Texas and Sinclair is here too, maybe they would get together.'

'This is a pretty thin lead.'

'I know, Boss, but we could check it out and if it turns out to be nothing, well, we can drop it, put it all down to gang violence.'

The older man thought for a while. He didn't think this was going anywhere but he didn't want to discourage the young analyst. 'Get in touch with the local sheriff's office, ask them to go and interview Quinn. See if anything sets the alarm bells ringing.'

Tyler jumped up from his seat, keen to get on with it. 'Right, Boss, I'll let you know what they find out.'

* * *

Mike Powell hadn't been with the sheriff's office for long. When he'd left the army and returned home, it was the only job that was really on offer. He'd needed the work and the sheriff was keen to get a veteran on board.

He'd stopped at the side of the desert highway to empty his bladder. There weren't any facilities in this area. Being the new guy, he got the jobs no one else wanted. He could easily spend all day out here, looking for speeding motorists, without seeing anyone. This was mostly a rural area and major crimes were rare. He sometimes wished he could spend some time closer to the city and get a little excitement.

The radio in his car came to life. 'Tango Two Seven Zero, this is Dispatch, over.'

'Shit.' He couldn't stop mid-flow.

'Tango Two Seven Zero, this is Dispatch, over.'

He quickly finished and zipped himself up, leaving a wet spot on the front of his trousers. 'Son of a bitch.'

'Two Seven Zero. Mike, you out there?'

Powell reached into the car and grabbed the mic for the radio. 'Dispatch this is Seven Zero.'

'What you been up to, Mike?'

'Sorry, Dispatch, call of nature. You got somethin' for me?'

'Yes, we have, you'll need to write this down.'

Powell pumped his fist in the air. At last, something different to do. He grabbed a pen and some paper. 'Okay, Dispatch, go ahead.'

'We've had a request for us to go to the Quinn ranch and interview a Josephine Quinn about an old friend of hers. You're over that neck of the woods, can you pick this up?'

'No problem, Dispatch, what's the friend's name?'

'Alison Sinclair. She may have been involved in a shooting at a motel in Houston.'

Powell wrote everything down. 'Is Quinn a suspect?'

'Negative, Two Seven, they just want to know if she has heard from, or seen Sinclair recently.'

Powell liked the sound of this. 'And Sinclair, is she a suspect?'

'Possibly, but not confirmed. Proceed to the ranch and see what you can find out. See if there's anything unusual and report back.'

'Roger, Dispatch, Two Seven Zero out.' It wasn't a drug raid or a major arrest but it would beat sitting in his baking hot cruiser all day. He closed the vehicle's door and put on his seat belt.

Chapter 14

Sinclair had woken at the sound of the cellar door being unlocked. She'd managed to snatch a couple of hours sleep on the concrete floor but her body now ached all over. Maybe it was the after effects of the drugs they'd given her. She got to her feet and tried to stretch the stiffness out of her joints.

The early morning sunlight flooded in and Bazarov stood, framed in the open doorway, at the top of the stairs. 'Please, Miss Sinclair. Come and join us.'

Sinclair stopped her stretching and climbed up the wooden staircase. This job had gone about as wrong as it was possible to go. Both her and Frank captured, no communication with London, she had to think. Whatever it was that Bazarov wanted her to do, she had no option but to go along with it – for now. As long as she was valuable, she and Frank were still in with a chance.

She stepped through the cellar door and followed Bazarov towards the kitchen. A guard, armed with an AR-15, tucked in behind her. 'Is he necessary?'

'Just a little precaution, we don't want you getting any ideas.'

'You've got my partner locked up in the barn. I'm not likely to risk anything, am I?'

'Better safe than sorry, Miss Sinclair. Sergei here is going to watch you for a little while. He likes blondes.'

Sinclair looked at her new shadow. Sergei was a squat, powerfully built, grubby man. He was unshaven and his greasy hair looked like it had been cut with a bread knife. He looked Sinclair up and down and gave her a toothless grin. Sinclair looked at Bazarov. 'If he tries to touch me, I'll kill him.'

Bazarov gave a snort of laughter. 'You hear that Sergei? You better keep your hands to yourself.'

Sergei's whole body seemed to shake as he let out a deep, rasping chuckle. Sinclair could see, somewhere along the line, he was going to be a problem.

The three of them entered the kitchen. Quinn was already there, sitting at the table with two cups of fresh coffee. 'Morning, Ali, are you okay?'

'I could use a coffee and a shower.'

Quinn slid one of the cups over towards Sinclair. 'Here you go. Just how you like it.'

Sinclair sat next to her and picked up the steaming mug. 'Thanks, Jo.'

Quinn leant over and whispered, 'I'm really sorry.'

Sinclair patted Quinn's arm. 'Don't worry, really.'

Bazarov placed both hands down on the table. 'So touching, ladies. Mrs Quinn, I'm disappointed. You didn't make me a coffee, and I thought we were friends.'

Quinn stood up, knocking over her chair. 'Fuck you.'

Sinclair righted the chair and guided her friend back on it. 'He's just trying to wind you up, Jo, don't give him the satisfaction.'

Bazarov smiled. 'I think our relationship has taken a turn for the worst, Mrs Quinn.'

'We don't have a relationship, you're a bottom feeder. You just use people to get what you want.'

'Doesn't everyone? You use the people who work for you to make the money that pays for all of your lovely things.' He waved his arm in the direction of the various works of art that hung from the walls.

Quinn stared into her mug, watching the steam rise. 'At least I don't kidnap their kids.'

Bazarov looked at Sinclair. 'I think your friend needs cheering up.'

'She'd be fine if you gave her the kids back and walked away.'

Bazarov shook his head. 'That's not going to happen. Now, we've got a busy day today. If I were you, I would get cleaned up and get your things together.' He turned and walked towards the door. 'Watch them, Sergei.'

Bazarov left them in the house and walked over to the barn. His men were busy loading equipment into the vehicles, preparing to pull out. They'd been here long enough. It was time to put this operation in motion. He spent a few moments checking on them before walking through to the back of the building.

McGill was in the corner of the workshop, handcuffed to a rack of shelves. He'd checked during the night for anything he might be able to use to break out but had found nothing. He'd slept a little but had now been awake for hours, trying to ignore his screaming bladder.

Bazarov opened the door to the workshop and walked in. 'Good morning, Mr McGill. I hope you slept well?'

McGill stood up and looked at him with the eye that wasn't swollen. 'What do you think?'

Bazarov turned to one of his men. 'Un-cuff him, let him

clean up, and feed him enough to keep him alive. We can't have our bargaining chip dying on us.'

'You're all heart. Don't put yourself out on my account.'

'I don't really need you, Mr McGill. I'm sure I could force Sinclair to do what I want without you. It's just easier to have you as leverage. Make no mistake, if I decide you are of no use, I will cut you up and scatter the pieces in the desert.'

The guard snorted a short laugh and looked at McGill with disdain. McGill's headbutt split the Russian's face and left him trying to staunch the blood that spurted from his nose. 'Keep that prick away from me.'

Bazarov glared at his pitiful-looking man and shook his head. 'Go and clean yourself up. You should join me, Mr McGill. I pay well and I could use a man like you.'

'Not even if my life depended on it.'

'What if Sinclair's life depended on it?'

'If you ever hurt her I'll do things to you your worst nightmares haven't even begun to conjure up.' He held up his cuffed hand. 'You gonna let me clean up, or what?'

A hint of a smile crossed Bazarov's face. 'I like you, Mr McGill. You get straight to the point.' He threw the handcuff key on the floor at McGill's feet.

The guard with the broken nose came back to the workshop. He now had tissue wadded up inside each nostril. Bazarov gestured to him. 'Watch McGill and get that key back. This time, stay out of his reach.'

Quinn and Sinclair walked up the stairs towards the bedroom with Sergei following a few paces behind. Sinclair whispered, 'We have to distract this guy somehow. I've got something hidden in my room that I need to get without him knowing.'

They reached the room and Sinclair went in. Quinn closed the door and stood outside with her arms folded. 'You can stay out here. She can't go anywhere.'

Sergei reached for the door handle and tried to push his way past. Quinn pushed him back. 'Did you hear me? I said, you stay out here.'

Sergei stepped back. 'Okay. You leave the door open.'

Quinn turned and went into the room, leaving the door ajar so Sergei could see inside. The sound of running water was coming from the shower and steam escaped into the room. Sergei stood opposite the door, watching, while Quinn sat on the bed.

The sound of water stopped, and after a few minutes Sinclair came out of the bathroom. She was dressed in fresh clothes and was towelling her hair dry. 'There, that's better.' She threw the towel onto the bed and pulled on a zip-up hoodie. She adjusted the hem and made sure it covered the bulge of the Glock that now sat, tucked into her waistband, in the small of her back. 'Right, I'm ready. Let's find out what Viktor wants.'

They walked down the staircase and out into the courtyard. Bazarov was sitting on the edge of the fountain, his hand dangling in the cool water. 'Ladies.' He lifted his hand and splashed water on his face and neck. 'They give you any trouble, Sergei?'

Sergei was, as usual, following on behind them. 'No Viktor. No trouble.'

'Good, good. I wish I could say the same for your friend McGill.'

'What have you done to him?'

'Relax, Miss Sinclair, he's fine. One of my men is looking a little bruised though.'

Sinclair laughed. 'That's Frank. He's a bit of a handful, isn't he, Viktor?'

'Yes he is. I don't blame him. I would be the same.'

'What do you want from me, Viktor?'

'I don't know how much you understand about my mission but I need the help of someone else in order to pull it off.'

'It's not a mission, Viktor, it's a crime. You're no more than a scumbag arms dealer and wannabe terrorist.'

Bazarov stood up and took two quick steps towards Sinclair. He raised his hand and extended a finger, pointing at her face. 'I'm more than a wannabe, Miss Sinclair. In a few days' time, everyone will know my name. I am going to make sure the Americans are too busy picking up the pieces of their own broken country to interfere in the affairs of others. I will be a hero to millions of people all over the world.'

'And if you have to kill a few hundred thousand innocent people to achieve that?'

'It's a price I'm willing to pay.'

'You're willing?' Sinclair was starting to raise her voice as she stood up to Bazarov. Quinn put her hand on Sinclair's arm. She was worried this would escalate further than anyone wanted it to. She knew that Sinclair wouldn't let it go and Bazarov was becoming more annoyed.

Sinclair looked into Quinn's eyes and saw the worry. She had to back off. There would be a time when she could take the gloves off, but this wasn't it. The few seconds of silence calmed everyone's tempers and diffused the situation.

Bazarov retreated and took a step back, Sinclair had got to him and he didn't like it. 'Follow me, ladies. It's time we left.'

'I want to see Frank first. I want to be sure he's okay.'

'I'm afraid that won't be possible.'

'Look, Bazarov, I've agreed to go along with whatever it is you want.' She held her arms out to the sides. 'Either I see Frank or you may as well shoot me now.'

Bazarov took a deep breath and looked up to the cloudless sky as if in prayer, this woman was infuriating. 'Very well, you can see him, but not for long.'

The three of them walked to the front of the house. Two four-wheel drives were parked on the driveway. The rear car had five men sitting in it ready to go. Bazarov pointed at the front vehicle. 'Mrs Quinn, if you would, please get into the car. Miss Sinclair, go and say your goodbyes to McGill.'

Sergei escorted Sinclair to the barn and into the workshop. McGill was looking better than the last time she had seen him. 'How are you, Frank?'

'The bed's a bit hard and the room service sucks but, other than that, I'm fine.'

Sinclair looked over at Sergei, he wasn't watching. He was too busy catching up with the other guards. She removed the Glock and gave McGill a hug. He put his arms around her while she tucked the weapon into his waistband and pulled his shirt over it. 'Wait until the right moment, Frank. We need to stop this and get Jo's kids back. If it goes wrong, don't worry about me.'

Sergei walked in. 'Okay, time to go.'

McGill let his arms drop to his sides. 'I'll see you soon, Ali.'

Sinclair walked out of the room backwards, aware that this could be the last time she saw him.

As soon as they were out of sight, McGill pulled out the Glock and slipped it into the side of his boot. He grabbed some electrical tape from the rack of shelves and wound it round the weapon and his leg. He pulled his combat trousers over his makeshift holster and stood up; it didn't show.

His Russian shadow appeared at the door with a pair of handcuffs. 'Put these on.'

McGill snapped the cuffs on his wrists. The guard gestured towards the barn door with his AR-15. 'Go.'

Bazarov was standing by the car waiting for Sinclair. He picked up a radio and pressed the transmit key. 'Open the gates, we're leaving.'

At the bottom of the drive the electric gates buzzed and opened.

Deputy Mike Powell pulled his cruiser off the road and turned into the opening to the Quinn ranch. As he did, the large wrought-iron gates opened and he drove through. He could see a line of vehicles parked up, close to the house. Two four-wheel drives and a couple of vans. They must be planning a trip. He stopped his cruiser and got out. 'Howdy, how are y'all this mornin'?'

Sinclair stopped, this was bad. As Powell approached Bazarov, McGill was pushed out of the barn door in handcuffs. The guard behind him was covering him with his assault rifle. Powell recognised the weapon, he'd used one himself. Sinclair tried to shout a warning but it was lost in the chaos of the next few seconds.

Powell reached down and clamped his hand round the grip of his own weapon. 'Freeze.' He wasn't quick enough. Before the end of the barrel could clear his hip holster, Bazarov had fired a single shot.

The bullet from Bazarov's Colt .45 hit Powell in the centre of his chest, smashing through his ribcage and ripping through his heart. For a split second he stood, frozen to the spot. Then, as if in slow motion, he fell backwards, dead.

Sinclair screamed, 'NO. You didn't have to do that.'

Bazarov swung his arm to point the Colt at her. 'Do not test me, Miss Sinclair. We have had enough delays. Get in the car.'

Quinn stuck her head out of the car's side window. 'Please, Ali.'

Sinclair looked back at McGill. He nodded and she climbed into the car with Quinn.

Bazarov walked over and joined his men. 'Hide the body and the car. By the time anyone comes looking for him we'll be miles away. You know what to do.'

The men nodded. As the two cars drove away and out of the gate, Sinclair watched out of the rear window as the Russians picked up the deputy's body and threw it in the boot of the police cruiser.

Chapter 15

anny Kinsella finished the dregs of his coffee and read the story he'd picked up from one of the obscure, local, state newswires he'd been monitoring. It was a story about a shootout in a motel in Houston. Not something he would normally have taken any further, but this one included an eyewitness statement about a blonde woman being one of the shooters. A quick search through local law enforcement threw up a report on a possible suspect, Ali Sinclair. From what he had uncovered, she wasn't a definite suspect, but was someone that the police and FBI were interested in speaking to, especially as she was also an escaped convict.

Sinclair's ability to blend in and survive on the run for the last year was, in some part, aided by the fact that the US authorities weren't actively looking for her. That had changed now. A BOLO had been issued – for police to be on the lookout for Sinclair – and it was only a matter of time until someone spotted her. She would have to stay hidden. If she tried to use the fake ID he'd arranged for her, there was a possibility she'd be picked up.

Now her freedom of movement was restricted there was little else she would be able to find out. With the FBI showing some interest it was time for her to get out. If they were going to get her home, they needed to act now before a national alert went out for her to be detained. He clicked on his email and sent a message to Carter with a link to the story. He should have arranged a meeting but there wasn't time.

Carter opened his mail and followed the link. The story didn't mention Sinclair or McGill by name but the facts gave them away. A man and a blonde woman, in Texas, take out a drug gang with ease. It had to be them. The information Danny had picked up from the BOLO filled in the rest of the details. Carter agreed with him, this mission was over. It was time for them to pull out and time for MI6 to live up to their end of the bargain. Sinclair needed to come home. He contacted Lancaster and arranged to see him straight away.

Carter walked through reception and out onto the pavement just as the black BMW pulled up outside. The window rolled down and he looked in. The driver was Lancaster's bodyguard from the Waterloo club. 'Good evening, Mr Carter.'

'Good evening.' He opened the back door and got in.

'I'm taking you to a meeting with Mr Lancaster, sit back, it won't take long.'

'Thank you ... sorry, I don't even know your name.'

'That's not important, sir, but you can call me Weston.'

'Thank you, Weston.'

They drove south of the river, past Vauxhall Cross and out of central London. The high-rise office blocks gave way to smaller buildings and tree-lined streets as they drove through the suburbs. After an hour, they pulled onto a side road and into the driveway of an old, detached house that sat behind a six-foot brick wall and an iron gate. Weston pulled up outside the front door as Lancaster stepped out.

Lancaster opened the BMW's door. 'Good evening, Simeon.'

Carter got out of the car and they shook hands. 'Evening, Edward.' The house was typically nondescript. Although it was large, it didn't stand out among the others in the neighbourhood and wasn't overlooked by any other property. 'I assume this is an old, safe house?'

'That's right. Let's go inside.' Lancaster led the way in and closed the door behind them.

The inside of the house was plain – functional. Carter recognised the standard decor from every other safe house he'd been in. 'I think I might have been here before, with a Soviet defector. Then again, it's hard to tell. They all look the same.'

They walked into the kitchen and sat at a table that looked like it had been there since the seventies. 'Just like old times, Simeon.'

'Yes, I think I recognise the table.'

They both smirked at old memories they thought they'd forgotten; some good, some bad.

Carter slid a brown envelope across the table to Lancaster. 'These are the main points of what I'm about to tell you, what you choose to do with the intell is up to you.'

'Boil it down for me, Simeon. What are we looking at?'

'McGill and Sinclair have found enough info to show that Bazarov is definitely targeting the Kraken.'

'Do we know what he's planning?'

Carter shook his head. 'It looks as though he's going to try hacking into the system from a test facility off the coast of Belize. Probably trying to harvest technical data to sell on the black market.'

'Is that the worst case?'

'I've looked at the options and Bazarov would need a lot more than he's got to enable him to do anything else.'

'What about Quinn?'

'It's hard to say whether she's being played or whether she's a willing participant. Sinclair thinks the situation with her husband and kids makes her a soft target. But then, Sinclair is a little biased.'

'How are McGill and Sinclair doing?'

'There is a possibility that they were involved in a shootout at a motel in Houston. It seems a local gang tried to roll them.'

'Any damage?'

'The gang are all dead. The problem we have now is the FBI are involved. I think it's time for my guys to pull out.'

Lancaster picked up the envelope and slipped it into his jacket. 'I agree. I'll pass this on to the PM and the MOD. I'm sure they'll postpone the Kraken deal and let the Americans know they have a security problem.'

'I'll contact McGill and tell him to pull Sinclair out. I'll work on getting her home.'

Lancaster stood up and headed for the front door. 'If there's anything I can do to help, Simeon, let me know. I have a feeling I'm going to need your team again.'

'There is something else, Edward. Something we found while we were snooping about.'

Lancaster took his hand off the door handle and turned to look at Carter. 'Sounds ominous.'

'It looks like we have a mole in Whitehall.'

'Not again, what did you find, Simeon?'

'There is a rumour that Bazarov has a government contact, someone who is referred to as Vadim.'

'I haven't heard that name before. No one in my department

is aware of it.'

'Exactly. Whoever they are, they must be pretty high up. You need to watch your back.'

'Like I said, Simeon, just like old times. I'll get some of my people looking for the name, see what they can find out.'

'I'll keep looking as much as I can, I'll let you know if I find anything.'

Lancaster opened the door. 'Weston will drop you back at your hotel. Thank you, Simeon, I'll be in touch soon. I have a feeling there's a new Cold War coming.'

Carter got into the BMW and closed the door. As Weston put the car in gear and drove away, Lancaster waved and turned to go inside.

The car pulled onto the main road and headed towards London. 'It's around an hour to your hotel, sir.'

Carter sat back in his seat. 'Thank you, Weston.'

* * *

The young FBI analyst didn't bother to knock this time. He threw open the door and rushed in. 'Sir, you need to see this.'

Thomas Johnson was on the phone and held up a hand to try and calm the analyst while he finished the call. Tyler hopped from one foot to the other, getting more and more agitated. 'Sir, this is important.'

Johnson nodded and pointed to the chair in front of his desk while he carried on with his phone call. 'Yes ... I agree ... I think it would be in all our interests if we—'

Tyler couldn't wait any longer. 'SIR, please.'

Johnson looked at the young man. This wasn't like him. He was normally quiet and didn't like to interrupt. 'I have to go, something's come up.' He put the phone on its cradle. 'What is it, Robert?'

Tyler placed several sheets of paper on the desk. 'It's the motel shootout, sir.'

'What have you found?'

'You remember we decided to ask the local sheriff to swing by the Quinn ranch to ask if she had seen Sinclair?'

'Yes, I remember. I also said don't spend too long on this.'

'Well, I wanted to chase them up so I phoned again this morning. They sent a deputy over there yesterday.'

'What did he find out?'

'That's the thing, sir, they haven't heard from him in over twenty-four hours.'

'Have they asked Quinn if she's seen him?'

'They tried to but there's no one at the ranch.'

Johnson got the feeling that Tyler might be on to something. There were too many coincidences and unexplained events. The last thing he wanted was his bosses asking him why he hadn't followed it up. 'I want you to get all of the data you've found into a file so we can track this.'

'Yes, sir. But that's not all.'

Johnson sat forwards in his seat. 'You've got more?'

Tyler passed over another sheet of paper. There was a photo in the top left-hand corner and the name Liam Quinn. 'That's Josephine Quinn's husband. He was reported missing at sea, with his children, over a month ago.'

'Why is the bureau looking at this?'

'Quinn is the CEO of a defence company. Let's just say they have some pretty high-profile friends in Washington.'

'Do we have any leads as to what happened to them?'

Tyler produced a fresh sheet from the printer. 'We don't

know what happened but this has just come in. A body has been found, washed up on the beach in Galveston, looks like it's him.'

Johnson read the report. This was shaping up to be the kind of job that warranted an investigation into why things hadn't been spotted earlier, the kind of investigation that ended with a scapegoat having to resign. He wasn't going to be that scapegoat. 'Get in touch with Halloran, he's down there. Tell him to get to the beach and see what he can find out.'

'Yes sir.' Tyler stood up and left the office, closing the door behind him.

Chapter 16

The yellow crime scene tape fluttered in the onshore breeze as Kurt Halloran ducked under it and worked his way towards the corpse that lay on the sand. A young police officer stepped in front of him. 'Hold it, buddy, back behind the tape. We don't need any sickos trying to check out the body.'

Halloran held out his own badge and ID, flashing it at the young officer. 'It's okay, son, I need to speak to your sergeant.'

The officer checked Halloran's credentials and shouted over to an older man who was standing next to the body, 'Sarge. The feds are here.'

Sergeant Ramirez was talking to the forensic team who had arrived to begin their examination of the scene. He resented the FBI butting in like this. He had enough experience to deal with a washed-up body. He took his time talking to the CSIs then left the corpse and joined the two men. Halloran flashed his badge again and introduced himself. 'Special Agent Halloran, FBI.'

The sergeant checked Halloran's ID and handed it back. 'You guys move pretty fast, we only called this in an hour ago.'

Halloran put his wallet back in his pocket. 'I was in the area.'

Ramirez looked him up and down. 'Yeah, you don't look

like you came from the office.'

Halloran was supposed to be on vacation; knee-length shorts and a Hawaiian shirt weren't his usual work attire. He was coming to the end of a week's fishing with some of his buddies when he'd got the call from the office. 'Top priority' they'd said. 'Get over there now.'

Washed up bodies didn't usually fall under the FBI's jurisdiction, or create this much urgency, but the office was insistent. 'The details aren't important right now. We'll fill you in later. Just check that it's Quinn and see what else you can find out.'

He took Ramirez to one side, out of earshot of anyone else. 'So, what have we got, Sarge?'

Ramirez held out a plastic evidence bag, inside it was a wallet. Halloran opened the bag and took it out. The wallet was coated in sand and still dripped sea water.

The sergeant opened his notebook and gave Halloran an outline of what he knew. 'Says in the wallet that he's Liam Quinn, washed up this morning, found by a woman walking her dog. When we ran his details through the NCIC we got a month-old missing person report and a request to contact the bureau with any information.'

Halloran checked through the wallet. Cards, driving licence, money – nothing out of the ordinary. 'Did he have anything else on him?'

Ramirez shook his head. 'Nothing else. No life jacket and no sign of wreckage from the boat. If the weather was bad enough to sink them, surely he would've had a life jacket on?'

'You think he might have fallen overboard and drowned because he wasn't wearing one?'

'It's possible, but where's the boat? We've had no reports of a drifting vessel of any kind, or even wreckage.'

'Does this kind of thing happen a lot along this coast?'

He gestured towards the water with his arm. 'Often enough, this isn't a lake. Tourists come down from the city and take to sea in their weekend boats. Most of them have no knowledge of tides, currents or the weather. They get caught out and are lost. We do normally find some evidence other than bodies though.'

'Maybe, now that he's washed up, the rest will follow.'

Ramirez nodded. 'Maybe, but the CSIs have found something.'

Halloran's senses prickled. He didn't like things out of the ordinary. There was rarely an innocent explanation. 'Found what?'

'It says on the NCIC that he was reported missing just over a month ago.'

'Yeah, that's what my office told me.'

'Well, the CSIs reckon he's been in the water for no more than two weeks.'

'So he could've been killed somewhere else then dumped at sea?'

'It's a definite possibility, but until they do an autopsy they won't know for sure.'

'Okay, Sarge, keep me in the loop and let me have the autopsy results.' Halloran put the wallet back inside the evidence bag and handed it over. He pulled his phone out of the pocket of his shorts and pressed the speed dial. 'It's him alright, Boss ... no ... no sign of anything else ... will do, Boss.'

He ended the call and took a last look at the body. If this was a simple boating accident, why hadn't any wreckage been found, where were the other passengers, and how had the body only been in the water for two weeks when he'd been missing for a month? This whole thing stunk.

As he walked to his car he stared out at the Gulf of Mexico at a small cargo ship coming into view, heading out to sea. Whatever had happened out there was no accident, and it had led to the death of Liam Quinn. This was a busy seaway; somebody must have seen something. The office hadn't filled him in on the backstory yet, but he had a feeling that it was about to ruin his vacation.

* * *

McGill didn't like being at sea, he never had; even as a Royal Marine where it was part of his job. The constant rocking motion was like being in a hammock that he couldn't get out of, and it made him feel like shit.

After Bazarov and Sinclair had left the ranch, the deputy's car was moved inside the barn, and the Russians had loaded all of their equipment into two container trucks that had backed up the driveway. Food, bedding, tools and machinery – everything they needed to set up and operate from Leatherback Cay – were loaded into the containers. Their weapons were concealed behind a false bulkhead that would defeat all but the most determined search. McGill was bundled into one of the vans and handcuffed to a seat for the journey to the ship.

When they stopped, they were on one of the wharfs of the Barbour's Cut Container Terminal in the Port of Houston. Tied up on the berth next to them was a small, five-thousand-ton cargo ship that belonged to QRL Global. The MV San Antonio was big enough to take the two containers on her deck and the two vans in the hold, but not much else. Once the ship had been loaded, it slipped its moorings, and set sail along the Houston Ship Channel. Three and a half hours from there to the Gulf of Mexico, and another three days to the island.

Once the ship was underway, Bazarov's men disappeared inside, probably to comfortable beds and Vodka nightcaps. McGill was left handcuffed to the seat in the back of the van. At least they'd left him some water and a bucket to piss in. He'd slept in worse places.

He checked the weapon that was taped to his leg, it was still securely in place and hidden. There was no reason for them to search him, no reason for them to suspect he was armed. The Glock would only come out when he had a chance of escape and, ideally, once he knew what had happened to Ali. She could look after herself but he didn't want to jeopardise her position. If it was possible, she would take out Bazarov, but if she didn't get that chance, Bazarov would bring her here to force Quinn to follow through with the job. That's when McGill could work on getting them out. On the other hand, if he found out she was dead, it would be down to him to kill Bazarov. Of course, he'd make him suffer first.

He picked up one of the bottles and took a drink. He'd always found the best way to cope with the nausea he experienced at sea was to sleep through it. Shuffling around, he stretched out, as well as he could with one hand cuffed to the seat, and closed his eyes.

Chapter 17

A Sheriff's cruiser pulled up to the front gate of Quinn's ranch. Sergeant Pete Novak got out, walked up to the gate, and peered through the railings. There were no signs of life. No movement, no lights and, more importantly, no sign of Mike Powell.

Since the deputy had been reported missing the previous day, the whole department had been searching for him. His last job was to come to the ranch but there was no evidence that he'd actually made it here. Thousands of miles had been covered by deputies in cars, the Marine Division were checking waterways, and helicopters searched the more inaccessible areas. Other sheriff's offices, city police departments and state troopers extended the search area outside the county but, up to now, nothing had been found.

Novak knew deputies didn't just vanish. If they went missing there was usually evidence, and they turned up pretty quick – even if they were dead. If Powell had been in an accident or his car had broken down, they would have found him. The fact that there was no sign of him at all made Novak uneasy; he was certain something had happened to Powell, something bad.

He got into his car and got on the radio. 'Dispatch, Tango

One Six Eight, over.'

'One Six Eight, go ahead.'

'I'm out at the Quinn ranch, no sign of Powell or anyone else. I need to get permission to go inside and have a look. Can we contact Quinn or get a warrant? Over.'

'Hang tight, Six Eight, checking.'

Novak grabbed his binoculars and went back to the gate. He scanned the house, the bungalow and the barn, looking for something to give him a reason to enter the property. The door to the barn was slightly open and he was sure he could see something in there, maybe a vehicle. He walked away from the gate and along the fence, trying to get a better angle, but he couldn't make it out. He heard another vehicle approaching and turned to see a black SUV pulling up behind his cruiser.

Kurt Halloran got out of the SUV and walked towards Novak. 'Afternoon, Sarge, Special Agent Kurt Halloran, FBI.' He flashed his ID and held out his hand.

Novak took his offered hand. 'Pete Novak, what can I do for you, Kurt? What are the Bureau doin' here?'

'I'm looking for Mrs Josephine Quinn. Has something happened I should know about?'

'One of our deputies has disappeared. He was on his way here to interview Quinn.'

Halloran had been filled in about the motel shooting and the missing deputy but didn't want to give too much away. It made him even more suspicious of the body on the beach and how it had got there. On its own it warranted a closer look, but coupled with a shootout in Houston involving Quinn's friend, and a missing deputy, this had all the hallmarks of major crime.

'He was sent over here at our request.'

Novak nodded. 'That's right. S'posed to be routine but no one has seen him since. What's goin' on, Kurt?'

'Quinn's husband was found washed up on the beach in Galveston. He's been missing for over a month but there's something not quite right about it.'

'I don't like the sound of that.'

'No. Me neither. You find anything here?'

'There's something in the barn but I can't make it out. Could be a vehicle.'

'You thinking probable cause, Sarge?'

'Yeah, in fact, I'm pretty sure that's one of our cruisers in there.'

'I'm with you there.'

Novak picked up his radio mic. 'Dispatch, Tango One Six Eight, over.'

'Go ahead Six Eight.'

'Reason to believe that Deputy Powell's cruiser is in the Quinn ranch. I'm gonna need backup and someone to open the gates, over.'

'Roger Six Eight, we now have a warrant, backup en route.'

'Roger, Dispatch, One Six Eight out.' He threw the mic onto the seat.

Halloran picked up Novak's binoculars and checked the house. 'That was quick.'

'Yeah, people high up gettin' twitchy. Quinn is connected to a lot of powerful people around here. I reckon they've been covering for her up to now, but with Powell going missing, well, let's just say they like protectin' their own asses more than Quinn's.'

It took an hour for the SWAT team to arrive at the ranch. Their black armoured response vehicles now blocked the

144

entrance. Officers clad in green combats and tactical vests readied their weapons as another worked on the gates. Novak and Halloran stood back; control of the situation was now out of their hands.

Halloran lit a cigarette and sat on the bonnet of Novak's car. 'I've got a feelin' that it's all about to hit the fan.' He offered a smoke to Novak.

Novak shook his head. 'No thanks. What do you think this is all about, Kurt?'

Halloran blew out a stream of smoke. 'Whatever it is, Pete, it's above our pay grade.' Halloran's phone rang. 'That's my boss. He'll want me to give him an update.' He walked away from Novak and answered the call. 'Yes, Boss ... they're about to make an entrance now ... I'll let you know what we find.' He ended the call and re-joined Novak.

SAIC Johnson replaced his telephone handset and looked across his desk at Tyler. 'Halloran's over there now, they're about to go in. How big do you think this is?'

The young analyst looked at the papers he had spread over the desk. 'I don't know, Boss, but it looks like a lot of things are connected. Quinn's husband, Sinclair, the missing deputy. If they are all involved, it's got to be big. Quinn has some major defence contracts. Maybe someone is trying to get to her.'

'I want you to go over everything. I don't like the look of this. I want to know what is going on and who is in on it. And find Quinn.'

'Yes, sir, I'll get right on it.'

* * *

Halloran and Novak watched as the gates swung open. The FBI agent dropped his cigarette butt and ground it out with his boot. 'Here we go.'

The two armoured vehicles drove up the drive with the officers from the SWAT team taking cover behind. There was no obvious threat but also no reason to take risks.

The first vehicle stopped at the house. The eight officers split into two teams of four and went through the archway into the courtyard. One team worked their way left and the other right, covering each other as they approached the main entrance.

One of the team members moved up to the door and placed a shaped explosive charge on the lock.

'Delta One and Two in position, over.'

'Roger, Delta One and Two, stand by.'

The second vehicle stopped at the barn. One of its teams of four took up position at the entrance to the bungalow, the other at the main door of the barn.

'Delta Three in position, over.'

'Roger, Delta Three, stand by.'

'Delta Four in position, there's definitely a police cruiser in the barn. Over.'

'Roger, Delta Four, standby.'

The radio operator looked at his lieutenant. 'All teams in position, sir.'

The lieutenant listened to his radio handset and gave a nod.

The radio operator turned back to his microphone. 'All Deltas, confirm status, over.'

'Delta One, check.'

'Delta Two, check.'

'Delta Three, check.'

146

'Delta Four, check.'

'All Deltas, stand by.'

The members of the four teams readied themselves, deep breaths, nodding to each other.

'Stand by.'

The adrenaline pumped through their systems, and their muscles flexed in anticipation. The thumb of Delta One's point man hovered over the detonator, ready to blow the lock.

'Stand by.'

Halloran and Novak stood at the gates, watching through binoculars as the operator gave the order.

'Go, go, go.'

There was a dull thud as the shaped charge blew the lock. All four teams breached at the same moment. Teams one and two burst into the house, clearing the open-plan space. They moved along the hallways and up the stairs, clearing every room as they went.

'Delta One, clear.'

'Delta Two, clear.'

Team three slid open the window into the bungalow, it was empty. They checked the bedroom and bathroom – nothing. 'Delta Three, clear.'

Team four poured into the barn and past Mike Powell's cruiser. They cleared the workshop and ascended the steel staircase into the offices – all empty. 'Delta Four, clear.'

The radio operator took off his headset. 'All clear, sir.'

'Bring them out.'

'Yes, sir. All Deltas …'

The men standing at the gate felt the rumble of the explosion a split second before the blast reached them. Halloran and Novak were knocked to the ground, dazed. Debris rained down on them. Halloran shielded his head and looked up the drive. All three buildings were now engulfed by an expanding, orange ball of flame.

For a moment there was silence, as they tried to comprehend what had just happened, then all hell broke loose. The drivers of the vehicles, injured, tried to crawl away from the heat of the fire. Other deputies ran towards the flames to try and rescue their comrades. The radio operator tried, in vain, to contact the SWAT teams. The lieutenant screamed into his radio, calling for backup and medics.

Halloran checked on Novak then got to his feet and surveyed the scene. It was like a warzone. There were more explosions as gas bottles exploded in the heat of the fire. Burning scraps of paper floated in the air, the roof of the barn was peeled back like the lid on a tin of beans, and the body of a SWAT team member hung from one of the windows.

Novak stood with his hands on his head, mouth hanging open. Halloran grabbed the first-aid kit from the sergeant's cruiser and took it over to him. 'Come on, Pete.'

Novak looked at him for a moment then seemed to snap out of it. He grabbed the kit and the two men ran up the driveway.

* * *

Special Agent Johnson sat with his elbows on his desk and his head in his hands. 'How the fuck did we miss something like this?'

Robert Tyler sat in the chair opposite and stared out of the door to the TV, which everyone else in the office was now crowded round. The scene on the screen was one of devastation. The news helicopter hovered over what was left of Quinn's ranch. Fire crews poured water on the smouldering wreckage of the buildings. One SWAT vehicle lay on its side, blown over by the blast, the other was buried under rubble. Paramedics carried out body bags and lined them up on the driveway, ready to be taken away by the waiting queue of ambulances.

Tyler shook his head slowly. 'I don't know, sir. There's no chatter on the net to hint at something like this, no intell, nothing.'

'The news channels are already calling it a terrorist atrocity. Saying we were duped and lured in. They'll have somebody's ass for this.'

Tyler held out his hands as if he were pleading with Johnson. 'But we weren't even looking for terrorists. It was supposed to be about a shootout in a Houston motel and Quinn's husband being killed in a boating accident. How'd we end up with this?' He gestured towards the screen.

Johnson took off his glasses and rubbed the bridge of his nose. 'I don't understand why they would target a ranch in the middle of nowhere. With this kind of expertise they could have taken out a shopping mall.'

'Quinn is the CEO of one of the world's largest defence companies. That might make her a legitimate target. Do you think she was in there?'

'I hope not. I don't want to see any more body bags.' Johnson looked at the notebook on his desk. 'Seventeen dead, two more not expected to live through the night, two with severe burns and four walking wounded. Jesus.' He forced himself to look up at the television. 'Okay, Tyler. Here's what we do. You drop everything, this is your only job now. Use as many other people as you have to. I want to know where we went wrong,

149

what did we miss?'

'But I'd swear we didn't miss anything.'

'Then find me the proof. Get me the info that shows we did everything right. Prove that this came out of the blue, and if someone else missed it, get me their name. I'm not gonna' let anyone throw us to the wolves.'

'I'll get right on it.' Tyler stood up and made for the door but before he was one step outside, Johnson called him back.

'Tyler.'

'Yes, sir.'

'Get Quinn and Sinclair's mugshots out to everyone. I want them found, no matter what.'

'Yes, sir.' He turned and went back to his desk.

Johnson picked up the phone and dialled Halloran's number.

'Yes, Boss.'

'You okay, Kurt?'

'A few scratches and some ringin' in my ears, other than that, I'm fine.'

'That's good to hear. They find anything yet?'

Halloran stubbed out his cigarette against the gate post. 'A little, it looks like the blast came from a large amount of Semtex, coupled with ANFO and gas canisters, a favourite of terrorists all over the world. Not much else to go on so far.'

'I want you to stay there, keep an eye on things, especially the other agencies. Someone must have known about something this big. Homeland Security, NSA, CIA. Let's see who turns up. Anything you need, Kurt, you contact me direct.'

'I'll phone you in a few hours, Boss. The crime scene guys should have something by then.'

Halloran watched as another body bag came out of the barn. Whoever had done this was no small-time operator. It took a lot of explosives and knowhow to pull off something this big. They had rigged it so the SWAT teams were all the way inside the buildings before they blew. They went for maximum casualties. Halloran had a feeling that this wasn't the main event. Quinn was caught up in something big, and things were about to get a whole lot worse.

He took out another cigarette and flicked open his Zippo. His hands were shaking; he was chain smoking and he needed a glass of something strong.

'You okay, Kurt?'

Novak had been standing beside him and he hadn't even noticed. Halloran lit his cigarette. 'Yeah. I could use a drink.'

'You and me both, buddy. When this is over we'll go and sink a couple.'

Halloran patted Novak on the back. 'That's a deal, Pete.'

Chapter 18

Danny Kinsella rushed through the hotel's reception and into the lift. He could have just phoned Carter but, and maybe he was being a little paranoid, this was the kind of thing security agencies were on the lookout for.

The lift stopped with a jolt on the third floor. The doors opened with a ping and he hurried out. Carter was in room thirty-eight at the end of the corridor. He tapped on the door; he didn't want to announce his arrival to the other guests. There was no answer. He tried again; still no answer. This time he hammered on the door, checking up and down the corridor for anyone watching. No one was interested in him. He heard the sound of the door being unlocked and when Carter opened it he pushed past him into the room.

'What is it, Danny? What's happened?' It was obvious to Carter that something serious was wrong.

'Close the door, Simeon.'

As Carter closed the door, Kinsella picked up the remote for the television and turned on the twenty-four-hour news channel. The sports correspondent was just handing back to the studio.

'What are we looking for?'

'Wait. It'll be on again in a minute. They've been running it all morning.'

The news anchor shuffled his papers and looked straight at the camera. 'Back to our main news story. A massive explosion in the United States claims the lives of at least seventeen people.'

The screen showed the footage, from the helicopter, of the carnage at the ranch.

'Authorities say that the death toll may still rise.'

The helicopter focussed on the body bags being loaded into the queue of ambulances.

'We have unconfirmed reports that a police assault was underway when the explosion occurred.'

The camera zoomed in on the two SWAT assault vehicles.

'Experts say that this bears all the hallmarks of a terrorist attack. The president will make a statement later today.'

The report ended with stock film of the US president giving a press conference.

Kinsella looked at Carter and gestured towards the television. 'That, is what's left of Quinn's ranch.'

Carter sat down on the bed, his hand on his forehead. 'What happened?'

'We knew the FBI was getting involved. They asked the local sheriff's office to assist. It seems they sent a deputy over to Quinn's and he hasn't been seen since.'

'You think Bazarov killed him?'

'It looks like it. A police car was found in the barn and the deputy is listed as one of the dead.'

Carter felt sick. 'It said the police were making an assault at the time.'

'That's right. The FBI was still interested in Sinclair and the

153

locals were looking for their deputy. When they couldn't get any answer at the ranch, they got a warrant and went in.'

'And the place was rigged to blow?'

'No one knows what actually happened, but the explosives didn't go off until the SWAT teams were well inside the buildings. Bazarov wanted to cause maximum damage and casualties.'

Carter dropped his head and stared at his feet. 'Are McGill and Sinclair on the list of the dead?' He looked up at Kinsella, willing the answer to be no.

'They aren't on the list so far, but there are two unidentified bodies.'

'Shit, I hope it's not them.' As he spoke, a picture of Sinclair appeared on the television. It was the photo from the motel shootout. They both stared at the screen and Carter stood up.

The news anchor came back on. 'Police say they want to speak to this woman in connection with the explosion but did not confirm if she was a suspect or a witness.'

He moved on to the next story and Kinsella switched off the television. 'They didn't mention her name or show a better picture.'

'They're not sure if it's her. They don't want to get caught up in a wild goose chase only to find out it's someone else. They'll sit on that info for now. We need to head this off before the news channels drop her in it.'

'What do we do?'

'You get back to your flat and keep an eye on how things are progressing. Let me know straight away if anything changes.'

'And you?'

Carter's phone bleeped, it was a message from Lancaster. 'I'll meet with Edward. He must have picked up on events.'

* * *

Carter sat in the window seat of a coffee shop round the corner from the hotel. It was only a short walk from Vauxhall Cross and Lancaster told him he would be straight there. When Carter had contacted his old friend, he'd used the code word that had begun all of this: Broadsword. It would let Lancaster know that it was important.

Carter stirred his coffee and watched out of the window as the city's young professionals hurried past, oblivious to the world around them. Things had changed since he was a young man coming to London for the first time. No one said hello or good morning any more. They barely acknowledged each other's existence. Most of them were more focussed on the device in the palm of their hand – their link to the virtual world. He was surprised more of them weren't mown down by the traffic, or blindsided by the cyclists who weaved between the cars and occasionally mounted the pavement to skirt round a red light.

The streets had lost all of their character. The shops were all famous high-street names, the same brands that could be seen filling the streets of most other major cities in the world. Even the coffee shops; he could remember when this one was a café, and your choice was tea or coffee with a bacon roll or a cake. Now, he couldn't keep track of the numerous types of coffee that were on the menu, there was no tea in sight, and the food was all expensive designer sandwiches and vegan friendly nut bars. People sat at tables for one, typing on their laptop keyboards. There were only a handful of tables with more than one person sitting at them, and most of the conversation was over mobile phones. This wasn't an ideal place for a meeting but it would have to do.

Lancaster stepped in off the street and walked to the counter. He didn't really want a coffee – what he really wanted was a large Scotch – but it would have looked strange if he hadn't ordered one. He picked up his cup and joined Carter at the table. 'It's been a bad day, Simeon. Don't make it worse by telling me we caused this.'

Carter checked that no one was trying to eavesdrop, and kept his voice low. 'I haven't heard from either McGill or Sinclair. I don't even know if they're still alive. What I do know is this. Wherever they are, if they're able, they'll be working to stop Bazarov. We have to give them time.'

'It's inevitable that the Americans will ask us for information on Sinclair. What do I tell them? "We've been operating in your backyard and may have caused this morning's attack"?'

'You don't have to tell them anything yet. Just give them a back story that covers her military past – that's not a secret. Remember, Edward, you approached me to recruit Sinclair and McGill so you could officially deny any involvement.'

Lancaster took a sip of his coffee and shook his head. 'I couldn't just abandon them like that.'

'We don't have to abandon them. Just drip-feed the Americans some information until we figure out how big this thing is.'

'You mean it could get worse?'

'I think this is a diversion. I think Bazarov has something else planned, something to do with Leatherback Cay.'

'But you analysed the information, said there was no threat. You thought Bazarov was just milking Quinn for information to sell on.'

Carter checked again for eavesdroppers. He was aware this

conversation was getting too in-depth for the location they were in. A young girl got up from her seat and pushed past their table on her way to the counter. Carter gave her a smile and waited until she was out of earshot. 'We came to that conclusion based on what we had, but this morning's events change that.'

'You can say that again, Simeon.'

'If we tell the Americans everything now they won't hold back. They'll steam in with all guns blazing.'

'But that would be a good thing, it would stop this dead.'

'Not necessarily, Edward. Bazarov may already be capable of launching whatever kind of attack he's planning. If the Americans get gung-ho and pile in, he could do something even more drastic before they take him out.'

'We could explain that to them. Tell them to hold off.'

'That's not likely to work. They've just suffered what the press are calling "a terrorist atrocity". Any clue to the culprit and it'll be Afghanistan and Iraq all over again.'

This time, Lancaster was checking for anyone paying too much attention to them. He needn't have worried. All the other customers were lost in their virtual worlds. Even so, both men were now leaning forwards, inches from each other. 'We all learned lessons after 9/11, no one is going to invade a country again just to get one man.'

'But it isn't a country, Edward, it's a private army holed up on a small island in the Caribbean. The Americans could carpet bomb it and kill everyone, including McGill and Sinclair.'

Lancaster sighed and stared into his coffee. 'I want to give them every chance to survive this but we can only protect them so far. We can't risk more deaths in the states if we have information that could stop them.'

'If the Americans take out Bazarov, we'll never know how vulnerable the Kraken is. That could cause us problems in the future. He could have sold that data on already.'

'What do we do, Simeon? I need your advice on this one.'

'Just tell the ministry to delay the Kraken contract. Tell them it's because of recent events and Quinn's involvement. Maybe that'll start the US looking into the possible threat. In the meantime, McGill and Sinclair can find out what Bazarov has in mind and get out of there. After that, a handful of cruise missiles could take care of the Russian.'

Lancaster nodded, mulling over his options. 'That makes sense. I can buy them a couple of days, but that's it.'

'That'll be enough. If they haven't been in touch by then, and things have moved on, we'll have to come clean and pass on the file to the yanks.'

Lancaster pushed his coffee to one side, it was cold anyway. He stood up and placed his hand on Carter's shoulder. 'Stay in touch, my friend. Things could change fast. We need to stay on top of it.'

Carter patted Lancaster's hand. 'I will. Take care of yourself, Edward.'

Lancaster walked past the counter and out of the door. Carter watched him disappear down the street and drained his own cold coffee, regretting it immediately and grimacing at the taste.

Outside, he fastened his coat and thrust his hands into his pockets. He knew Sinclair and McGill were still out there somewhere. He had to do everything to bring them home. He looked right, in the direction of his hotel. The best place for him to be now was with Kinsella. As soon as anything happened, Carter needed to know straight away. He turned left and set off towards Danny's flat.

Chapter 19

The Lone Star Golf Resort and Spa was four hundred acres of lush green fairways and woodland a few miles south west of Houston. An oasis of green surrounded by the sunburned brown scrub, and flat, featureless farmland of the plains. An exclusive resort where Houston's great and good, and above all wealthy, came to relax. Rich white men played a few holes while their wives were pampered in the spa. Powerful men spent weekends with their mistresses and bored trophy wives had secret liaisons with their younger boyfriends.

Admiral James D. Garrison was a fully-fledged member of the elite. The second son of a Texas oil billionaire, he'd risen to the top of the US Navy – more down to luck and his father's contacts than any real talent. He was a man who liked being in a position of power and enjoyed, to their full extent, the privileges and perks that came with it. After a stint as a member of the joint chiefs, he'd retired and decided to run for office. Backed by his family's money, his ambitions were as big as anyone's could be. Governor, Senator, maybe even President Garrison. There was no holding him back – until the scandal had broken.

James Garrison had a penchant for younger blonde women.

It was well known by other members of the political class and covered over effectively by his inner circle. Unfortunately for Garrison, his close friends weren't as close as he'd thought, and it was only a matter of time before he went too far even for them. The event that had brought Garrison's political ambitions, and his already crumbling marriage, crashing down around his ears, had involved an eighteen-year-old girl and a father who couldn't be bought off.

As part of his political campaign, his team had created a backstory showing him as a devoted family man, a pillar of the community and man of the people. He was shown attending charity dinners, supporting his local, minor league baseball team and going to church with his wife and grown-up daughters. He became a patron of several community projects and a passionate supporter of military veterans. He was everything that a budding politician needed to be.

Hannah Danvers, on the other hand, was a rising star of the high school political society: a group of young men and women who wanted to be the leaders of the future. They were willing to help out in campaigns to build up their experience and understanding of the democratic process and give up their spare time to fill envelopes and volunteer at fundraisers. It was at one of the party fundraisers that Garrison's true character was finally exposed to a wider section of the voting public.

Hannah was impressed by Garrison. She saw him as a future president and she wanted to be on his team. She was ambitious and saw herself working in the Whitehouse one day. So, when Garrison had invited her to his room to help him sort out some files, she was all too keen to go. It had never entered her head that the admiral, already drunk, had something entirely different on his mind.

When Hannah had entered his hotel room, she was a young woman who believed she was helping a good man trying to improve the lives of others. When she'd left, sobbing and with her clothes in disarray, she knew exactly what Admiral James D. Garrison was.

She hadn't told anyone at first, how could she? No one would have believed her anyway; he was rich, powerful – a member of the establishment. Her father hadn't seen it that way. He'd known something was wrong, the spark she'd once had was missing, and he'd pushed her until he got to the truth.

Garrison's inner circle had closed ranks, to begin with, but Hannah's father wasn't going away and the rape story gained traction. As more and more details of the admiral's life surfaced, a growing number of his friends had simply walked away, unwilling to tarnish their reputations by being associated with him. His family made an attempt to settle out of court, to pay off Danvers, but he was having none of it. He had wanted to see his daughter's attacker sent to prison for a long time.

Garrison's highly paid lawyers, however, knew their way around the system. As part of a plea bargain, they entered a plea of guilty to the lesser charge of simple assault. Taking out the sexual element reduced the offence from a felony – with a potential sentence of twenty years – to a misdemeanour. Garrison was fined a few thousand dollars and served one year in the county jail.

He'd managed to avoid serious jail time but his political career was over, as was his marriage. Without the powerful positions and influence that she'd used to her advantage, his wife, who had tired of his drinking and affairs, had no reason to put up with him any longer, and walked out.

Although he was let off lightly by the justice system, the media had crucified him. They dug into his past. There were allegations of other assaults, fraud, and bribery when he was in office, but there was no real evidence. The admiral's contacts weren't saying anything and he had no conscience; he'd shown no remorse. After a while the story died away, and on his release, he went back to his privileged life as if nothing had happened.

He now spent his time at cocktail and dinner parties, a new circle of friends gathered around him. Willing to forget his past and put up with his boorish behaviour, hoping to climb the social ladder.

Hannah Danvers wasn't interested in parties, she retreated into her shell. She rarely left the house for fear of someone recognising her, the ambitions she'd had were gone; her young life in tatters. After two suicide attempts she was now a resident in a clinic, a retreat, determined to rebuild her life.

Garrison had his own retreat. Every couple of months he spent a few days at Lone Star, rubbing shoulders with the same people who had publicly shunned him during his fall from grace. They couldn't cut him out for too long though, he was one of them after all. He would get in a few rounds of golf, play poker, drink bottle after bottle of vodka, and occasionally pay for an expensive escort to join him. Young and blonde of course.

On this particular morning, Garrison, nursing his usual hangover, had a reserved tee time with a high court judge. He wasn't really in the mood to play but it was useful to have a judge as a friend, as he'd already found out. He picked up his golf bag, took a deep breath of morning air, and whistled as he made his way across the car park to the first tee.

Bazarov drove the SUV up to the security barrier of the golf resort and showed the guard his reservation. The guard looked at the two newcomers. 'Is this your first time staying with us,' he looked at the names on the booking form. 'Doctor Belov?'

'Yes, it is.' Bazarov leant forwards, closer to the guard. 'To be honest, I'm really rubbish at golf.'

'That's not a problem, sir. You can book lessons with our pro. He'll get your handicap down. He's quite popular with the ladies who come here. Maybe your wife would like to book a lesson too?'

Bazarov looked at Sinclair then back to the guard. 'Oh, we're not married. Alison's a nurse at my clinic. We're checking out your facilities for a patient of mine who's looking for somewhere to recuperate.'

Sinclair smiled at the guard. 'I'm just here for the spa.'

The guard laughed. 'I'm sure you'll both have a great time and your patient will be more than welcome here.'

'I can see that.'

The guard handed the reservation back through the car window and pressed the button to raise the barrier. 'Welcome to the Lone Star Resort.'

'Thank you.' Bazarov smiled and waved as he drove under the barrier and towards the hotel. He put his hand on Sinclair's knee. 'Thank you for your help, Miss Sinclair. We make a good team.'

Sinclair grabbed his wrist and twisted. Her other hand pushed against his elbow, putting maximum pressure on his joints. Bazarov was forced against the steering wheel and the car slowed to a halt. Sinclair looked straight into his eyes. 'Let's get this straight. I'm not here to help you, I'm here to help my friends. If I even think that you've hurt them, all deals are off and I'll enjoy watching you suffer.'

The guard at the gate watched as the car stopped, something looked wrong. He opened the door of his hut and took a step towards the SUV.

Bazarov was in pain. From this position Sinclair could pop his shoulder joint right out of the socket; it wasn't something he wanted to experience. He gritted his teeth. 'Okay, you've made your point. You need to let me go now. The guard back there will be wondering what's going on. If our cover gets blown and I don't make it to the island, all your friends are dead.'

Sinclair looked in the wing mirror. The guard was watching and slowly walking towards them. She released the Russian's arm and he sat back in his seat, rubbing his shoulder. 'Thank you. Now, let's get on, shall we?' He put his foot on the gas and the car continued up the track.

The guard watched for a moment and returned to the gatehouse shaking his head. It looked like they were arguing – a lovers' tiff. He chuckled to himself. Lots of people brought their mistresses here and he'd heard some wild excuses over the years, but checking out the resort on behalf of a patient was a new one.

Bazarov parked the car and they each pulled out a suitcase, wheeling them noisily across to reception. Bazarov held open one of the doors. 'Ladies first.'

'Fuck you.' Sinclair opened the adjacent door and walked up to the desk.

Bazarov checked for anyone watching, he didn't like being made to look a fool. If he hadn't needed Sinclair for this part of the operation he would have killed her back at the ranch.

His original plan was to grab Garrison from his room and bundle him into a car; it wasn't the best plan but it was all he'd been able to come up with at the time. The first problem with it was that a group of men arriving here would stand out. Most guests were single men or couples, not groups. Most of his men wouldn't easily blend in with the sophisticated guests at the resort. Then there was the potential problem of someone raising the alarm during the kidnap. He and his men could face the possibility of having to shoot their way past security. The police would be tipped off and the whole operation would be at risk. Once they were on the island any police involvement wouldn't matter, but he had to get Garrison there or it was over.

Sinclair arriving on the scene had given him a flash of inspiration, a new plan. An older man with a younger woman wouldn't raise any eyebrows here. The plan to get Garrison out of the hotel depended on Sinclair's cooperation. He would have to put up with her shit a little bit longer.

At the desk the receptionist smiled and asked them for some photo ID. 'It's hotel policy for guests who are here for the first time.'

'No problem.' Bazarov handed over a driving licence in the name of Doctor Uri Belov – consultant cardiologist at a private clinic in Houston.

'Thank you, Doctor.'

Sinclair handed over the fake credentials she'd been given at the motel. Today she was posing as a senior staff nurse at Belov's clinic.

'Thank you, Miss Sutherland. Welcome to Lone Star. You'll find information on all of our facilities in the pack in your room. Your rooms are adjoining, as requested, and if you need anything just give me a call.' The receptionist slid two key cards across the desk and flashed another sincere looking smile.

'Thank you,' Bazarov looked at the receptionist's name tag, 'Christine.' He picked up both key cards and handed one to Sinclair. 'Shall we?'

They rode the lift up to their rooms in silence. Bazarov took the key card from Sinclair and opened her door. 'I'll keep this for now.' He walked into her room and unplugged the telephone from its socket. 'Don't want you getting any ideas. I'll put it back later tonight.' He unlocked the door that connected their rooms and went around to his, taking the phone with him.

Sinclair checked for anything that might help her contact Carter to let him know what had happened. There wasn't anything. It was a typical hotel room: bed, bathroom, free shampoo, and minibar. The connecting door opened and Bazarov walked through it.

'I think we'll keep this open. Make sure you don't go missing.' He locked the main door to Sinclair's room. 'And don't answer the door.'

He wasn't going to let Sinclair out of his sight. She was going to have to go through with this and look for an opportunity to get away once they were on the island. She picked up the remote and turned on the TV. The news was still focussing on the explosion at Quinn's ranch; it was the first time either of them had seen it. She pointed at the screen. 'What the fuck is that?'

'Just a little diversion, keep them busy while we take care of Garrison.'

Sinclair looked back at the screen, shaking her head. 'Somebody's going to take you down, Bazarov. I just hope it's me.'

He switched off the TV. 'That's enough entertainment, we've got plans to go through before tonight.'

'We don't need to go through the plan again, I get it. We're drugging and kidnapping this guy so you can do whatever with him.'

Bazarov sat in the chair opposite Sinclair. 'Garrison isn't a nice guy, he's no innocent. You're wasting your time feeling any compassion for him.'

'He might be an arsehole, but I'll bet he hasn't killed seventeen people already this morning and I don't imagine he's planning to nuke anyone.'

'I'm only doing what's necessary to get what I want.'

'And what is that? What do you want?'

'I want things to return to the way they were. I fought for the Red Army during the great days of the Soviet Empire. We were the most powerful country on Earth. Since the end of the Cold War, no one fears or respects us. I belong to a group who want to see those days return. We want to show the world that we are still powerful, we want to bring NATO and the Americans to their knees.'

'You know they won't negotiate with terrorists.'

'So we will level their cities, and then they will dance to our tune. This isn't going to be a quick hit. We are not going to strike them and run away. We are going to hold this over the West until they bow to us.'

Sinclair watched Bazarov as he began to get worked up, pounding his fist on the arm of the chair to drive his point home. The guy really believed this shit. 'And what if they nuke you first?'

'They won't have time to react to this. The missiles are too close. It'll be worse than having them in Cuba. The mushroom clouds will be hanging over them before they realise what's happened.'

Sinclair knew she had to stop this. Bazarov was acting like a bad Bond villain. She could kill him right here but she had no way of knowing what he had ordered his men to do if that happened. How much damage could they do without him – without Garrison? 'If you're so powerful, why do you need a burned-out politician with you?'

'Let's just say he'll make things a whole lot easier.' He stood up and turned towards the door. 'Get some rest. It's going to be a long night.' He walked through to his own room and left the door open behind him.

Sinclair lay back on the bed and closed her eyes.

Garrison sat in his room. His round of golf with the judge had turned into a long day of networking, but he'd made some valuable new contacts and you can never have too many of those. Now he needed to lie down and have an hour's sleep to recharge his batteries. One of his favourite parts of a stay at the resort was eating in the restaurant and then moving on to the bar. It was an opportunity to flirt with some of the female guests who were here alone. Sometimes he got lucky, and he wasn't going to pass up the chance of that.

* * *

Sinclair applied the finishing touches to her makeup and checked herself in the mirror. She was wearing red, high heeled shoes and a short, tight fitting red dress that accentuated her figure. Her scarlet lipstick stood out in contrast against her pale skin, and her blonde hair rested lightly on her shoulders. A pair of fake diamond earrings and a bracelet completed the look. It was a long time since she had dressed up to go anywhere and she had to admit that she looked good.

During her time on the run she'd put on the weight that she'd lost in prison, and the cage fighting had kept her toned. At any other time she'd be pleased with the way she looked, but this was different. She was only dressed like this to attract a particular man so he could be kidnapped. Even though Garrison was a nasty piece of work, that fact didn't sit well with her. In this situation he was an innocent.

Bazarov came into the room and looked her up and down. 'He's going to think he's hit the jackpot when you start coming on to him.'

Sinclair sprayed some perfume on her wrists and neck. 'Let's just get this over with.'

'You remember the plan?'

'I'll get him up here and drug him. The rest is your problem.' She picked up a small handbag and gestured towards the door. 'Are you ready?'

'I'll be right behind you.'

Sinclair opened the door and set off down the corridor towards the lift. Bazarov followed her. They were posing as co-workers who were having an affair, but when they got to the bar they wanted it to look like there was a problem between them. That would give Garrison the chance to step in and chat-up Sinclair. She would start flirting with him just to make sure he got the message.

The lift doors opened on the ground floor and the two of them entered the restaurant. Garrison was already there, showered and dressed up to the nines in his best ladykiller outfit. Cream trousers and a white polo shirt underneath a dark blue blazer that bore the US Navy crest on the pocket. He wore a large gold championship ring, from his football days in college, to show potential conquests he was athletic and strong, or at least used to be. A chunky gold watch studded with diamonds, and the pre-requisite medallion around his neck advertised his financial credentials. He thought it made him look irresistible. Sinclair thought he looked like a sad old man trying to recapture his youth. Flirting with him wasn't going to be easy for her but luring him upstairs wouldn't be a problem.

They picked a table that was in Garrison's line of sight but far enough away that he couldn't hear their conversation. Bazarov pulled out a chair for Sinclair and they set about portraying an image of a romantically involved couple. To begin with their conversation appeared to be normal. They ordered their meal and some wine. She touched his hand now and again. Everything looked fine.

Garrison couldn't take his eyes off Sinclair from the minute she walked in. She was exactly his type. It was a pity she was with someone. Although she wasn't wearing a wedding ring, so maybe he was still in with a chance. Lots of young mistresses were brought here by older men and some of them were into a bit of extra fun. Especially with men who had money.

As the evening wore on, Bazarov appeared to be getting annoyed by something, and occasionally raised his voice before looking around the restaurant and dropping back to a whisper. Sinclair looked upset and, after a while, dabbed at her eyes with her napkin.

Garrison watched discretely, it was beginning to look like a full-blown fallout. That would give him the chance he was looking for, the chance to put his predatory skills into practice. What he didn't know, what he couldn't know, was that he was being played. He was being pulled into a trap that his contacts and his money couldn't get him out of.

The whole restaurant fell silent when Bazarov banged his fist on the table. He looked up at the other diners, threw his napkin on his empty plate, stood up and stormed off. Sinclair was left on her own, the whole room looking at her. She put her hand over her mouth as she too stood up and hurried away from the stares, trying to hide her embarrassment. Garrison gulped down his glass of wine and followed her out.

Sinclair stood outside the main entrance taking deep breaths and wiping her eyes. Garrison opened the door and approached her. 'Are you okay?'

This was another decision point for Sinclair. She could tip off Garrison, fill him in on the plan – tell him to run, but she couldn't help thinking about Frank, Jo and the kids. She could always tell Bazarov that Garrison wasn't interested in her and she couldn't get him up to the room, but he wouldn't believe that. Even if he did, he would get the admiral another way and she would've blown any chance of the others getting away. If she could buy time, Frank might escape and get in touch with Carter. She had to go through with this for now. She smiled at Garrison. 'I'm fine thanks, just needed a little air.'

'I couldn't help seeing what happened, an argument with your husband?' Garrison was fishing for information.

'Oh, he's not my husband, he's my boss.' She began to reel him in.

'Walking out on a beautiful woman like you, he must be an asshole.'

Sinclair laughed. 'He's a married asshole.'

'Right, I get it. He's not willing to leave his wife?'

'Something like that. How stupid am I?'

'He's the stupid one. I'll bet his wife doesn't look as good as you.'

Sinclair looked at her reflection in the window. 'I'm nothing special.'

'You're the best-looking thing in here tonight.' He gave her a wink.

'You certainly know how to flatter a girl.' She held out her hand. 'I'm Alison.'

Garrison took her hand and lifted it to his lips. 'I'm James Garrison. Admiral James D. Garrison. Retired.'

Sinclair did her best to look impressed. 'An admiral, wow. I must admit,' she looked around as if she was divulging a great secret, 'I do like men in uniform.'

Garrison could sense an opportunity here. 'Would you like to have a drink, Alison, in the bar? You can tell me all about your problems. I'm a good listener.'

She didn't want to appear too keen. It might warn him that something wasn't quite right. 'Thank you, but I think I'd better just go up to my room. Anyway, he'll be in the bar drinking himself into a coma.'

'Well why don't you show the loser you're fine without him?'

'I'm not sure that would be a good idea, what if he causes a scene or gets violent?'

'Don't you worry about that. I'm well known here. He'll be thrown out before I am and, if he gets violent, I can take care of myself.'

She had him. He was doing everything he could think of to get her inside with him. All she had to do now was get him up to her room. 'Okay, Admiral. Why not? Let's show him.'

Garrison's charm had paid off. All he needed to do now was seal the deal over a drink. 'Please, call me James.' He opened the hotel door and offered his arm.

Sinclair slid her arm into the crook of his elbow and they walked into the bar.

Bazarov was sitting on a stool at the end of the bar looking, to everyone else, like a rejected lover. He stared at his vodka as he toyed with the glass, seemingly lost in his thoughts. It was all an act. He was alert to his surroundings, watching the reflections in the mirror that hung behind the bar. He emptied his glass and slid it across to the barman for a refill as Garrison and Sinclair came in, arm in arm.

The couple made for a table as far away from Bazarov as they could get. Garrison pulled out a seat and Sinclair nodded to him as she sat down. 'Thank you, James.'

Garrison clicked his fingers towards a waitress. 'A bottle of your best champagne.'

The waitress wrote down the order on her pad. 'Yes, sir.'

'And a large bourbon, on the rocks.'

'Yes, sir, coming right up.' She hurried away towards the bar.

Garrison sat down and leaned forwards, towards Sinclair. 'Now, Alison. Tell me how a beautiful woman like you got tied up with a guy like that.'

Sinclair took him through the back story that she and Bazarov had cooked up on the way to the resort. She was a young nurse who'd come to America looking for a new start. Bazarov played the consultant living in a loveless marriage, although she now knew that was a lie. Garrison listened just enough to look like he cared, throwing Sinclair compliments occasionally, before steering the conversation back to his favourite subject. Himself.

The waitress appeared with more drinks and Garrison downed yet another glass. If he drank any more Sinclair would have to carry him upstairs. It would save them having to drug him but wouldn't fit with the plan. She finished her wine, put her hand on Garrison's forearm, and winked at him. 'I think it's time I was in bed.' She nodded to Bazarov and headed for the lift.

Garrison couldn't believe his luck. He threw his last bourbon down his throat and got quickly to his feet, almost overbalancing. He steadied himself and set off in pursuit of Sinclair, focusing on the sway of her hips as he followed her to the lift.

The lift doors opened with a swish and they both got in, Garrison making sure he held on to the handrail to stop himself falling over. He'd drunk a little too much but he could hold his liquor. As long as he stayed upright she'd never notice. He didn't want to ruin his chances by looking like a drunken idiot.

Sinclair watched him holding on, he could barely stand up. At this rate she was going to have to hold him up just to get him to the room. The man was nothing more than a drunken waster, convinced he had a way with women. She didn't want to imagine what he'd done to some of the women he'd tricked or forced into his bed. Drugging and kidnapping this guy didn't seem like such a bad thing after all.

The lift doors opened on the third floor and Sinclair took Garrison's arm, guiding him down the corridor towards her room. He, of course, was convinced it was the other way round – he was a strong man with a beautiful woman on his arm; she was powerless to resist his advances, putty in his hands.

They arrived at her room and Sinclair opened the door. Garrison grabbed her from behind, manhandling her into the room. He kicked the door shut and forced her up against the wall, his hands all over her. She pushed him off and gave his face a hard slap. She really wanted to punch him, but a swollen eye wouldn't suit the story. Garrison took two steps backwards, trying to hold his balance. 'So, you like it a little rough, do you? Well, that's fine by me.' He unfastened his belt and dropped his trousers to his ankles, just as Sinclair reached out and injected the drugs into his flabby neck.

Garrison put a hand up to his neck. 'What the fuck?' His voice was slurred, a combination of too much bourbon and the fast-acting tranquiliser that was rushing through his bloodstream. His ears began to buzz and the room was spinning. He blinked to clear his blurred vision. He stepped towards Sinclair and tried to grab her but, with his trousers around his ankles, he could only waddle across the room like a toddler taking its first steps. He lost his balance, fell forwards, and landed, unconscious, only half on the bed.

Sinclair lifted Garrison's legs and heaved them onto the bed. Working quickly, she removed the rest of his clothes and laid him on his back. The room had to be staged for the plan to work smoothly. She took off her dress and put on a bathrobe, messed up her hair and smeared her lipstick. It needed to look like Garrison had had a kind of seizure, or heart attack, while they were in bed together. Something that would cause a scandal for the hotel, something they would want hushed up. She picked up the phone and dialled zero.

The receptionist rushed into the bar and straight over to Bazarov. 'Doctor, there's a telephone call for you, it sounds urgent.'

Bazarov followed her to reception and took the call. 'Hello, this is Doctor Belov.'

'It's done. Now it's your turn. Sell the story and let's get out of here.'

'Don't panic. Monitor his vitals and I'll be right there.' He put down the phone and turned to the receptionist. 'I need your help, Christine. It seems that Admiral Garrison may have had a heart attack upstairs.'

'I'll call 911 straight away.'

Bazarov held up his hand. 'No. Listen, you don't really want people knowing about this, do you?'

'What do you mean?'

'You don't want flashing blue lights outside while the other guests watch Garrison being loaded into the ambulance.'

Christine thought about it for a second. The important guests who came here did so for privacy, any emergency call would make it into the papers and shine a spotlight on them. 'No, I'm sure the hotel management would prefer some discretion.'

'I'm sure they would. There's also the matter of a man with Garrison's reputation being found in a room with a young woman he may have forced himself upon.'

Christine didn't like the sound of this. 'But they were in the bar together.'

'They were, but they left separately.'

'Oh my god, what do I do?'

'You don't panic, Christine. My clinic has a helicopter. I'll phone them and get it out here. We just have to get Garrison over to your helipad, it's far enough from the hotel that no one will notice, they'll just think it's another guest arriving.

He'll be getting treatment at my cardiology clinic in no time.'

'That sounds like a good idea, Doctor, thank you.'

'That's quite alright, Christine. Now, do you have wheelchairs for the use of guests?'

'Yes, we do, Doctor.'

'That's good. Go and get one and meet me up in the room.'

'Okay, yes, right, I'll do that.' She disappeared through a door behind reception.

Bazarov walked over to the lift and pressed the call button. When he reached the room, he knocked on the door and Sinclair let him in. 'Are they going for it?'

'So far. The girl in reception is panicking just enough, but not so much that she has called her bosses, yet.'

'We'd better get this over with quickly.'

Bazarov took his mobile phone out of his pocket and pressed the speed dial number. 'Get here now. The helipad is behind the hotel. We'll be there.' He closed down the call and put the phone back in his pocket.

There was a knock at the door. Bazarov answered it and Christine came in pushing a wheelchair. 'Will this be okay?'

'Yes, thank you, Christine.'

The receptionist looked over at Garrison, lying naked on the bed, and over to Sinclair. She didn't look like she'd been forced into anything. 'Are you okay?'

'Yes, I'll be fine.' She waved her hand towards Garrison. 'Let's just get this guy to a hospital as quick as we can.'

Bazarov was checking Garrison's pulse. 'Alison, you get dressed. I'll need you in the helicopter with me.'

'Yes, Doctor.' She grabbed some clothes and went into the bathroom.

'Christine, you give me a hand. We'll get him dressed and

178

into the chair.'

Fifteen minutes later, the three of them were coming out of the freight elevator and out of the back entrance of the hotel, pushing the unconscious Garrison in the wheelchair. Bazarov stopped and put his hand on Christine's arm. 'Thank you for your help, Christine. You get back to reception. We'll take it from here.'

'Maybe I should let my boss know what's happening, just in case.'

'I would wait until morning. We'll call and let you know how Garrison is doing later on; then you can give them a full update.' Bazarov set off towards the helipad with Sinclair pushing the wheelchair.

The helicopter was coming in to land. The young receptionist watched as they loaded Garrison on board and took off again. She thought it was strange that an air ambulance would say QRL Global on the side. Maybe she should call her boss right away.

Chapter 20

K urt Halloran stubbed out his cigarette and walked into the Lone Star Golf Resort. In the room behind reception, two other agents were trawling through hours of camera footage looking for Sinclair and Bazarov. Halloran stuck his head into the room. 'Anything?'

'Nothing that tells us much, they only have cameras in the public areas.' The agent pointed at the image on the screen. 'This is definitely Sinclair but we're not sure who the guy is yet.'

'Stay on it, take a copy of everything.'

Christine sat in the manager's office next door, alone. Halloran had isolated her in there with a pad and pencil to write down everything she could remember about the previous night's events. As he entered the room she looked up, frightened, a rabbit caught in the headlights. He tried to reassure her to help her relax. 'It's okay, Christine, you're not in trouble.'

'I didn't know they weren't who they said they were.'

Halloran sat opposite her and turned the pad round so he could read it. 'Is this everything you remember?'

'Yes, I didn't really see much of them. They came down for a meal and appeared to fall out, then Garrison appeared and

180

he and the woman sat in the bar for a few hours until ... well, you know the rest.' She looked down at her hands clasped in her lap. 'I should've noticed something.'

'It's not your fault, Christine. It looks like we're dealing with professionals here. They knew exactly what they were doing, don't worry about it.'

'Do you know who they are? What they want?'

'We have an idea.' He ripped the page off the pad and stood up. 'Thanks for this, it'll really help.' He smiled at her. 'You did as much as you could. If you hadn't gone along with them they would have killed you.'

Halloran stood beside his car and lit another cigarette. He pressed the call button on his phone and rang his boss. 'It's definitely her, we need to know who the guy is ... They took off in a QRL chopper, so Quinn is caught up in this somehow ... Right, I'll hang on here and see if anything else comes to light.' He took another lungful of smoke from his cigarette, immediately coughing it out again in several rasping, hacking coughs. He really needed to stop, but now was definitely not the time.

Special Agent in Charge Thomas Johnson put down his phone and summoned Robert Tyler to his office. The analyst knocked on Johnson's door and opened it. 'You want me, sir?'

'Yes, Robert. Close the door and take a seat.'

Tyler did as he was asked. 'Is this about the Quinn ranch?'

'It's all tied up together. Kurt is sending some pictures from the hotel. I want you to identify the guy with Sinclair. First the ranch and now a kidnapping, he must be on our database somewhere.'

'I'll get the facial recognition software on it. It shouldn't take long if he's known to us.'

'Let me know as soon as you have his name. I'm going to speak to an old friend at the CIA, maybe he can find something out. Some of this has deniable op written all over it. There's no way the British would lose track of an asset like Sinclair, even in prison.'

'You think she's gone rogue and they know?'

'Maybe she's still working for them. Escaped convict would make one hell of a cover story.'

* * *

Danny Kinsella clicked on the folder icon on his screen and checked the log of his network search. His applications were systematically trawling through the networks of US law enforcement organisations and news agencies for a mention of Lone Star. Among the spurious hits that came to nothing, a story jumped out at him. An emergency call had been made from the Lone Star Golf Resort to local police, reporting the possible kidnapping of a guest. It was the name that attracted his attention. He grabbed the survivors list he had printed out for the Apocalypse Protocol. There, halfway down, was former member of the Joint Chiefs, Admiral James D. Garrison.

Kinsella went into his spare bedroom and switched on the bedside lamp. Carter was lying on the bed fully clothed. Kinsella had convinced him to lie down and get some sleep a couple of hours earlier. The long nights scanning the net for information and the constant worry about McGill and Sinclair had taken their toll. Carter was looking old. Kinsella bent down and shook him gently. 'Simeon. Simeon, you need to see this.'

Carter opened his eyes and blinked at the light. 'What is it, Danny?'

Kinsella handed him the printout of the kidnapping report. 'Things just got a whole lot worse.'

Carter put on his glasses and read the report. He recognised the names. They'd been trying to find out what Lone Star referred to since Sinclair had found the documents at the ranch. Garrison was on the Joint Chiefs when the Kraken and the Apocalypse Protocol were being developed. In those days he was on the survivors list, one of the men with his finger on the nuclear trigger.

Kinsella handed him the list. 'I've now got the full list. Garrison is halfway down. Look at the name at the bottom.'

Carter checked the list. At the bottom was Josephine Quinn. 'Jesus, what is she doing on it?'

'Like I said before, this was put together to test the control systems for the Kraken. It isn't the actual list. Quinn was a young engineer at the time. She helped develop it.'

'So Bazarov now has Quinn and Garrison and he could launch a nuclear attack?'

Kinsella nodded. 'All he has to do is get them both in front of a control terminal and he can use their bio data to take over the system.'

'I have to tell Edward. He has to get the Americans to lock them out.'

'It can't be done, Simeon. The Apocalypse Protocol is a backdoor. It was designed specifically to ensure that control of the missiles didn't fall into enemy hands after an invasion. It can't be locked out.'

'You're telling me there's no way to switch it off?'

'Once the protocol is implemented, all US control panels are disabled. Control passes to the panels in the other countries that have bought into the system.'

'But no other country has it yet.'

'Exactly, there is only one of those panels in existence. It was used to test the process for handing over the nuclear trigger to another country. Even destroying the panel doesn't stop the missiles from launching. The launch can only be stopped from the panel that started it.'

Carter took off his glasses as he realised, with horror, what Kinsella was telling him. 'That other panel is at Leatherback Cay, isn't it?'

'Yes, it is.'

'Surely there's something they can do to stop him? Switch the whole system off, disable the missiles, something?'

Kinsella pointed at the time and date on the printout. 'This kidnap took place yesterday. They've had enough time to get Garrison to the island. I might be too late already.'

'What the hell are we going to do, Danny?'

'You have to get hold of the Americans yourself, Simeon. Fill them in on the details. Lancaster's hands are tied by his bosses. They'll sit on the info. They won't want our involvement known, it might cause a diplomatic incident. We have to bypass them. You must have some friends in the CIA left over from the old days.'

'I have a few that I can contact, off the record. They still have enough swing in Washington to get access to the executive.'

'I think off the record is good. Don't forget about Vadim. If we accept he is connected to Bazarov, he must know about all of this. Yet, I haven't been able to find out anything about him. That means two things.' Kinsella held up his right forefinger. 'One. He's high up. High enough to get rid of any data that might point to him and high enough to get rid of us if he thinks we're a threat.' Kinsella held up a second finger. 'And two. He's willing to see this operation go ahead either for money or to cover his own arse. That makes him extremely dangerous.'

Carter nodded. 'You're right. I'll start tracking down my contacts. Lancaster will understand, that's why he's using us in the first place.' He got out an old address book. 'I knew this would come in handy someday.'

'I hope your old friends can do something, Simeon. Otherwise, the only hope we've got is Sinclair and McGill. We don't even know if they're still alive.'

Chapter 21

Copperhead Bay was a deep-water harbour situated at the northern end of Leatherback Cay. A long spit of land protected its eastern side with a man-made breakwater curving west to complete the harbours shelter. A small lighthouse sat on the end of the breakwater and lit the way to the harbour's single jetty. The port facilities were arranged along a thin strip of land between the bay and a steep cliff face. The jagged, jungle covered mountains rose up from the northern end of the island and sloped down to the lagoon that covered most of the island's southern half.

The MV San Antonio sailed into the harbour and manoeuvred itself to come alongside the jetty. Bazarov's men threw the ropes to the shoreside dock workers who manned the island for QRL. They secured the cargo ship to the dockside bollards and prepared to unload. As far as they were concerned, this was business as usual.

McGill felt the change in the ship's motion and heard noises coming from the deck above. If he was going to do something, this was probably his best chance. He shuffled along the bench in the back of the van as far as his cuffs would let him, and reached across the front seat. A bundle of maps and instructions, from Bazarov to his men, lay on the dashboard. At full stretch McGill could get his fingertips to them. He pulled them closer, inch by inch, until they slid off the dashboard and into his hand.

There was a metallic clang as the clips on the door to the hold were turned and the door opened. Someone was coming to get him. He worked quickly, taking the paperclip from the papers and opening it up. The footsteps on the metal ladder got louder as Bazarov's henchman came closer. McGill bent the end of the paperclip into an L shape and worked it into the lock of his handcuffs. It was a party trick he'd learned years ago, but he'd never expected to have to use it for real. He looked out of the window at the guard who had now reached the bottom of the ladder and was approaching the van. He focussed on his cuffs and, after a few seconds, the lock opened. He pulled up the leg of his trousers and began ripping at the tape that was securing the Glock to his boot. He picked up the blanket they had given him and wrapped it around the weapon. As the side door of the van opened, McGill pulled the trigger and shot the guard in the chest.

He grabbed the documents, shoved them in his pocket, and jumped out of the van. The shot was muffled but still loud enough for someone to hear, he had to get out. The man lying at his feet stared up at him with wide, questioning eyes; blood frothed around his mouth as he tried to breathe. There was no need to finish him off, he wasn't a threat any more and McGill didn't want to risk being heard, or waste a bullet.

He reached down and pulled off the man's combat jacket. In the pockets there were extra magazines for the Glock and the assault rifle that all the guards carried. McGill put the jacket on and slung the assault rifle over his shoulder. On the guard's webbing belt hung a holster containing his Glock and a Russian Kizlyar knife. McGill unfastened the belt and placed it around his own waist. He looked down at the man – he felt no sympathy for him: this was business. As the guard coughed up his dying breath with a spray of blood, McGill took off towards the upper deck.

At the top of the hold's ladder he turned the clips on the hatch and opened it just enough to peer through the gap. Everyone was busy – either securing the ship or preparing the containers to be lifted by the dockside crane. He pulled up his collar to hide his face, kept his head down and slipped through the door. He stopped, with his back to the superstructure on the dark side of the ship, away from the shouting dockers and guards. He checked left and right, there was no one watching or patrolling, they weren't expecting him to escape. He took two steps forwards, climbed over the guardrail, and hung down the side of the ship. After one more check below, he dropped the remaining fifteen feet into the water.

He stayed beneath the surface as much as possible, working his way along the length of the ship and over to the jetty. He looked up, it was twenty feet to the dockside. He had to climb up and get away before the Russians realised he was gone.

At regular intervals along the dock, metal ladders reached up from the water. McGill put his weight on one of the rungs and tested it. There was no creak of rusted metal – it was solid – and he climbed, carefully, checking for movement above as he went.

Stopping, with his body in darkness and his head just clearing the top of the ladder, he surveyed the scene. The waterfront floodlights created multiple shadows behind wooden crates and tarpaulin covered piles of equipment that sat on the dock. The crane was lifting the first container from the ship, and swinging it over onto a large, flatbed railway truck, to be transported around the coast to the test facility. The top of the ladder was well lit but all the dockers were watching the container as it hung from the crane, none of them were looking in his direction.

He completed the climb onto the jetty and rolled behind a large drum of cable. Crouching down, he worked out his options. There weren't enough of Bazarov's men for them to launch a manhunt through the jungle. Once he was away from the docks, they were likely to concentrate on keeping him away from the facility. Alone in the jungle he couldn't do anything to disrupt their plans. As long as they thought that, it suited him fine.

Water ran from his clothes and trickled in rivulets across the concrete, he needed to find some shelter and build a fire to dry off. He looked up at the cliff face; it looked climbable, but only if there was nothing else. He would use up too much time and energy he didn't have going that way. He could follow the railway tracks but there was a chance he'd be spotted. His best option was the train. If he could hide on board until it was clear of the cliffs, he could jump off and set up camp close to the test facility compound. The engine pulling the trucks was small so he didn't think the speed of the train would be a problem. Once he was set up, he'd monitor the buildings until Sinclair arrived – if she wasn't here already.

He stayed low and kept to the shadows, closing in on the railway tracks. As he reached the back of the train there was a sudden commotion on board the ship. From the look of it, they had discovered his handiwork in the hold. He climbed under the chassis of the truck and readied his Glock, if all else failed he'd have to shoot his way out.

Bazarov's guards ran down the gangplank, torches scanning the jetty. The beams lit up the cliff and the surface of the water. McGill watched as they systematically searched along the dock and found the puddle behind the cable drum. He looked down; water was still dripping from his jacket and forming small pools on the oily railway sleepers. He needed to move but it was too late. As he lowered himself to the ground, two guards approached. They shone their torches under the chassis of the train, beginning with the engine, moving towards the rear and McGill's hiding place.

He shuffled backwards, away from the probing lights, trying to melt into the framework. With the Glock in his right hand he sucked in a lungful of air and held his breath.

As the guards' torchlight hit the underside of the truck, one of the dockers began shouting, half in English, half in Spanish. 'Peligroso, danger ... you move, ahora ... now.' He pointed up at the second container, which was now being lowered onto the rear truck, and back at the searchers. 'You, danger.'

Bazarov's two goons decided they weren't being paid enough to risk being crushed under the container. The pair backed off and McGill breathed out, loosening his grip on the trucks metalwork. He watched as all the guards came together at the end of the gangplank. Several of them shook their heads and one pointed upwards at the cliffs. McGill was right. They didn't have enough people to carry out Bazarov's instructions and a manhunt at the same time. He wasn't worth the effort.

Once the containers were secured, the workers on the jetty rounded up the guards and shepherded them into a carriage at the front of the train. The engine fired up and the truck jolted as the train pulled away. They moved out of the reach of the dockside floodlights and McGill's eyes adjusted to what little light there was. He could make out the cliffs on one side, and the sea on the other, as the train trundled the five miles around the coast to the test facility.

After a short but bumpy ride, McGill began to see the floodlights flickering through the foliage that covered most of the island. The buildings of the test facility were surrounded by a razor wire topped security fence. Outside the fence were lattice floodlight towers that lit up the test facility and the surrounding area. The main gate was manned by armed guards and a second entrance beside it was opening up to allow the train access. As the train slowed, McGill dropped down from his position under the truck and onto the railway tracks. Once the train had moved over him, he rolled off the tracks and disappeared into the jungle.

The train carried on to the compound's station. The dockers from the jetty reappeared and a small fleet of forklift trucks began unloading the containers' contents. McGill watched as wooden crates and tarpaulin covered pallets were taken inside the large warehouse next to the tracks. Most of the crates had military markings on them, probably weapons of some sort. Some of the pallets were piled high with ammunition boxes and others with tinned food. Bazarov was well stocked to hold out for some time. McGill couldn't get close enough to make out any real details but, even at this distance, he did recognise a worrying shape. In a raised position, just outside the compound fence, he could make out the unmistakable outline of a Rapier surface to air missile launcher. Bazarov was expecting, and ready to repel, an aerial attack.

McGill couldn't do anything yet, there were too many people about and he still had to confirm if Bazarov and Sinclair were on the island. He needed shelter, fire, and food. He'd checked the pockets of his jacket when he'd taken it off the guard and all he had found was ammunition. The webbing belt had the Glock and the knife but also a small pouch that he hadn't checked yet. He opened the flap on it and removed a small tin box that contained the kind of survival equipment you might find in a store that catered for weekend warriors and survivalists. Some of it was pointless in this particular situation, but you never knew what might come in handy later. As his most urgent need was warmth, he was happy to see a flint and striker in the box. At least he could get a fire going and dry out his clothes. With any luck he would find a small cave or rock overhang where he could hide out. He left the guards and dockers to finish their work and walked back through the jungle towards the cliffs.

* * *

Simeon Carter sat in an office on the second floor of the US Embassy on Grosvenor Square. He'd arrived early to make sure he made it through security in plenty of time. He stood in line to be searched in the security hut outside the main entrance then made his way up the steps past the throng of people trying to apply for a visa. His identity was checked before he was escorted to the office of William Easter, an old friend from the Cold War days. There was no nameplate on the office door but Carter didn't need one. He knew Easter was chief of station for the CIA in London.

Carter stood up as Easter entered the room. 'Bill. You haven't changed a bit.'

The veteran spy patted his stomach, which hung over his

belt and strained the buttons of his shirt. 'If only that were true, Simeon.'

They shook hands warmly and Easter gestured for Carter to take a seat. The American sat opposite him on a leather couch. 'How can I help you, Simeon? I was surprised, but pleased, when you called. I thought you were out of the game?'

'Maybe I am. Maybe it's just a social call, an invitation to a party.'

Easter smiled. 'I know you too well, Simeon. You don't do parties.'

Carter sat forwards in his chair. 'Can we talk?'

Easter knew what his old friend meant. He was asking if the room was bugged, if their conversation was being recorded and could come back to bite them on the arse. 'You're free to talk in here. No one is listening.'

'Good. What I'm about to tell you could cause some political fallout, but we have to get past that.'

'Sound's bad.'

'As bad as it gets, Bill.'

Easter stood up and pressed a button on the intercom that sat on his desk. After a couple of seconds his secretary's voice answered, 'Yes, Sir?'

'Hold all my calls please, Gina. No one comes in here, no matter who it is.'

'Yes, sir.'

Easter sat back down on the couch. 'Okay, Simeon, you have my full attention.'

'I'm sure you've heard about the explosion in Texas, the dead officers?'

'Of course. We're trying to figure out who's responsible. Whether or not this is a terrorist attack.'

'There was also a shootout in a motel in Houston and the kidnapping of Admiral Garrison from a golf resort. They are all linked.'

'And you know this, how?'

'We have an asset on the inside. Her name is Ali Sinclair.'

Easter walked over to his desk and picked up a plain, red folder. He handed it to Carter. 'The FBI in Houston have asked us to find out everything we can on a woman called Sinclair. They say she used to be one of yours but is currently an escaped convict. They came to the conclusion she was mixed up in all three of these events.'

Carter opened the folder. It contained mug shots of Sinclair, the photographs from the motel, and stills from The Lone Star's CCTV footage. 'They're right. She escaped from a Mexican prison and we tracked her down, put her in undercover. We thought this was no more than a possible security leak. A threat to the secrecy of the Kraken deal. We were wrong.'

'How wrong? What's the threat here, Simeon? It's already gotten pretty bad. The politicians are screaming for someone's ass over this.'

Carter held up one of the stills from the file. 'The man with Sinclair at the resort, the one you can't quite make out, it's Viktor Bazarov.'

'Holy shit. What the fuck is he doin' in the US? He hasn't raised any alarms, we thought he was in the Middle East.'

'We believe he is now in QRL's test facility on their private island in the Caribbean. He has access to a control panel for the Kraken and, in Quinn and Garrison, he has the means to launch a nuclear strike.'

Easter ran his hands through his hair, he was stunned. 'You

194

waited until now to tell us this?'

'Like I said, Bill, we have to avoid the political fallout. We have to take care of this before we start analysing who should have told who what, and how soon.'

Easter picked up his phone. 'I've gotta tell the Pentagon. They'll order in an airstrike, bomb the shit out of the place.'

'You can't do that. We don't know how close Bazarov is to launching, he may have started a countdown already. Destroying the test facility won't stop it. The other thing we don't know is if the island is his only option. Killing him might set off something else. Another attack we know nothing about. If you destroy the island you may lose any chance you have of preventing this.'

'Then what do we do?'

'You can't go through the normal channels, it'll take too long. If the CIA raise the alarm, the brass will want to know where the info came from and why it didn't come to light sooner. They might even think it's some kind of hoax, the delay could be fatal. You must make an assault on the island. Marines, SEALs, whoever you have in the area. You get them in there, as quickly as you can, and help Sinclair. She has backup from a guy called Frank McGill. A good man, ex-marine, but he's not enough to take out Bazarov's private army on his own.'

'How can Sinclair halt the countdown?'

'She's on the inside. She'll know that she needs to get Quinn and Garrison to safety and protect the control panel. She's all you've got.'

'Okay, Simeon. I'll get in touch with the FBI in Houston. There are two guys there I've worked with before, Johnson and Halloran. They've done all of the leg work on this, put all of the pieces together. If they flag up the potential threat, it'll look like they figured it all out and should bypass all the political shit.'

Carter stood up and fastened his coat. 'One more thing, Bill. You need to tell your people that Sinclair and McGill are our assets. I don't want them taken out by friendly fire.'

'I'll do everything I can, Simeon, I promise you that.'

'Thank you, Bill.'

They shook hands and Easter opened the office door. 'This looks like it could get very messy. Here's hoping we all get through it okay.'

'Goodbye, Bill.'

Easter's secretary escorted Carter down to the first floor and out of the embassy's main entrance. He thrust his hands into his pockets and set off for Kinsella's flat. All they could do now was monitor traffic over the various networks and try to follow events.

Chapter 22

The red, Quest Kodiak seaplane flew over the compound as the sun was coming up. McGill watched it from his vantage point on a rocky outcrop overlooking the lagoon and the test facility. He watched as the Kodiak grew from a small dot on the horizon, stayed low over the buildings then looped round, and descended towards the surface of the lagoon. Its floats created rooster tails of spray behind it as it touched down on the water. The plane decelerated and the pilot began manoeuvring it across the lagoon towards the small pier that jutted out from the shore opposite the compound gate.

McGill couldn't make out the faces of the people in the aircraft, but it must be Bazarov, Quinn and Sinclair. He climbed down from his rock observation point and kicked soil over the dying embers of his fire. Time to get closer and see what's going on down there. He picked up his assault rifle and set off for the compound.

The pilot jumped out of the Kodiak and tied it to the bollards on the small dock. A guard climbed out of the front passenger seat, followed by the other passengers from the rear. Bazarov and Quinn first, and then Garrison, who was now in handcuffs and wearing an ill-fitting blue boiler suit. He tried to pull away from the guard and complained as loudly as he could through the duct tape that covered his mouth. The guard attempted to push him along the dock but Garrison decided to put up a fight. Bazarov stepped towards them and pointed his .45 at the admiral's head. 'Stay quiet and do as you're told or die right here, right now.'

Despite his attempts at bravado Garrison's eyes gave away his fear. He lowered his head, not wanting to look at the weapon, and meekly allowed the guard to lead him away.

Sinclair clambered out of the plane and stretched her arms. 'That's not exactly club class.' She put her hands in her pockets and sauntered along the dock after Quinn. She stopped as she drew level with Bazarov and turned her head. 'You didn't have to do that. He's terrified already.'

Bazarov tucked the .45 into a shoulder holster and took off his jacket. He pulled a white handkerchief from his trouser pocket and wiped his forehead. 'I don't need your advice. I don't need you.'

'Then why bring me here?'

'Your only value now lies in keeping Mrs Quinn calm. If you give me any problems, I'll bury you in a hole.'

'You're such a charmer, Viktor.' Sinclair smirked.

Bazarov was beginning to lose patience with her. He waved one of the guards over and pointed at the two women. 'Escort them inside and lock them in.'

Sinclair looked at the guard then at Bazarov. 'I want to see Frank, now.'

The Russian jabbed his finger at her. 'You're in no position to make demands, Miss Sinclair.' He clenched his fists – annoyed that he kept letting her get to him. He turned on his heels and stormed off.

The guard gestured towards the compound with his assault rifle. Sinclair put her arm through the crook of Quinn's elbow. 'Shall we?'

They followed Bazarov across to the compound, the guard bringing up the rear. As they entered the building, Bazarov leaned over to Quinn. 'I want this all set up and ready as soon as possible. I'll send for you in one hour.'

The guard led them down the corridor and into what looked like a cheap hotel room. There was a bed, couch, wardrobe, desk and an en-suite bathroom. The guard closed the door and locked them in.

Sinclair began checking for anything that might help her. 'Come on, Jo, we've got one hour till he comes back. What's the easiest way out of here?'

Quinn sat on the bed. 'I don't know, Ali, I've never thought about it.'

'Well you need to think now, if you ever want to see your kids again.'

'This whole building is made from concrete. The walls are a foot thick. There's no way you're digging your way out.'

'What about the ceiling?'

'It's false. It was put in when we turned these parts into accommodation for our engineers. Above it are all the cables and ventilation shafts, that kind of thing. You're not thinking of crawling through the ventilation, are you?'

'All I need is to get out of here. I'll take my chances after that.' She pulled a chair over to the corner of the room and, standing on it, pushed up one of the tiles that made up the false ceiling. Above it there was a gap of six feet to the concrete roof. Running along one end, close to the roof, was a three feet wide ventilation shaft. Hanging beneath it was a wide metal tray that supported various cables. She could see there was a gap between them where they ran through the wall. A gap she could fit through.

She jumped down off the chair. 'Listen, Jo. I can get through the gap in the wall but I need you to tell me what's on the other side.'

Quinn thought for a moment and pointed to her left. 'That side is just a storeroom.'

'That's good.' Sinclair went into the bathroom and turned on the shower. 'I want you to cover for me. If anyone comes in just tell them I'm in there.'

'What do I do if they look?'

'Don't put yourself at risk. Just tell them I got out.' Sinclair climbed back onto the chair and reached up to the cable tray. She lifted herself up and tested its strength. 'I think it should be okay. I won't be on it long.' She swung her legs up, climbed onto the tray and leaned down through the hole in the ceiling. 'All hell's gonna let loose when they find out I've gone. Hopefully I'll have found Frank by then. You just sit tight, okay?'

Quinn smiled and nodded. 'Be careful, Ali.'

Sinclair replaced the tile and began her crawl along the cables towards the dim light coming through the gap. With no false ceilings in the other rooms, the light from one was bleeding through to the others. It was just enough for her to see where she was going. She shuffled towards the light and up to the gap in the wall.

She put her head through the gap and looked down into the neighbouring room. It was about eight feet long, six feet across and looked like a prison cell. Judging by the contents of the shelves that lined the walls, this was the cleaners storeroom.

She gripped the edge of the cable tray and swung down, dropping as quietly as she could to the floor. There was no obvious lock on the door so she turned the handle; it opened a fraction.

The corridor outside was lit up but deserted. She opened the door a little more and looked both ways. Quinn had told her the control room was to her right. That must be where Bazarov and his men were, not a good idea to go that way just yet.

She knew there was more accommodation on the other side of the building. That was the most likely location of Quinn's kids. She needed to find them and hide them somewhere safe. Next, she had to find Frank. Without him, stopping Bazarov would be even more difficult. She needed someone she trusted to watch her back. She didn't want to think that Frank was dead but she had to accept it was a possibility. She closed the door behind her and made her way along the corridor.

Sinclair checked room after room on the other side of the facility. From what Quinn had told her, this part of the building was all accommodation. It must be where the kids were being held. The rooms were all empty so far; Bazarov had got rid of anyone he didn't need. Sinclair hoped that he'd had them shipped off to the mainland but she knew that wasn't likely. Some of the occupants had obviously been dragged out with no notice and many in their sleep. Unmade beds, cold cups of coffee and discarded towels and clothes added to the spooky, abandoned atmosphere. It was like the Marie Celeste.

As she reached the end of the corridor she could hear voices, children's voices, coming from one of the rooms. She put her ear up against the door. The kids were talking about their mom and wondering where she was. There was no way to tell if there was a guard in there with them. She opened the door of the neighbouring room. Moving a chair over to the corner, just as she had to escape her own room, she lifted the ceiling tile and climbed onto the cable tray.

She took her time, sliding towards the kids' room. Their voices grew louder as she pushed through the gap in the wall and stopped directly above them. She still couldn't make out any noises that pointed towards the presence of a guard. She reached down and lifted the ceiling tile a couple of inches. She could see the two boys sitting on the bed, hand in hand, comforting each other. Aiden, the younger boy, was crying while Tom tried his best to convince his little brother that everything would be fine. There was no one else in the room.

Sinclair lifted the tile out of the way. The two boys looked startled and Sinclair held her finger to her lips to keep them quiet. 'Are you alone, boys?'

Tom nodded.

'Okay. I'm coming down.' Sinclair swung her legs through the hole and dropped to the floor.

The two boys backed away, unsure of who this dirt-streaked woman was. Sinclair listened at the door, there was no noise out in the corridor. She checked the handle; the door was locked. The accommodation had started life as offices and each door had a good quality mortise lock, which Sinclair didn't have the tools or the time to pick. She turned to Tom and Aiden who were now standing in the far corner, frightened.

'It's okay, boys. My name is Ali, maybe your mum has mentioned me before? I'm the British girl she knew from Mexico.'

Tom and Aiden both nodded. Quinn had told them about

Ali, told them how she had gone to prison to help her, that she was a true friend. Sinclair beckoned them over to her. She knelt down and took their hands. 'We have to get out of here and find your mum.' She looked into Aiden's eyes. He was scared but nodded. 'We have to climb up to the ceiling to escape. Is that okay?' She looked at Tom. He was doing well to hide his fear and even managed a little smile. Sinclair returned the smile. 'You're both very brave, it'll be an adventure.' The two boys nodded in tandem and Sinclair grabbed the chair.

Tom was first up into the ceiling void. He was tall for his age and only needed a little boost to reach the tray. Aiden was a different matter. He was quite short and Sinclair had to put him on her shoulders and push him up through the hole. Tom grabbed Aiden's hands and between them they manhandled him onto the tray. Sinclair pulled herself up and, after sliding the ceiling tile into place, led the boys down into the next room.

Moving quickly and quietly, they made their way along the corridors. Sinclair had to find a hiding place for them. Ideally, she would have liked to get them outside, but the building was locked up tight. After trying a few doors they came across one that opened out to concrete steps and down to a basement. They descended the steps and crept along a walkway that ran between air conditioning and chilled water plants. At the back of the basement was another door that led to a small maintenance room. Tools lined the walls and steel cupboards stood at either end. Sinclair opened one of the cupboards, it was full of oil, cleaning fluid and fuel; everything flammable. She quickly emptied it and knelt down with the boys once more. 'Listen guys, I'm going to get your mum. I want you to stay here. If anyone comes through that door, you get in this

203

cupboard and shut the door. Can you do that?'

The boys nodded, still unsure what was happening. Sinclair ruffled their hair and smiled, reassuring them as much as she could. She knew they must be confused and terrified. It made her even more determined to make sure they got through this, no matter what.

She checked the rows of tools that hung on the wall, hoping to find something she could use as a weapon. There were no knives or other bladed weapons so she settled for a large screwdriver and a hammer. She tucked them in her belt and headed back through the plant room to the concrete steps. She checked the corridor for any guards, closed the door behind her and made her way towards the room where Quinn was waiting for her.

Chapter 23

Bazarov walked through the double swing doors into the control room. One half of the large, open space was full of equipment wrapped in protective plastic sheeting; moth balled after previous projects and not needed to take control of the Kraken.

In the other half of the room, Quinn's remaining engineers were in the final stages of setting up the Kraken control panel. They looked nervous, eyes darting between their work and Bazarov. When the Russian and his men had first arrived on the island, the engineers and scientists had assumed this was just another QRL project. Now, surrounded by armed guards and with Garrison handcuffed to a chair in the corner, they knew this was something entirely different.

In front of the control panel, mounted on the wall, a giant screen displayed a map of the United States; green icons flashed around the coastline. They now had visibility of the Kraken system. The launch silos, installed in the seabed, were all operational and ready to be taken over.

One of the engineers had finished checking the paperwork he had fastened to a clipboard. 'That's as far as we can go. We need Mrs Quinn for the next step. She created the Apocalypse Protocol – she's the only one who knows how to activate it.

We can't do anything else without her.'

Bazarov waved him away. 'You don't need to worry. Just make sure it all keeps working until I'm ready.'

The engineer backed away and re-joined the huddle of white-coated lab staff. Sergei came through the double doors, past the huddle, and joined Bazarov. 'There's been a problem on the ship, Viktor.'

Bazarov turned to look at him. 'What kind of problem?'

'McGill escaped. He killed Uri. He's loose on the island somewhere. I'll find him.'

'No. We haven't got time to look for him now. Vadim will be here soon and I don't want anything to get in the way of the launch. Just make sure McGill doesn't get inside. He can run around out there as much as he wants.'

'I'll brief the men.' Sergei turned to leave but Bazarov called him back.

'Go and get Quinn first. I want her here, setting this up.'

Sergei nodded then left through the double doors.

Sinclair climbed back into the roof void above the cleaning cupboard and crawled through to the room Quinn was still in. If she could get Quinn out and hide her with the kids, Bazarov couldn't launch any missiles. That would give the military time to get there and stop him.

She reached down for the ceiling tile and at that same moment the door to the room below crashed open as Sergei burst in. Sinclair withdrew her hand and stayed motionless, listening.

Quinn was surprised by the sudden intrusion and jumped up from the bed, letting out a shrill scream. 'Don't you knock? What do you want?'

Sergei stood in the doorway, his rifle slung over his shoulder.

'Viktor wants you in the control room, now.'

Quinn hesitated, glancing towards the bathroom. 'Ahh … Okay. Let's go then.'

Sergei held up his hand, palm outwards. 'Wait. Where's Sinclair?'

Quinn gestured with her head. 'She's in the shower. We don't need her for this, let's go.'

She took two steps towards the door but Sergei was going nowhere. He walked over to the bathroom door and stood, with his head cocked to one side, listening to the sound of running water coming from within. He banged on the door. 'Sinclair?' There was no answer. 'Sinclair, open the door or I'll kick it down.'

Quinn started to panic. If Sergei discovered that Sinclair had gone it could blow any chance she had of finding her children. 'Leave her. We should go. Viktor wants me right away.'

Sergei listened for a few more seconds; he wasn't interested in anything Quinn was saying. He unslung his assault rifle and drove his boot against the door. With a crack, and a splintering of wood, the flimsy lock gave way and Sergei entered; his assault rifle pulled into his shoulder as he swept the steam-filled room. No one was in there. He approached the shower and, after a slight pause to listen once more, ripped down the curtain. He lowered his assault rifle. 'Fuck.' He knew they should have locked her up.

He stormed into the bedroom. Quinn backed away but Sergei grabbed her and threw her on the bed. He raised his weapon, aiming at her forehead. 'Where is she?'

Quinn held out her hands – an attempt to fend him off. 'She's gone and you won't find her.'

After a few seconds, which seemed like an age to Quinn, Sergei lowered his rifle and stood back to consider his options. He clenched and unclenched his teeth, the muscles in the side of his face flexing, his eyes full of menace. Quinn inched across the bed away from him. 'If you hurt me, Bazarov won't get what he wants. Do you think he'll forgive you for that?'

Sergei paced across the room, murmuring to himself. He knew Quinn was right. If he did anything to jeopardize the operation, Viktor would put a bullet in his head.

He slung his weapon over his shoulder and kicked out at the chair. 'Fuck.' The chair smashed against the wall. He grabbed Quinn's arm, pulled her off the bed and propelled her through the open door into the corridor.

Sinclair had held her breath purely out of instinct – Sergei wouldn't have been able to hear her anyway. She was relieved he hadn't decided to look harder for her. If he'd thought about it, the ceiling was the obvious way for her to get out. The Russian could have raked the tiles with bullets and that would have been the end of it.

She had to get outside the building. Quinn would be okay for now: Bazarov needed her too much. The kids were hidden and, unless a detailed search was carried out, would remain that way. Sinclair had to find Frank – if he was still alive. The two of them needed to work together. That was the only chance they had of stopping this in time.

Quinn stumbled as Sergei dragged her along the corridor by her arm and pushed her through the swing doors into the control room. She overbalanced and went sprawling across the floor in front of Bazarov. He bent down and helped her to her feet. 'You must be more careful, Josephine. We don't want you coming to any harm when we are so close to fulfilling our goal.'

She pulled herself free of his grasp and backed away. She rubbed her arm where Sergei had gripped. 'Don't touch me.'

Sergei was standing by the doors, looking nervous. This was the second time he'd come to Bazarov with bad news. He stepped forwards. 'Sinclair's gone.'

Bazarov stopped what he was doing and turned to face Sergei. 'What do you mean gone? Gone where?'

Sergei held up his palms and shrugged his shoulders. 'I don't know, Viktor. I don't understand how she got out of the room.'

Bazarov shook his head. 'Who are these people? McGill kills Uri and disappears. Now, Sinclair vanishes. I thought I'd hired the best.'

Sergei was beginning to fear for his safety. 'It's not my fault, Viktor. I said we should put a guard on her.'

Viktor Bazarov wasn't a man who enjoyed being told by an underling that he was wrong. His reputation as an unforgiving, brutal boss was well deserved. It was only the amount of money he paid that kept men working for him. He drew close to Sergei and looked him in the eyes. 'I want you to go outside and set up a cordon around the building. I want McGill kept out. Then, I want Sinclair found.' Bazarov prodded his finger into Sergei's chest. 'I'll hold you personally responsible if it isn't done. Do not let me down again, Sergei. Do you understand?'

'Yes, sir.' Sergei hurried out of the control room, eager to get away from the threat of his boss.

McGill lay under the foliage next to the compound fence and watched as Sergei appeared and gathered the guards together. After lots of pointing and shouting the men dispersed around the building. The only guards left near the fence were controlling access through the gate. To McGill, it looked like they were concentrating on keeping him out of the compound. They'd decided he wasn't a threat as long as they kept him out of the building. He could now move around the island almost unhindered.

As he watched the Russians setting up their cordon, he became aware of the sound of an engine. Not the single tone of a car or truck engine, but a low rumbling throb that he recognised well. It was the sound of a large, transport helicopter.

He raised himself up on his knees so he could see the compound's helipad. QRL used large choppers to ferry people over to the mainland. A direct flight to the States was outside the aircraft's effective range so it was necessary to fly to Belize City first then catch a flight to the US from the airport. All large items of equipment had been brought in by sea, but Bazarov had travelled by seaplane from Texas to avoid crossing borders. Whoever was landing now wasn't worried about that.

The helicopter came into view. It was a civilian version of a Chinook. It flew over McGill's position as it approached the helipad. He could feel the throb of the engines in his ribs. The Chinook's twin rotors created a dust storm as the downdraft blew across the compound floor. Its wheels touched down on the helipad and the pilot cut the engines. As the rotors slowed, the tailgate at the back of the aircraft dropped open and the choppers lone passenger made his way down the ramp.

Bazarov walked out of the main entrance and across to the helipad. The new arrival was a tall man who looked to be around forty years old. Only the flecks of grey hair around his temples hinted that he was in fact in his mid-fifties. He wore a plain, white shirt and cream trousers. A light brown blazer was slung over his shoulder and mirrored aviators covered his eyes.

McGill couldn't see the man clearly and had no idea who he was, but he recognised his type. He was wealthy and had power, but the power he had wasn't enough. He wanted more. His type lived a life of privilege governed by greed. They competed with each other to see who could amass the biggest fortune like it was a game. They never paused to consider the effect they had on others. The world was full of them: politicians, bankers, CEOs. They sat in their comfortable offices and directed men, like McGill, to do the dirty work. They didn't usually get their own hands dirty. This man was taking a big risk to be on the spot when the shit hit the fan.

His body language was confident, assured. He walked upright, unworried by the possibility of an attack. He considered himself to be the big dog, the alpha male, no one was going to threaten him; he was in charge and giving the orders.

Bazarov welcomed the passenger at the edge of the helipad. They obviously knew each other, but the Russian was fully aware of his place in the pecking order, almost bowing as they shook hands. Whoever the new arrival was, he was obviously Bazarov's boss. McGill watched them chat for a minute before they walked away from the helipad and into the building.

The office that Bazarov led his boss into was just inside the main entrance. It had a modern, light-coloured wooden desk at one end with a comfortable couch opposite. On the left-hand wall was a small drinks cabinet, this was the room where QRL did their VIP meet and greets before setting off on a tour of the facility.

211

Bazarov poured two large glasses of Scotch and handed one to his boss. 'It's better if you stay in here until launch time, Vadim. Out of sight and out of the way.'

Vadim took the offered glass and inhaled the aroma of its contents. 'Is there a problem I should know about?'

Bazarov shook his head. 'Nothing that can't be controlled. I just don't want you in harm's way if things get violent.'

'Is that a possibility?'

'I'm afraid not everyone shares our goals. They may need persuasion.'

Vadim drank his Scotch in one gulp and handed over his glass for a refill. 'And will I be able to maintain my anonymity? What if someone recognises me?'

Bazarov filled up the glass and handed it back. 'Quinn and her staff were never going to leave this island anyway. Your identity will be safe.'

Vadim smiled. 'You are a bastard, Viktor.'

'You wouldn't have hired me if I wasn't.'

'Very true, Viktor, very true.' Vadim held up his glass. 'A toast. To success.'

Bazarov clinked his glass against Vadim's. 'Success, and the new Soviet Union.'

Sinclair was hiding in the next room. She'd tried to get out of the building but the cordon of guards outside had put a stop to that. When she had seen Bazarov and the other man heading straight for her, she'd ducked through the closest door and was now crouched in a corner listening to their conversation. She hadn't recognised Vadim, his face wasn't familiar, but his accent was definitely English. Upper class, privately educated, inherited money English. This was the mole that London were trying to track down. If only she was armed. She could kill them both now and save everyone a lot of trouble.

Bazarov drained his glass. 'Stay in here out of sight. I'll come and get you when it's ready to go.'

Vadim nodded. 'Be quick, Viktor.' He stood up and helped himself to another Scotch.

Sinclair heard the door open and a single set of footsteps leave the room. Finding out Vadim's true identity wasn't a priority for her; time was running out. She had to find a different way to get outside.

She looked up; the ventilation system and cables didn't come through this room, she'd have to take her chances along the corridor. She opened the door and checked for guards, they were all outside manning the cordon. She sneaked past the other office door and made her way towards the basement where she had hidden the Quinn boys.

Sergei picked out three of the guards and brought them inside. He had to redeem himself to Bazarov. Finding Sinclair was all he cared about now. He positioned one guard next to the entrance, cutting off Sinclair's exit and the whole of the control room side of the building. The other two guards tore apart every room, one by one, as Sergei patrolled the corridors looking for signs of movement.

Beds and office desks were overturned by the two searchers; cupboards were emptied and their contents spilled across the floor. Ceiling tiles were ripped down – Sergei had a feeling he'd figured that one out too late. They worked their way through the building – Sinclair's options were running out.

She had made it to the maintenance room down in the basement. Tom and Aiden Quinn were nowhere to be seen: they'd done exactly what she'd told them to do. She tapped on the door of the steel cupboard. 'It's okay guys, it's Ali.'

Sinclair opened the door and the two boys climbed out. She crouched down and took their hands in hers. 'Well done, Tom. You too, Aiden. If I didn't know you were in there, I'd never have guessed.'

Aiden smiled. He'd always liked hide and seek. 'Where's Mom?'

'She's doing some work in another room. You'll have to stay here a little bit longer. Okay?'

The two boys nodded. Tom was beginning to look worried but Aiden was enjoying the game, unaware of the danger they were in.

Sinclair checked the rest of the room. There was no way out other than the single door she had come through. 'I have to go and help your mum now. Remember, if you hear anyone coming through the door and down the steps, you hide back in the cupboard. Can you do that for me?'

Tom smiled and put his arm around his younger brother. 'We'll be okay. We're good at this. Aren't we Aiden?'

Aiden smiled. 'The best.'

Sinclair didn't like leaving them alone again but they would be much safer away from her. 'That's my brave boys.'

She left the maintenance room and went into the main part of the basement. In the corner of the room she could make out some light coming from behind one of the large air conditioning plants. The ceiling lights were dim and didn't cover that area so there must be something else: another room, a fire escape, a window. She ducked under the handrail, which ran along the side of the central walkway, and clambered over pipes and ducts to check it out.

Behind the machinery was a small window, six feet from

the floor. Sinclair stepped up onto a pipe, which ran around the wall, and rubbed some of the grime from the glass. The window was at ground level on the outside and just large enough for her to squeeze through.

From the look of the frame and the catch, the window had been painted several times but hadn't been opened for years. Sinclair turned the handle and tried to push it open but it was jammed – the years of paint holding it shut. Using the screwdriver out of her belt, she scraped some of the layers of paint off the wood and worked the screwdrivers tip into the gap beside the handle. The window started to give a little. She worked her way along the frame; the gap widened as she went. The paint split and began to flake off until, with a loud crack, the window gave way.

Outside the window was an overgrown area littered with old wooden crates and lumps of metal that must have been left over from the construction of the facility. Sinclair gripped the frame and pulled herself through.

It was a tight squeeze and there wasn't much to hold on to but she gradually shuffled her way through. Once her upper body was clear she turned over onto her back, so she could push with her legs, and looked directly into the muzzle of an assault rifle that was pointing at her forehead. The guard on the other end of the weapon tried to crack a smile but it was more of a grimace. 'Out.'

She could have dropped back into the basement and made a run for it, but that would have brought more guards and put the boys at risk. She couldn't take that chance. If the guards had orders to kill her, they'd already be dragging her corpse through the window. They must be taking her to Bazarov. That would give her time to plan something else. Two more guards arrived and Sinclair held out her hands. 'A little help would be good.'

The two new guards grabbed an arm each and dragged her into the open.

Chapter 24

McGill crawled through the undergrowth and up to the fence to get a better view of the entrance. He could've done with his binoculars to help him make out details, but they'd been left back at Quinn's ranch; he'd have to manage without. The guards were patrolling around the concrete walls, each guard in view of the next. There was no way in or out while they were there; he had to find something to distract them and pull them away from the building.

McGill heard a shout coming from the rear of the building. Two of the guards left their posts and disappeared around the corner, out of sight. Something was going on, something that was enough to distract them. If he could find out what it was, maybe he could use it to his advantage.

The rest of the guards didn't move up to fill the gaps in the line. That was good news for him. It meant he didn't have to move them all away from their positions to get through. He looked at his watch. He needed to know how long they would leave the gap open – how long he would have to break in. One minute passed, then two, it was looking good. The longer they were away, the better. Three minutes passed then McGill's heart sank. When the guards came back into view,

Ali was walking between them.

'Shit.' While McGill was pleased to see Sinclair was still alive, he doubted she would stay that way for much longer. He didn't know what they had planned for Ali, but Bazarov didn't have any reason to keep her around. McGill's timeline had just shortened. He had to get her out, give the Russians something else to worry about. If he could rig up an explosion to distract them, that might work. First, he needed to get a look at the whole building, especially the back. If Sinclair had managed to get out of the building there, that could be his way in. He crawled away from the fence and into the undergrowth.

Jo Quinn sat at the Kraken's control terminal typing in commands. As she did, each of the symbols on the wall display turned red. The west coast was now complete. Quinn carried on typing and the eastern seaboard launchers changed colour one at a time: Florida, Georgia, Virginia, New Jersey; only Maine was still green. Quinn typed the last line of code and hit enter. The last icon turned red, the new fire missions were ready to be transmitted to the Kraken.

A white-coated engineer ticked some more boxes on his clipboard. 'That's phase two complete, Mrs Quinn.'

Quinn looked up at Bazarov. 'We're ready for phase three, the two-stage approval process. When we've completed that we'll have total control of the missiles and can send your target details to the launchers. The US authorities may know something's happening, though.'

'They'll never figure it out in time. Even if they did, they can't stop the countdown. Right?'

Quinn nodded. 'That's right. It can only be stopped from here.'

Bazarov looked pleased; the plan was entering its final stage.

'Thank you, Josephine.' He pointed at Garrison. 'You first.'

Garrison sat up in his chair, his handcuffs rattling against the steel frame. He looked at Quinn, unsure what to do. 'What if I refuse?'

Bazarov freed him from his shackles and stood him up. 'James, the first thing I need is your fingerprints.' He pulled a large knife from his jacket. 'Whether they are attached to you or not, makes no difference to me.'

Garrison's bravado once again faded away. He was ashamed of himself. Maybe if he wasn't such a coward he could have done something to prevent this from going any further. He walked over to the console, his head bowed. 'What do I have to do?'

Quinn took his hand and gave it a reassuring squeeze. She guided it onto a scanner. 'Just put your hand on here, the system will do the rest.'

As soon as Garrison's hand touched the scanner the glass plate lit up and took an image of the palm of his hand. The blue light seemed to shine through his pale skin. Within a couple of seconds, a picture of a younger Garrison had appeared on the main display along with all of his details. Everything from name, rank and number to age, height and hair colour.

Quinn pressed another key on the panel and a box on the screen flashed. 'Can you give me your code word please, Admiral?' She paused, her fingers hovering over the keys.

Garrison shook his head. 'I … I can't remember it. It's been a long time.'

Bazarov aimed his weapon at Garrison's face. 'Let's stop this game, Admiral. This is your last chance. Cooperate or die, your choice.'

'Prometheus. It's Prometheus.'

Bazarov lowered his aim. 'Thank you, Admiral.'

Quinn typed the code word into the box and another line of flashing text appeared. 'Now, if you'd look into the eyepiece.'

She tapped what looked like a telescopic sight. Garrison bent forwards and placed his eye against the rubber cup at one end. A white light flashed and Garrison pulled back, blinking.

Bazarov nodded towards him. 'You can go and sit down again.'

Garrison returned to his chair, relieved that he wasn't being handcuffed to it this time. If he kept quiet, maybe he would live through this.

* * *

Sergei opened the door to the basement, it was one of the last rooms they had to clear. He held the door open and sent his two men in to carry out the search. Descending the steps, they let their eyes adjust to the darker conditions, then carried on along the walkway.

In the maintenance room, Tom and Aiden got inside the cupboard as they heard the men approach. They held each other, holding their breath. One of the searchers approached the door and, with his Glock at the ready, turned the handle.

Sergei heard a shout from the man he had left by the exit. 'They have her, Sergei.'

Bazarov's number two clenched his fist. Now he'd be back in the good books. He shouted to his men in the basement. 'You two, out.'

The two guards ran up the stairs and all three of them rushed along the corridor to the main entrance.

Sinclair stood just inside the door, hands on her head,

flanked by the Russians who'd found her. Sergei approached and stood right in front of her, his face an inch from hers. Sinclair could feel the Russians foul breath on her skin. Sergei looked deep into her eyes. 'You're mine now.' He pulled back his fist and rammed it hard into her ribs.

Sinclair doubled over, breath exploding from her lungs. She collapsed on the floor, trying to suck in air as the guards stood over her.

* * *

Josephine Quinn was looking through the eyepiece as the scanner took an image of her retina. Slightly blinded in one eye, she looked up at the display. Her picture and details were next to Garrison's. They both had three green lights beneath them, showing that the checks had been successful; their identities were confirmed. One more password was now required to load the firing mission and begin the launch countdown. Quinn stared at the flashing box on the screen that demanded her input.

Bazarov turned towards her. 'What are you waiting for, Mrs Quinn? Enter the password.'

Quinn didn't move. 'I can't do it.'

'I'll remind you that the safety of your children depends on this. Should I ask Sergei to go and fetch them?'

Quinn was in turmoil. Her maternal instinct to protect her children was overpowering, but she couldn't be responsible for the deaths of hundreds of thousands of innocent people.

Bazarov slammed the desk. 'Mrs Quinn.'

The swing doors to the control room burst open as Sinclair was thrown through them. She careered into a desk and fell

221

to the floor, bloodied and winded.

Bazarov backed away from Quinn. 'Miss Sinclair. I'm so glad you could join us.' He gestured to his men. 'Pick her up.'

They picked up Sinclair and pushed her into a chair opposite Quinn. She had blood running from cuts on the side of her face and the corner of her mouth. She coughed and spat more blood onto the floor. 'Hello, Jo. How've you been?'

'Oh my god. What have you done to her?'

'Nothing yet, Mrs Quinn. You can keep it that way by entering the password.'

'Don't do it, Jo. The kids are ...'

Sergei smashed Sinclair's head into the desk. She was dazed, almost losing consciousness. Bazarov pulled out his knife and drew it across the side of her neck. Blood oozed from the wound and the Russian positioned his knife to cut again.

Quinn reached out to try and stop him. 'No. I'll do it.'

Quinn's hands trembled. She looked at Sinclair, at the knife resting on her friend's throat and the blood running onto the desk. She clenched her fists and tried to steady herself. There was nothing else she could do. She keyed in the final password and hit enter. 'God forgive me.'

Bazarov released Sinclair and sheathed his knife. 'Thank you, Josephine.'

They all looked at the screen. The pictures of Garrison and Quinn had been replaced by large numbers that had begun to count down. One hour till the launch of the missiles. The read-out underneath gave updates on the status.

COMMUNICATIONS CONFIRMED: MISSILE GYROS ACTIVATING.

Each of the missile icons now had its new target's latitude and longitude beneath it. Just a series of numbers, but each one corresponded to a location within the US: Washington, New York, Chicago, Los Angeles; every missile aimed at a major city.

Bazarov nodded to his men. 'Take everyone into the lab next door, and one of you stay with them, no one leaves.' He couldn't kill Quinn until the mission was complete, he needed her to fix any problems.

The guards gathered Quinn, Garrison and the remaining engineers together and shepherded them out through the double doors and into the other lab. Sergei grabbed Sinclair and followed them but Bazarov stopped him. 'Not her, Sergei. Follow me and bring her with you.'

Quinn turned around, noticing that her friend was being led away in another direction. 'Ali. No. Where are you taking her, you bastard? You said you'd leave her alone.'

'I didn't promise you anything, Josephine. I'm afraid your friend here has caused us far too much trouble. I don't need her any more. Sergei is going to take her outside and put a bullet in the back of her head.'

'NO.' Quinn bolted towards Sinclair but a guard grabbed her around the waist and dragged her off into the lab. The doors closed behind them, her futile screams echoing down the corridor.

Bazarov and Sergei led Sinclair to the office where Vadim was waiting. Bazarov opened the door and all three entered the room. Vadim was sitting on a couch, cradling his glass in his left hand and holding a large cigar in his right. 'Viktor. Everything is going to plan I hope? No last-minute fuck-ups?'

'We almost had a problem. Let me introduce you to Ali Sinclair.' He waved to Sergei who pushed Sinclair to the floor in front of Vadim.

'Miss Sinclair is an agent of the British Government. Sent here to find out what I was up to.'

Vadim looked down at Sinclair. 'So, you're Ali Sinclair. Have we been infiltrated, Viktor? Remember, I need my anonymity.'

'It's not a problem, Vadim. The British thought they'd stumbled across some espionage, an attempt to steal information about Kraken. They have no idea what is really happening. By the time they figure it out, it will all be over.'

'Excellent. I do hope she won't survive long enough to blow my cover.'

Sinclair got to her knees and held up her head. 'I'll remember your face and I'll see you dead.'

Vadim laughed. 'You won't see the end of the day. Nothing personal. Strictly business, you understand.'

Bazarov nodded to the door. Sergei lifted Sinclair and pushed her out of the room.

Sinclair walked with her hands on her head along the length of the outside wall. She didn't look at the other guards who formed the cordon, she kept her eyes focussed ahead of her. She wasn't going to give them the satisfaction of seeing her fear. Sergei walked two paces behind her with his assault rifle pointing between her shoulder blades.

They reached the rear of the building where Sinclair had climbed out of the window.

'Stop.' Sergei barked at her. 'Get on your knees.'

Sinclair knelt among the old crates and metal waste. She dropped her hands to her knees. This was it, this was where she was going to die: on her knees in the dirt. She always thought she'd go down fighting but, when it had come to it, there was no point. She was going to die either way.

Sergei shouldered his assault rifle and took out his Glock.

'I told you I'd kill you, bitch.'

'Just get on with it you prick.' A million thoughts ran through her mind. This must be what they meant by your life flashing before your eyes.

Sergei cocked his weapon and chambered a round.

Sinclair looked up at the sky. Vapour trails from commercial airliners crisscrossed the cloudless blue sky. Normal people going about their normal lives, oblivious of the shitstorm that was about to be unleashed. A flock of birds flew overhead, heading for the jungle canopy. She took a deep breath and closed her eyes.

McGill squeezed the trigger. The sharp crack of the shot chased the bullet through the foliage but Sergei would never hear it. The round struck him just above his right ear and blew a hole the size of an orange in his skull as it exited on the left. Sergei dropped to the floor like a puppet with its strings cut, already dead.

Sinclair spun round. Sergei's eyes were frozen open – a look of surprise, asking a question that would never be answered. She picked up his assault rifle and checked for any other threats. A noise to her right caught her attention and she brought her aim round, ready to fire.

McGill knelt beside the fence, his rifle still aimed at Sergei. The fence on that side of the compound had been neglected where it was overgrown by the encroaching jungle. McGill had cut the wire ties from the chain link and been able to lift it up enough to scramble under. He stood up and ran over to join Sinclair, giving her a hug, thankful that he'd been in the right place at the right time. 'Jesus, Ali. That was close.'

Sinclair fought back tears of relief. She was beginning to think that McGill was her guardian angel. She definitely owed him a drink – if they survived that long. 'I'm gonna need therapy after this one.'

'Like you didn't need professional help before.'

Sinclair pulled away from McGill and gave him a playful punch in the chest.

McGill checked for any sign of followers; the other Russians must have heard the shot and thought Sinclair was dead. He dragged Sergei's body into the undergrowth and threw some palm fronds over it. 'Let's get the fuck out of here, Ali. We need to put a plan together.'

'Right behind you, Frank.'

Chapter 25

Before Kurt Halloran had joined the FBI, he served in the US Marines. He served in the first Gulf War and Afghanistan before injuries had slowed him down enough to win him promotion and a desk job. He'd called it a day after that, but still served in the reserves and retained his rank. When his boss, Johnson, had received the call from Easter, filling them in on the threat that the British had found, he'd called his contact at the Pentagon. They hadn't hesitated, and Johnson was soon calling Halloran into his office.

'Grab your kit, Kurt, you're going on active service again.'

Secretly, Halloran felt a buzz of excitement. He missed the adrenalin rush of combat. He knew a lot of people thought that made him a bit of a psychopath, but it was the one thing that made him feel alive.

Within the hour he was in the back of a plane heading for the US Navy assault ship, USS America, currently stationed in the Caribbean. During the flight he re-read the documents he'd been given, to make sure he had it all in his head. The British had flagged up the possibility of a nuclear launch being initiated from a test facility. Bombing the place was a no go. It would wipe out the only way of stopping the countdown. His job was to brief a marine team and launch an assault on the island.

The British had two operatives in situ but their status was unknown. No one had heard from them for some time and it wasn't clear if they were alive or dead. His main role during the assault was to get control of the nuclear trigger and secure Josephine Quinn and Admiral Garrison. If he could get the Brits out too it would be a bonus.

The events of the last few days were falling into place now. He'd always had a nagging feeling that they were part of a much bigger story, but he hadn't had access to the information to put it all together. The FBI had wasted time looking for the mysterious woman from the motel and the golf resort. Now it looked like she'd been on their side from the start. He was being sent on this mission to help the agency cover things up. Make it look like they were in control all along. Someone would get a rocket up their ass after this but that could wait. First, they needed to stop this guy, Bazarov, from launching his attack on the US.

He looked out of the window as the plane approached the ship and started its landing pattern. By the time the plane lifted off again, he would be briefing the marines and getting ready to climb into the Knighthawk helicopters that would fly them in to their target. He studied the photographs of the two British operatives; he had to be able to recognise them quickly. He felt sorry for them. As always, it was people like them and him who paid the price for other people's fuck-ups. They were soldiers and knew the risks, but it sounded to him like the British had dropped their people in the shit and left them to it. The poor bastards weren't in with much of a chance.

Halloran's briefing didn't go into details of the backstory – the events of the last few days – it wasn't necessary. All the marines needed to know was who they were up against and what the objective was. Halloran took them through the expected size and quality of Bazarov's private army. He took them through a map of the island and walked them through the blueprints of the facility. Last, he showed them the photos of Sinclair and McGill. 'These two guys are friendlies. McGill is a marine, just like us. If you see them, give them all the help they need.'

Two Knighthawk helicopters were now in position on the flight deck of the USS America and ready to go. Halloran finished his briefing and the marines gathered together their equipment. He checked his assault vest, spare magazines, sidearm, and radio. He put on his throat mic and carried out a radio check with his team.

This was it, plans had been made and gone over, weapons were checked and letters to loved ones written. Now it was time to focus on the assault, all other thoughts pushed to the back of his mind. He picked up his M4 carbine and followed the other men out of the briefing room and up to the flight deck.

The Knighthawks' pilots completed their own pre-flight checks and fired up the engines as Halloran and the marines climbed on board. One final radio check confirmed approval for the mission, and the two helicopters lifted off the flight deck and headed west.

* * *

Sinclair and McGill sat in a small clearing, one hundred metres from the compound fence, their weapons laid out in front of them. They had two assault rifles, three Glock

229

semi-automatics and two Kizlyar knives. Enough for the two of them. The big problem they had was ammunition. They had gathered everything they had taken from Sergei, and the guards they had killed. Once they'd loaded the ammunition into magazines, they had one each for the Glocks and four for the assault rifles. McGill loaded one into his AR-15 then passed two to Sinclair. 'We don't have much ammo, Ali. If you can pick any up from the guards you take out, all the better.'

Sinclair loaded a magazine into her assault rifle and drew back the cocking handle. The spare magazine went in her pocket. 'If we don't get any backup we're pretty much fucked.'

McGill discarded the third Glock and put the other one into his hip holster. 'Carter will be doing everything he can to get the Yanks to assault this place. Hopefully they'll know we're here, otherwise they could be just as dangerous to us as the Russians.'

'It'd be a real shame to make it this far only to get taken out by our own side.'

McGill nodded. 'Wouldn't be the first friendly fire we've been in, Ali.'

Sinclair stood up and slung her assault rifle over her shoulder. 'So, we go for the anti-aircraft missiles first?'

'We have to. It'll use up some of the time we have but there'll be no backup arriving if that thing is still operational.'

Sinclair looked at her watch. 'I reckon we've got about forty minutes to stop the countdown. Let's get to it.'

McGill climbed to his feet and they headed through the foliage towards the Rapier launcher.

They approached the anti-aircraft installation from slightly different directions, knives drawn. They had to keep this as quiet as possible to begin with, and save ammunition. Once they were ready to assault the building they would need it to be very loud, but not just yet.

The Rapier system's launcher and control trailers were positioned in a clearing on some raised ground, with a clear line of sight over the most obvious line of attack – east across the compound and out to sea. Behind them, the mountains provided cover and made it very difficult to fly in from that direction.

A generator hummed at the back of the clearing and helped to cover any noise Sinclair and McGill made. Beside the generator were a fuel dump and some wooden crates. It looked like the two men who were manning the position, didn't think they would be needed to shoot anything down. They were sitting on a log, well away from the generator and the trailers, playing cards and smoking. Their weapons were leant up against a tree and there were empty beer bottles lying on the floor at their feet.

Sinclair was closest to them and would lead the attack. She inched closer and closer, staying as quiet as possible, but at the same time ready to explode into action if she was spotted. Six feet from the men she came up to a crouching position, her knife in her right hand. She nodded to McGill then covered the remaining distance in two steps. She clamped her left hand around the nearest guard's mouth and drew her knife across his throat. Arterial blood spurted onto the other guard as the man tried to stand up. Sinclair wrapped her legs around him and clung on to his back as he struggled for the last few seconds of his life. He dropped to his knees, backwards onto Sinclair, and bled out.

The other guard didn't have time to react. By the time his friend had stood up and sprayed him with blood, he too was in a fight for survival. McGill wrapped his left arm across the man's throat and drove the knife into his back. He pulled him backwards off the log and, withdrawing the knife, turned him over and plunged the blade into his heart.

Wiping their blades clean, they re-sheathed them and set about searching the corpses for ammunition. Each guard only had the magazines that were in their assault rifles. It wasn't much but it was better than nothing and was a big increase in Sinclair and McGill's current stock.

'No need to hide the bodies, Frank. This'll all be over before anyone has time to find them.'

'And hopefully we'll still be alive at the end of it.'

The two of them rushed over to the fuel dump. There were large forty-gallon barrels of diesel and petrol alongside smaller jerrycans, and four long crates containing spare missiles. They quickly moved the smaller containers and the crates over to the missile launcher, stacking them up around it.

McGill opened one of the smaller cans and poured petrol over their stack and the large drums. He took out his flint and scraped sparks onto the fuel. It lit almost immediately into a bright fireball. 'That should take a few minutes to blow. Gives us time to get round to the window.'

Sinclair picked up her weapon and they set off into the jungle.

It only took them a couple of minutes to reach the back of the building where Sinclair had had her escape from death. Sergei's body was still hidden where they'd left it. They pulled up the rusty chain link fencing and crawled beneath it to enter the compound.

Checking for anyone patrolling, they kept low and ran over to the basement window. Sinclair curled her fingers around the frame and pulled it open. She looked into the dimly lit machinery room for any movement but there was none. Lying on her back she slid in, feet first, through the window and dropped down on one knee, covering for McGill. 'Okay, Frank. All clear.'

McGill pushed his way through the gap. It was more of a tight fit for him and he wouldn't have been able to defend himself in that position. After one last big push, he was through and joined Sinclair. 'Bit of a squeeze that.'

Sinclair smiled. 'You should stay off the cakes, fat boy.'

McGill raised his eyebrows. 'Thanks.'

They both clambered over the pipework to the walkway. When they reached the maintenance room, Sinclair put her hand on McGill's shoulder. 'I want to check on the boys.'

'Okay. Be quick.'

Sinclair opened the door and tapped on the side of the metal cupboard. 'It's me, boys.'

Tom and Aiden Quinn opened the door and looked at her. 'Can we come out yet? Where's Mom?'

They looked frightened; this was no longer a game for them.

'You just need to hide for a little longer. Mummy will come and get you. You'll hear some loud bangs and some shooting but you're safe here. Do you think you can hide a bit longer?'

The boys both nodded.

'That's my brave boys. Now, back in the cupboard, I'll close the door.'

The Quinns got as comfortable as they could and Sinclair closed the door. She left the maintenance room and re-joined McGill on the walkway.

'Are they okay, Ali?'

'As well as you would expect in the circumstances.'

'That's good. Now, let's get ready.'

They moved quickly along the walkway and up the concrete steps. Pausing at the top, McGill held on to the handle. 'You ready for this?'

Sinclair nodded. 'As ready as I'll ever be.'

Chapter 26

Bazarov and Vadim watched the large display as the countdown continued. The text on the screen flashed as each stage was reached.

GUIDANCE CODES CONFIRMED: MUZZLE HATCHES OPENING.

'Only twenty minutes to go, Viktor. Nothing can stop us now.'

Bazarov took out a silver hip flask and unscrewed the lid. 'Almost time for the start of the new era, Vadim. The new Soviet era.' He took a drink and passed it across to Vadim.

Vadim held up the flask in salute. 'And the downfall of the Americans.'

Just as the flask reached his lips, the first of the small petrol containers, which were packed around the Rapier launcher, ruptured.

The explosion started a chain reaction. The first jerrycan burst open in a ball of fire that damaged the other containers. They, in turn, split, and spilled more fuel onto the flames. Explosion after explosion rocked the launcher until the fuel inside one of the missiles gave in to the intense heat. The whole thing went up: petrol containers, missile fuel, warheads. The shockwave bent trees and set fire to foliage as the bright orange mushroom of flame headed skyward.

Back at the building all the guards ducked at the same time, as the ear-splitting noise of the blast reached them. All of them ran to the front of the compound to try and see where the artillery onslaught was coming from.

The jungle was in flames. It looked like a scene from a Vietnam War movie; US helicopters napalming a fishing village. Debris, thrown up by the explosion, started raining down on them: lumps of burning wood, sharp fragments of twisted metal and pieces of missile. The guards ran for cover, convinced they were under attack. They were.

Bazarov instinctively ducked as the noise reached the control room. He'd been under artillery fire in Afghanistan but it wasn't something you got used to.

Vadim dropped the hip flask. Of course, he'd never been in combat. 'What the fuck was that?'

Bazarov walked over to the swing doors and looked through the window. The guard who had been watching Quinn and Garrison appeared in the corridor. Bazarov pointed at Vadim. 'You stay here. I'm going to check.' He pushed open the door and joined the guard.

As soon as McGill heard the sound of the first blast he looked at Sinclair and they nodded to each other. They checked their weapons and left the basement. They had to get to the other end of the building as quickly as possible without taking any stupid chances. The only people inside who weren't a threat were the Quinns, Garrison and two or three scientists and engineers. Everyone else was a target to be dropped on sight. There would be no rules of engagement here. No warnings or second chances. Two bullets for each man and move on.

They moved along both sides of the corridors. One of them

moving forwards, checking that doors were locked before covering the other's advance. They didn't need to speak, they knew each other so well it was like they were telepathic. Each knowing instinctively what the other was thinking. McGill on one side and Sinclair on the other, door by door, leapfrogging their way towards the control room.

Vadim didn't like what he could hear outside. The explosion had rocked the building. It wasn't some minor problem, this was serious. He wasn't renowned for his bravery and hadn't got to his current position of power by putting himself at risk. He regularly put other people at risk, that bit wasn't a problem, but not himself.

He moved to the other side of the room and started looking for a way out. Buildings like this always had an emergency exit, no matter how secure they were. It wasn't a nuclear bunker, it was a lab. He checked along the walls and behind the plastic-wrapped equipment. There was no obvious fire door or escape route but, in one corner, he came across a black painted steel ladder that rose up to a hatch in the ceiling. Checking the doors for Bazarov returning, he started the twelve feet climb up the ladder.

The hatch at the top was made of thick steel and didn't move an inch when Vadim pushed against it. He looked for a lock or latch that would release it. To the right of the ladder was a grey, metal box with a large, red handled, switch mounted in the centre. After another nervous check of the doors he grabbed the handle and turned it.

There was a buzz and an electrical hum as the metal hatch rattled and slid out of the way. Above him, the ladder extended another four feet into a space that was like a small shed. Daylight leaked through louvres in the walls on three sides, with a door making up the fourth wall. He climbed the rest of the ladder and turned the door's aluminium handle. It opened with a creak and Vadim found himself standing on the roof of the lab.

The view from the roof didn't look good. The debris from the explosion littered the compound and the roof. The jungle still burned and Bazarov's men were running around trying to put out small fires closer to the building. It was time for him to leave.

Vadim looked for a way down from the roof, but the only ladders he could see would put him back inside the compound amongst Bazarov's men and the flames. That wasn't somewhere he was keen to be. The parapet around the roof was only a foot high and, on the left-hand side, the edge was only eight feet from the outside fence. He didn't relish the idea of jumping but, in this case, self-preservation overcame his natural cowardice. The lush green jungle foliage had grown right up to the fence and should cushion his fall, if he managed to jump that far.

Over in the lagoon the red seaplane was still tied up to the small jetty. That was his way out, he could fly it. It was no different to the light planes he'd learned to fly during his short military career. He took a few big steps backwards and gave himself every chance to make the jump from the roof. After a couple of deep breaths to get the adrenalin flowing, Vadim sprinted to the parapet and launched himself towards the trees.

Bazarov stood at the main door and looked at the chaos outside. Where the hell was Sergei? He needed his right-hand man now. They'd obviously underestimated McGill's ability to cause them trouble. His priority now was to make sure the launch went ahead then he would get him and Vadim out of there. He told the guard standing next to him to get the chopper warmed up and ready to fly. They would be leaving in less than twenty minutes.

He took his Colt from the shoulder holster under his arm and strode back to the swing doors. As he turned the corner, he heard a sound behind him. He spun round and saw Sinclair coming at him with an assault rifle tucked into her shoulder. He dived through the doors just as the 5.56mm rounds splintered the wood of the door frame. He bolted the doors from the inside and pulled a heavy desk in front of them while he shouted to Vadim. 'Take cover. Sinclair's alive. She's in here with McGill.'

Bazarov fired a volley of shots through the door's window and retreated into the room. 'Where are you, Vadim? We need to get out.'

Vadim was already on his way to the seaplane and well out of earshot. Bazarov caught sight of the daylight coming from the roof hatch. He fired two more rounds through the door, to keep Sinclair's head down, and sidestepped his way to the ladder. As he looked up he could see the open door to the roof and it dawned on him. Vadim had bailed on him; abandoned their mission at the first sign of trouble. 'Bastard.' He'd always had his suspicions about Vadim. This confirmed what he had thought all along. Vadim wasn't committed to the cause like he was; he was just in it for the power.

Bazarov looked over at the control panel. He had to destroy it. At least then no one could stop the launch. More text flashed on the screen.

MUZZLE HATCHES OPEN: ARMING GAS GENERA-TORS.

He walked over to the desk and took aim at the keyboard. The swing doors shuddered as something heavy slammed into them from the outside. Before Bazarov could pull his trigger, the window shattered and the muzzle of an assault rifle came through the gap. Bullets whistled through the air past his head. He hit the floor and crawled to the other side of the room, taking cover behind a large metal equipment rack.

He checked his automatic, three rounds left. He didn't have a spare magazine, he hadn't been expecting a firefight on his own. Bullets pinged off the steel rack and the swing doors began to give in to the onslaught from the corridor.

He stood up and waited for a break. As soon as the shooting stopped, he stepped out from behind his cover and fired his three remaining bullets, in quick succession, at the control panel. There was no time to check what damage had been done. He dropped his weapon and sprinted towards the ladder to the roof.

McGill slammed the fire extinguisher into the doors and they finally moved enough for Sinclair to slide through the gap. She pulled the desk out of the way and McGill followed her.

Sinclair looked at the damaged console and at the clock on the screen. 'Only ten minutes, Frank. Get Jo in here. She has to stop this. I'm going after Bazarov.' She ran across to the ladder and climbed up through the roof hatch.

Chapter 27

Vadim knelt at the edge of the jungle that bordered the compound. Sweat ran into his eyes and stung the multitude of cuts he had picked up during his jump from the roof. He dabbed at his face with the sleeve of his shirt and wiped his eyes. He'd known that coming here was a bad idea as soon as Bazarov had suggested it. Vadim wasn't an idealist – he was in this for the money and the power. Resurrecting a strong Soviet Union was a way to get that. Right now, all he cared about was getting clear. He didn't want to die and he wouldn't survive in prison. Taking that kind of risk was what he paid Bazarov to do.

He looked through the fence to where Bazarov's men were running around like cockroaches suddenly exposed to daylight. They weren't looking for him. Burning debris was raining down on their heads – they had bigger fish to fry. The lagoon's jetty and the Kodiak were only one hundred yards from his position. If he could make it to the seaplane, he could get away. It was only a short flight to Cuba and he had friends there.

He crawled out from his hiding place, looking back at the compound as he went. No one was even looking in his direction. He got to his feet and, keeping his head down, ran to the jetty. He untied the rope from the wooden bollard and got into the pilot's seat.

After two attempts the engine spluttered into life and he steered the Kodiak out on the lagoon. He lined up the nose of the aircraft to give himself plenty of room and increased the power. The engine's revs approached the red line and the seaplane's floats skimmed across the surface before lifting into the air. Vadim pulled back on the joystick and the Kodiak climbed as it flew over the compound. He looked at the chaos below and smiled to himself. He was a survivor; that's how he'd become so successful.

Sinclair exited onto the roof and watched the small red plane climb into the air over the rising pall of black smoke that hung above the island. She considered firing off a few rounds to try and bring it down but she didn't have the ammunition for that. Her priority was taking down Bazarov. After everything he'd done there was no way she was letting him out of her grasp. Vadim could wait for another day. She was sure she'd see his face again.

She skirted around the edge of the roof looking for Bazarov. She was sure he would have had an escape plan in place. Now that Vadim had flown the coop, Bazarov would be in full self-preservation mode.

When Sinclair reached the other side of the roof she saw something. Standing at the far corner of the building was a figure hiding behind packing crates. She could see enough to recognise Bazarov's jacket. She took aim but it would be an almost impossible shot. She could only see the edge of his shoulder and arm. The best she could do was wound him, but the most likely outcome was that she would just warn him she was there.

In the distance Sinclair could make out two shapes approaching over the ocean. They were moving too slowly to be jets. She thought she could make out spinning rotor blades – at least she hoped she could. With any luck this was an assault team coming in. They'd take care of the guards, Frank, Jo and the boys would be safe, she had to stop Bazarov.

The Chinook on the helipad was starting up its engines and the Russian was waiting before he made a dash for it. Sinclair still had time to catch him. She slung her weapon across her back and climbed on the ladder that led down the back of the building.

* * *

The two Knighthawk helicopters came in low, over the lagoon, and flew over the compound. The door gunner opened up with the mini gun, cutting through Bazarov's men and sending the few who remained running for cover. They weren't paid enough for this, all they wanted to do now was survive, but the marines had other plans.

Ropes rolled down from both sides of the Knighthawks and green clad men slid to the ground, dispersing across the compound. When Halloran touched down, the helicopters peeled away and headed for the other side of the lagoon, away from the firefight.

Two of the guards made a run for it but Halloran's men cut off their escape. As the Russians turned their weapons towards the Americans, the marines' M4s dropped them where they stood.

By the time Sinclair reached the corner of the building where Bazarov had been standing, the firefight at the front of the building was in full flow. She recognised the sound of the Knighthawk's multi-barrelled mini gun and was glad she was nowhere near it. Bazarov had used the assault as a distraction and taken his chance to make a run for the Chinook.

As the marines closed on the Russians, the rest of the guards made one last dash for safety. All six of them stood as one. Two faced up to the marines and opened fire; they were dead before their magazines had emptied. The other four ran off: two in one direction, two in the other. Dust kicked up as M4 rounds hit the dirt around them but they didn't stop. One by one they dropped as the marines zeroed in on them. After only five chaotic, bloody, minutes, all of the guards lay dead.

As soon as the shooting stopped Sinclair set off through the undergrowth to follow Bazarov. She caught sight of him as he reached the edge of the helipad. The Chinook's tailgate was down and the aircraft was ready to fly. She brought her weapon up to her shoulder and fired off three quick shots. Her aim was rushed and her heart was pounding. The shots were wide of the mark and Bazarov dived for cover.

She had to stop him escaping. She loaded her last magazine into the assault rifle and unloaded into the helicopter. Bullets tore through the fuselage and smashed into instruments. One of the crew slumped in his seat, a gaping wound in his neck. The pilot took a round to his shoulder and blood seeped through the fabric of his flight suit.

Sinclair threw her assault rifle to one side, all of her ammunition spent. She and Bazarov stood up in unison and sprinted for the helicopter's tailgate as the pilot, who had decided it was time to leave with or without his passenger, turned the throttle. Bazarov made it inside and was immediately thrown forwards as the pilot fought with the controls of the stricken aircraft and tried to take off. Sinclair dived, full length, and landed on the tailgate as it closed and the Chinook's wheels left the ground.

Chapter 28

McGill sprinted out of the control room and smashed his boot into the lock on the door of the other lab. It wasn't a solid door and it gave way easily under the force of McGill's kick. The wood around the lock split and the door swung open. Jo Quinn, Garrison, and two engineers cowered in the far corner, not knowing what to expect. McGill lowered his weapon and gestured with the barrel. 'Everyone, get in here. Switch this thing off before it's too late.'

They all hesitated, like deer caught in the headlights of a car that was about to kill them. None of them were accustomed to the violence that was all around them.

'NOW.'

McGill stepped forwards and pulled Quinn to her feet, pushing her through the door. Garrison, shocked into action, used a chair to climb stiffly to his feet, and the two engineers followed on behind.

When they arrived in the control room, Quinn was working frantically on the keyboard. 'Help me. I need power for the scanner.'

The fingerprint scanner's power unit was now a collection of scattered electronic components and shattered plastic.

Bazarov's bullet had hit the mark. Quinn typed in the lines of code that would abort the launch, but they would still need the fingerprint and retina scans to halt it.

While Quinn typed, one of the engineers ripped the plastic wrapping off another equipment rack. The other engineer grabbed a toolbox and joined him in searching for the right tools.

'HURRY.' Quinn was almost finished. 'James, get over here.'

Garrison felt like a spare wheel. He didn't know what he was supposed to do so just stood next to Quinn like an enthusiastic schoolboy during a science experiment.

One of the engineers pulled a handful of wires from the rack and ran to the console. 'This should do the job. Uses the same voltage.' He stripped the insulation from the new power supply's cable and began jointing it to what was left of the old one. He threw the power switch and, after a flash and a spark, the scanner's blue light stuttered to life.

Quinn hit the key on the console. 'Now, James, hand on the scanner and look through the scope.'

Garrison did as he was told and his details, once again, appeared on the screen.

Quinn typed another line of code then copied Garrison's actions. Hand on the scanner and looking through the scope. The blue light dimmed and went out.

'NO.'

The engineer picked up a screwdriver and franticly pounded the top of the power supply. After another spark, the blue light flickered back on and scanned Quinn's prints and retina. Her details flashed up on the screen next to Garrison's. She turned the key in the console and slammed her hand down on the red abort button.

The flashing launcher icons on the map had all returned to a steady green. The countdown clock was frozen at twenty seconds.

LAUNCH ABORTED: MUZZLE HATCHES CLOSING.

McGill puffed out his cheeks and visibly relaxed, his muscles and teeth unclenching. The engineers high-fived and Quinn held her trembling hands up to her face.

Garrison bent over and picked up the hip flask that Vadim had dropped earlier. He sniffed the contents and took a sip. 'That was too fucking close.' He held out the flask to the others. 'Drink, anyone?'

The others started to laugh with relief but McGill had no time for laughter. This wasn't over yet. 'Jo. Your kids are in a cupboard in the basement. They're safe. I've got to go after Ali.'

Quinn touched his arm. 'Thank you, Frank.'

Outside, the marines were crouched down, a few yards from the building's main door, as one of their number attached two small charges of C4 plastic explosive. He stepped away and into cover, his thumb hovering over the trigger. Halloran made sure that none of his own men were exposed to the blast and nodded. The marine's thumb dropped. The C4 blew and, with a loud thud and a cloud of dust, reduced the door to a pile of smouldering wood and twisted steel.

They heard the explosion in the control room. It was followed by the sound of boots running along the corridor. Garrison checked through the window in the door and saw the marines closing in. 'Thank God, here come the marines.'

Quinn turned to McGill. 'Frank, you're dressed like one of Bazarov's men. If the Americans see you like that they might think you're one of them and kill you.'

'I can't let them take me prisoner, I've got to help Ali.'

'Please, Frank. They'll shoot first and regret it later.'

McGill weighed up his options. Quinn was right. It was easy for the marines to make a mistake in the heat of battle. He dropped his weapons and took off his jacket. He knelt down, facing the door, and put his hands on his head.

Quinn and the engineers stood in front of McGill, shielding him. The first man through the control room door scanned the room then took aim at McGill, but Garrison stepped forwards, spreading out his arms. 'It's okay, boys. I'm Admiral James D. Garrison.'

The marine recognised Garrison from the briefing Halloran had given.

Garrison pointed at McGill. 'This man is on our side, he's friendly. We don't want any blue on blue incidents here, son. Who's your commander?'

The marine lowered his aim and turned to the doors. 'SIR.'

Halloran made his way through the group of marines and into the control room. 'I'm Special Agent Kurt Halloran, FBI and US Marine reserves.'

Garrison held out his hand. 'Good to see you guys. I'm Admiral Garrison and this is Josephine Quinn. I take it you knew we were here?'

Halloran took Garrison's hand. 'Yes, Admiral. The brass will be happy you're both unhurt.' He looked at McGill and gestured for him to stand. 'You must be Frank McGill.'

McGill nodded. 'I need you to help me find Sinclair. She went after Bazarov on her own. He was heading for the chopper.'

Halloran turned to his men. 'Go with him. Bring back Bazarov.'

McGill picked up his weapon and set off running up the corridor. He led the marines out through the smouldering hole where the door used to be and across the compound towards the helicopter pad. Before they were halfway there, the twin rotors beat the air and blew up dust as the Chinook climbed unsteadily, rocking and dipping as the pilot struggled to control it.

McGill watched it go. There was nothing more he could do. If Sinclair was on the chopper with Bazarov, she was on her own.

* * *

In the back of the aircraft Bazarov and Sinclair faced each other square on. Each of them held a knife, waiting for the other to make the first move. Sinclair was up on the balls of her feet, balanced, counteracting the movement of the Chinook. Bazarov was much older and more flat-footed, but he was ex-Spetsnaz and no mug when it came to hand-to-hand combat. She knew that Spetsnaz were famed for their ability with bladed weapons. It was a big part of their training.

Bazarov steadied himself against the airframe. 'It was a valiant effort, Miss Sinclair, but you're finished now.'

Sinclair smiled. 'On the contrary. You're the one who's finished. Your whole plan was a disaster. Your boss ran off and left you, and all of your men are dead.'

'I'll live to fight another day. There's no stopping us, Miss Sinclair. The East will rise again. This is just the beginning.'

'If you think you're going to be around to see it, Viktor, I can assure you that you're wrong. It doesn't matter if I die. All that matters is that I kill you first.'

'We'd better get on with it then.'

Bazarov raised his knife and rushed towards Sinclair. She was surprised by his sudden attack but her balance and speed easily spun her out of his reach.

'You're getting old, Viktor. Not as good as you used to be.'

She had to keep him off guard. He was dangerous and, although she was good in a fight, knives weren't her speciality. She stayed on her toes and danced round him, jabbing in punches and slashing with her blade.

Bazarov kept his distance as much as he could. Sinclair was right, he wasn't fast on his feet any more. His age and his old combat injuries were against him. All he had left was power and experience. He blocked most of Sinclair's punches. The attacks he couldn't evade didn't land cleanly or hurt him too much. Sinclair could punch but he'd had much worse. Her knife attacks weren't getting through either. The slashes that were making contact weren't getting through the layers of clothing he had on.

Sinclair had to get through his defence. She threw two quick punches and drove her shoulder into his ribcage, which knocked him backwards against the airframe.

Bazarov absorbed the attack and drove the point of his elbow into Sinclair's spine. Her knees buckled and he threw her across the hold like a soft toy. She landed hard and her knife bounced away from her. The Russian followed up with a powerful kick to her ribs.

She felt one of her ribs crack and pain shoot along her body. It looked like she was about to end her unbeaten streak. She tried to get to her feet but Bazarov stood on her left hand with all of his weight, pinning her to the floor. Sinclair screamed as one of her fingers broke.

The Chinook's pilot was losing his fight with the bucking aircraft and his own blood loss. His vision was darkening, his senses failing. They'd travelled most of the distance to the mainland but now they were coming down. 'Sir. I can't hold it. We're going to crash.'

Bazarov looked through the cockpit window. There was a beach about a mile ahead of them; if the chopper came down there they could all die. They weren't too high up; he'd take his chances in the sea, but first he had to kill Sinclair. 'Open the tailgate.'

He grabbed a handful of Sinclair's hair and dragged her to her feet. 'Unfortunately, Miss Sinclair, you die in the crash.' He raised his knife above his head, ready to strike the fatal blow.

'I don't think so.' Sinclair brought her right hand up, with all her remaining energy, and drove her fingers, upwards, into Bazarov's eye socket.

Bazarov screamed. His eyeball ruptured and was forced out of its socket. He let go of Sinclair, and his knife, clasping his hands to his face. Sinclair dropped to her knees. She picked up his knife and stabbed him in the inner thigh, severing his femoral artery.

The aircraft tipped and Bazarov slid down the wall. Propped up, with his legs sticking out in front of him, fluid from his destroyed eye ran down his cheek, and blood spurted between his fingers as he vainly tried to stem the bleeding from his leg.

Alarms sounded in the cockpit and the helicopter rocked wildly. Sinclair came to the same conclusion as Bazarov had. She would take her chances in the sea. She ran to the back of the aircraft and looked out of the open tailgate. She thought it was about thirty feet, but it was hard to tell. It was definitely

252

high enough to do some damage if she didn't land right. She took a deep breath, had one last look at Bazarov, and jumped out.

The Chinook hit the beach hard, tailgate first. The nose slammed into the hard, packed sand, and the chopper crumpled and tipped over on its side. The twin rotor blades hit the ground and shattered; fragments flew off in all directions – some embedding themselves into the ground and others flying into the air.

Sinclair surfaced, coughing and gasping for air. The jump from the tailgate hadn't gone to plan and she'd hit the surface like a sack of potatoes rather than an Olympic diver. She looked at the wreckage on the beach for any sign of movement. The last thing she wanted to see was Bazarov limping away to freedom. She didn't have the energy to chase him down – even in the state he was in.

She started the swim towards land. Just as she thought she saw someone moving in the wreckage, a huge fireball ripped through the fuselage, blowing it to pieces and killing everyone on board. Lumps of metal, and fragments of airframe and engine, flew high into the air. Sinclair felt the heat of the explosion hit her and she dipped below the surface again as pieces of wreckage splashed down around her.

When the metal rain had ended, she resurfaced and continued her swim to the beach. By the time she got there, the fires had died down and people were approaching the crash scene. She was exhausted and bloodied. Her broken rib and fingers screamed every time she moved. She dragged herself out of the water and up the beach where she lay down in the sand and passed out.

Chapter 29

Simeon Carter waited in the coffee shop for Edward Lancaster to arrive. They hadn't spoken much since the Kraken affair. They both thought it would be best to let things lie for a little while. Everything Carter and his team had done was unofficial and possibly illegal. The last thing Lancaster wanted was to drop them in any more shit.

Some people were looking for scapegoats for the whole affair, others wanted prosecutions, but Carter had managed to use his contacts to erase all mention of his team from the records. If anyone wanted to go after them, they would have to go through him first.

Lancaster had taken care of the official side of things. Denying that MI6 had had anything to do with the operation, and challenging his detractors to come up with evidence. Of course, they wouldn't find any. The Americans were as keen as MI6 to keep this quiet.

Questions were asked in parliament about what the government had known, and when, but they were able to plausibly deny everything. The opposition tried to score political points from it but the government weren't aware of the facts; they hadn't been kept in the loop. The Americans, of course, insisted that they never lost control of any nuclear missiles, and played down the possibility of the explosion at Quinn's ranch being terrorist related.

Everything died down, politicians moved on to the next crisis, and the newspapers found someone else to go after. Now it was time for Carter to look after his people.

The coffee shop door opened and Lancaster walked in. He ordered himself a medium latte and joined Carter at the table. 'Good morning, Simeon. It's good to see you again. How have you been?'

Carter took a sip of his coffee. 'I'm okay, Edward. How are you doing? Are we all in the clear now?'

Lancaster checked for any eavesdroppers and nodded. 'As far as the hierarchy are concerned, none of your team are wanted for anything in connection with Kraken or the Apocalypse Protocol. It's all been hushed up.'

Carter was relieved. The thought of anyone being hauled over the coals, because of something he'd got them into, filled him with dread. 'Sounds like the best thing for everyone, Edward.'

'How's your team holding up?'

'Danny is okay. He's spending time trying to track down this guy Vadim. It's important we find out who he is.'

Lancaster nodded. 'I agree. Have you had any luck?'

'Nothing yet, Edward. Whoever he is, he's kept himself well hidden. Sinclair is the only one who can identify him and prove he's our mole. We need her home. We need her safe.'

'How is Sinclair? Have you spoken to her at all?'

'The embassy in Mexico are able to pass on messages to her but I haven't spoken to her personally. We need to get her out of there. I promised her I'd bring her home.'

Lancaster was genuinely sorry for Sinclair but his hands

were tied. 'It was unfortunate that the beach they landed on was on the Mexican side of the border.'

Carter banged his fist on the table. 'Unfortunate?'

Other customers in the café stopped their chat and looked at the two men. Carter looked around apologetically.

'She saved all of our arses, Edward, and we just abandon her? We let the Mexicans cart her off back to prison?'

Lancaster gulped another mouthful of coffee. 'We're doing everything we can. As you said, we need her to identify Vadim. The Americans are on our side but it's hard when we've denied the operation ever took place.'

'You're forgetting one big problem though, Edward.'

'What's that?'

Carter lowered his voice and leaned forwards. 'Frank McGill.'

Lancaster's expression changed to one of worry. 'Have you heard from him?'

'Nothing so far. I don't know where he is. I've tried going to his house but he wasn't there. I don't even know if he's still alive, but if he is, we should worry.'

'Do you really think he would try something?'

Carter chuckled. 'Frank McGill killed the drug dealers who murdered his wife, all of them, the whole gang, and he didn't do it quickly. Now Sinclair is the closest thing he has to family, and he'll do whatever it takes to protect her.'

Lancaster knew he couldn't afford to have a man like Frank McGill coming after him. All of the security in the world couldn't protect him all of the time. 'I want you to track him down, Simeon. I want him on our side.'

'Why is that, Edward? Usually you'd be better off getting rid of someone like him.'

Lancaster finished his coffee. 'McGill is very useful for off the book wet work. His link with Sinclair makes them a perfect team. Combined with you and Danny, that's a team I think I'm going to need.'

Carter knew what Lancaster meant. He wanted a team that wasn't linked to the government or the official security services. In the current environment of leaks and witch hunts, Lancaster needed people who could work freelance.

Lancaster passed a brown A4 envelope to Carter. 'I've got some work for you and your team, Simeon – if you're interested. In the meantime I'll do everything I can to get Sinclair out.'

'And if I'm not interested?'

'Then I might not be able to help Sinclair as much as I'd like to.'

Carter took the envelope and tucked it inside his jacket. 'The game never really changed, did it, Edward?'

'We're all pawns, Simeon. You know that.'

Carter picked up his cup and looked at the cold dregs of his coffee. 'I'll speak to you soon, Edward. Watch your back.' He stood and shook hands with his old protégé then turned and left the café.

Outside on the pavement, Carter zipped up his jacket and put on his gloves. It looked like he was coming out of retirement. There was a new Cold War on the horizon. Russia was flexing its muscles and the West seemed to be turning a blind eye. A resurgent Russia against a West weakened by financial crisis, and seemingly incapable of keeping anything secret. Throw in the various terrorist factions and the whole world was a much more dangerous place than it had been a few years ago.

He made his way along the streets to Danny's flat. The way things were now, it would be best for him to stay at Danny's full-time. He had to be close to Lancaster in order to be effective as an unofficial resource.

* * *

Lost in his thoughts, Carter was back at the flat before he knew it. He unlocked the door and went in. It was unusually dark inside. Normally, Kinsella would have enough lighting so he could see his keyboards. He was rarely off them when he was at home – no matter what time of day it was. Sometimes, it was like living in a data centre.

Carter reached over and threw the light switch by the door. When the light came on, the scene in front of him wasn't really a great surprise. He had half expected it every time he had come home for the last couple of months.

Danny Kinsella was sitting in a wooden, kitchen chair with a terrified look on his face. Opposite him, lounging on the sofa, was Frank McGill. He was dressed in jeans and a non-descript black, leather jacket. In his gloved hand was a silenced Glock 19.

He beckoned Carter into the room. 'Come in, Simeon. Take a seat.'

Next to Kinsella was another kitchen chair. Carter took off his coat and sat down.

'Nice to see you, Frank. I wasn't sure if you were back in the country or not.'

McGill held his arms apart, palms up. 'Well, now you know.'

Carter patted Kinsella's forearm. 'It's okay, Danny. Frank isn't going to hurt us, are you, Frank?'

McGill held up his Sig. 'What makes you so sure?'

'Because you're not a psychopath, Frank. Some people might think you are, but you're not. You don't kill innocent people.'

'You don't know me that well, Carter. I will kill someone who hurts my family, they deserve it. They aren't innocent.'

'Danny hasn't done anything to hurt you or Sinclair.' He turned to Kinsella again. 'Why don't you go and make us all a coffee, Danny?'

Kinsella didn't move – he just stared at the armed madman on the couch. Unlike Carter, he wasn't used to dealing with situations like this.

McGill gestured with his head towards the kitchen. 'Go on, Danny. You're in no danger. I've got no quarrel with you.'

Relieved, Kinsella gladly left the room and disappeared into the kitchen leaving the two men to it.

When the kitchen door closed, Carter looked at McGill. 'So, Frank. What is it that you want? Revenge?'

'If I was just out for revenge, you'd be tied to that chair.'

'Well, I should be thankful for that at least. Although, I imagine if I don't help you, I could still end up on your shit list.'

McGill leant forwards, his elbows on his knees. He appeared a little more relaxed, or maybe he was exhausted. The past months catching up with him. 'I want you to get Sinclair out of prison, and home, like you promised. That's all.'

'That's what I want too, Frank.'

'Then do something about it. You told me she would come home, you lied. Worse than that, I told her she'd be fine. You made me a liar.'

'No one wanted it to end like it did. It was …' He hated himself for it, but he was about to use Lancaster's phrase from earlier. 'Unfortunate.'

McGill visibly flexed at Carter's use of the word and sat up straight. 'Unfortunate? You fuckers abandoned her again.' He slid forwards on the couch and pointed at Carter with his Sig. 'I told you what I would do if you double crossed her.'

Carter had the same feeling that he'd had when he first met McGill: that this was a man who would kill him at the drop of a hat and not lose any sleep over it. 'It wasn't a double cross, Frank. If she'd landed in Belize, she'd be here, with us, now. As soon as the Mexican authorities had her, it was out of our hands. They wanted to parade the recaptured prisoner. They had an election coming up.'

'Well, I'm going to put it back in your hands.'

Carter didn't like the sound of that. The last thing he needed was McGill going off on a one-man crusade; a loose cannon. 'What do you have in mind, Frank?'

'Once I'd left the island I went over to Mexico. I wanted to see what I could do for Ali. I've spent the last two months scoping out the prison. I've found a way to get her out but I need equipment, weapons, and some backup.'

'Okay, Frank. I can help you to get organised but I have another option for you.'

McGill sat back in his seat, relaxing a little. 'And what would that be?'

'We let the diplomatic process run its course first.'

McGill shook his head. 'Where would that get us? It hasn't done any good so far.'

'I appreciate that, and I understand if you don't trust any of the civil servants and politicians, but they are on our side and are doing everything they can. The Americans are putting pressure on the Mexican government. The foreign secretary herself is pushing for Sinclair to serve out her time here.'

'She shouldn't be serving time anywhere after what she's done.'

'I know, but if we get her transferred here, we can release her ourselves. Lancaster will bend over backwards to get her home as long as we stay in his good books.'

'That sounds like you're trying to threaten me, Simeon. Blackmail me at least.'

'You haven't been in this game as long as I have, Frank, but you must know how it works. We do something for him, and he does something for us.'

McGill hated this kind of shit. He just wanted people to do what they had promised. None of this tit-for-tat, you scratch my back and I'll scratch yours, bullshit. 'Ali has already risked her life for him. Time he paid her back.'

'Leave that side of things to me. I know my way around the political maze.'

Danny Kinsella came through the kitchen door with a tray of mugs. 'Is it safe to come in, or do you guys need a little more time?'

McGill looked at Carter. Deep down, he knew Simeon was doing everything he could to help Sinclair. McGill was just looking for someone to transfer the guilt to. He'd always told Ali that everything would be fine, and it wasn't. He'd told her that she would come home, and she hadn't. The guilt he felt was causing him physical pain. He unscrewed the silencer from his weapon and put it away. 'It's okay, Danny, you can come in now.'

Kinsella placed the tray on the table. 'Help yourselves to milk and sugar.'

McGill put two sugars in his black coffee and sat back in

his seat. 'So, what's this "something" Lancaster wants me to do to keep me in his good books? I'm assuming it involves me getting dropped in the shit again.'

Carter stirred his own coffee. 'You do thrive in that environment, Frank.'

'And, if I agree to do this, you'll do everything possible to bring Ali home?'

'I give you my word.'

McGill thought for a moment, whatever happened, he needed Carter's help to get Ali out of that prison. 'Okay, let me see the details.'

Carter picked up the brown envelope and threw it across to McGill. 'Have a read of that and tell me what you think.'

THE END

Bonus Content

Ali Sinclair returns, with Frank McGill and the rest of the team, in *Hunting Ground*. A high octane, race against time to stop the conspiracy and bring down Vadim. The following is a teaser to whet your appetite.

Hunting Ground: Prologue

The stained enamel bath in the derelict apartment was full of water that had been brought up from the river. The bottom of the bath was covered in a layer of rocks and the sediment, moss and algae that floated on the water's surface was now mixed with blood and hair.

Justin Wyatt was strapped to a board that was balanced at the tap end. He'd lost count of the amount of times the board had been tipped up and his head had impacted on the bottom. How many times had he held his breath until his lungs were crying out for air. Breathing in water and falling into unconsciousness only to be brought back up again.

He broke the surface, vomiting the filthy water back out of his body and gasping to breathe. His face was swollen, and blood streamed from his nose. They had shouted at him over and over, 'Tell us what you know, and we'll let you live.' He doubted that.

Two hours ago, he was breaking into an office with a stolen key card, looking for some information, following up a tip. He needed some sort of evidence to back up the story he'd been told. He'd been naïve, though. He knew there was a risk and he was prepared for that, but he thought that, if he was caught, he could talk his way out of it, pretend he was a burglar. The company was respectable, at least on the surface. He assumed they would just hand him over to the police.

He couldn't have been more wrong. The story he had been told, everything he had found out, was true. The conspiracy he'd uncovered was far too big to be derailed by someone like him. Now, he was sure he was going to die. His priority now was to keep his mouth shut, to protect the ones he loved. He just hoped he'd left enough of a trail for them to follow, the ultimate treasure hunt. He would bring these people down one way or another. That would be his greatest achievement, that would be his legacy.

He tipped back into the water again, his head smashed into the bottom of the bath and blood clouded in front of his eyes. He couldn't take much more of this. Surely, he'd be dead soon. His vision darkened but, again, he was brought back up, coughing and spluttering.

There was no questioning this time. Instead, one of his captors was on the phone. 'Yes, sir… No, sir. We don't think he knows anything… He would've told us by now… We'll do a background check on him and find out who he is, who he lives with. If he won't talk, maybe they will… Yes, sir. We will. It'll look like suicide.'

Wyatt didn't want to die, but he didn't want anyone hurt because of him. The man put the phone down and walked back into the bathroom. He looked at Wyatt then nodded to his accomplice. Wyatt, once again, plunged into the water, his head bleeding, his lungs screaming. He didn't have the strength or the will to fight anymore. He stopped holding his breath and slipped into oblivion. This time, he wouldn't be lifted back up.

Hunting Ground: Chapter 1

Callum Porter walked along the rain slicked pavement of Rue Saint-Joseph, from the tram stop on Rue du Pont-Neuf, towards his apartment in the Carouge district of Geneva. He'd moved into the Swiss city's "little Italy" shortly after he landed the job at the bank and was quickly accepted as part of the community. He'd always loved it here. It had a different atmosphere to the rest of the city. The shops, the architecture, the bars that came to life after dark. It was safe and clean, compared to other cities he'd been in, and only a 10-minute ride to the city centre. Perfect, until now. The last few days had been a blur. Every sight and sound conjuring up memories that stabbed at his heart.

His apartment was on the top floor of a three-story building which was set back from a tree lined side street off the main road. He quickened his pace as the rain started to come down again and soon turned into the apartment block and up the two stone steps into the entrance hall.

Inside the building's traditional architecture, was a modern design with clean, minimalist lines and glass and chrome trim. Water ran from Porter's rain coat as he unfastened it and left small puddles on the faux marble floor. He walked over to the mail boxes which ran along the left-hand side of the entrance and checked for any deliveries. As usual, it was empty. He didn't receive much mail; he did most of his business online.

The single lift in the foyer was on the opposite wall to the mail boxes but he preferred to use the stairs that were next to it. The only time he used the lift was when he had some heavy shopping to carry. He walked across the foyer and climbed the stairs.

On the third floor, the door to the stairs opened onto a single long passageway with doors on both sides and a window at either end. His apartment, 317, was half way down on the left. Simple glass and chrome wall lights switched on as he approached to light his way. There was no-one else around and it was quiet, his neighbours would still be making their way home too. He pulled out his door key, slid it into the lock and opened the door.

The inside of the apartment carried on the minimalist décor of the rest of the building but, here and there, were items of furniture that didn't quite fit in. Things that Porter had picked up in the antique shops and street markets in Carouge. An old wooden set of drawers jutted out into the hallway, spoiling the simple straight line that led from the front door to the kitchen. On the left-hand side of the corridor was the door to the single bedroom. Inside it was a free standing, pine wardrobe, next to the built in one, which cut down on space and made the room look cramped, but he preferred the eclectic look.

Opposite the bedroom door was the entrance to the living room where a well-used leather settee had replaced the more angular, modern couch that was there when he moved in. Two brightly coloured, seventies chairs made up the rest of the suite that was arranged around a well-used wooden coffee table.

Porter stepped into the living room and switched on the light. He let out an involuntary yell at the sight of a man standing next to the window. Porter's fight or flight response was screaming at him to turn and run. 'Who…who are you? What do you want? I don't have anything. Get out of my flat.'

Frank McGill held his hands out, palms up. 'Calm down Callum, I'm not here to hurt you. I'm here to help.' He motioned towards the couch. 'Have a seat.'

Porter's mind, again, screamed for him to run, but his legs wouldn't move. He had the feeling that this intruder would only chase him down anyway. He looked at McGill. This man spoke with authority, he was obviously used to taking charge in situations like this and used to imposing his will, violently if necessary. Porter took two steps to the right and sat down.

McGill was unkempt. He wore black leather boots, blue jeans and a faded green combat jacket. His hair was messy, and he had a few days growth on his chin. No one would pay him any attention, he wouldn't stand out in a crowd on the street. He looked homeless, the kind of man that most people ignored as they rushed about their busy lives, unaware of the plight of people who lived on the street. If asked to describe him later, Porter would have said everything about him looked average. Average height, average build, no striking features, not memorable at all.

McGill sat down, opposite the couch, on one of the seventies chairs. He sat forwards, elbows resting on his knees. 'You don't know me Callum, but I've been watching you for a few days now. Whenever you left your office for lunch, when you were on your way home, I was there.'

'I never saw you, how is that possible.'

McGill smiled. 'It's what we do for a living, son.'

'Who is we? Your obviously British. MI5, MI6?'

McGill nodded. 'Something like that, but you don't need to

know the details.'

'I don't suppose you've got any ID. you can show me.'

McGill raised an eyebrow. 'You're gonna have to trust me. The people I work for aren't big on ID.'

'What do you want from me? I haven't done anything, I just work in a bank.'

McGill pulled a black and white surveillance photo from his jacket and placed it on the table in front of Porter. 'It's not you we are interested in, Callum. I came here to speak to this man.' McGill pointed to the photo. 'Can you tell me who he is?'

Porter picked up the photo and sat back on the couch, staring at it. After a few seconds of silence, he took a deep breath and let out a sigh. 'His name's Justin Wyatt.'

McGill could sense that the man in the picture meant something to Porter. 'We need to speak to him, Callum, it's for his own safety. Do you know where he is?'

Porter looked around the flat as if he was checking for anyone who might overhear them. Checking for more intruders. 'How did you find me? We weren't public about our relationship.'

'We tracked down Justin by identifying you. Do you know that he contacted the British Consulate?'

'He told me that he was planning to talk to the authorities in case something bad happened, but I didn't know he had.'

'He made an anonymous phone call. He gave enough detail to get us interested and said he had more. He didn't want to give up too much as he swore there was a mole in the British Government.'

Porter couldn't believe what he was hearing. He always assumed that Justin was blowing his stories out of proportion.

He thought the trouble he might get into would mean arrest, maybe imprisonment. 'But, if it was anonymous, how did you know it was him?'

'We traced the phone he used to make the call to the Consulate and scanned through CCTV images of the area. We didn't know his name, but he was the only person to use the phone in that timeframe. You showed up in other CCTV images with him and we put two and two together, you were easier to find. You weren't trying to hide in the way he obviously was.'

'And then you were sent to find me? To find Justin.'

McGill nodded. 'We were hoping to leave you out of it. I asked a few questions, hung around in the right areas. I followed you for a few days, hoping to see you together and I could follow him, but you never met up with him again.'

Porter looked down and ran his fingers over the image in the photo. He was struggling to speak, he would never get used to saying it. 'That's because he's dead.'

McGill let out a sigh of frustration. 'I'm sorry about that, Callum, I really am. What happened? Can you tell me about it?'

'They found his body in the river. He'd been washed downstream and dragged along the riverbed and rocks. They had difficulty identifying him but found his wallet near-by.'

'How did you find out about it?'

'They put a small report in the paper. A few sentences on page eight. They said he jumped. They said he killed himself.'

McGill could hear anger in Porter's voice. 'But you don't believe that, do you, Callum?'

Porter felt at ease with McGill. He was glad to be finally unburdening himself. Telling someone else his secret. 'The night before his body was found, he told me he was going to break into some guy's office. He was convinced that he was involved in something big, something that would change the world, he said. He was looking for evidence. I thought he was exaggerating.'

'Did you tell anyone that? Have you spoken to the police?'

Porter's face was ashen. 'No, I was too scared. They might have come after me next. Besides, like I said, we always kept our relationship secret. It's still frowned upon in some circles. I didn't want to attract attention.'

'It might already be too late for that. We found you. They will too, sooner or later.'

'Who are they? What if they found him through me too? What if he's dead because of me?'

McGill had to calm Porter down. It was obvious that the young man was afraid. His hands were trembling, and he struggled to put a sentence together. McGill spoke to him calmly and quietly, as he had to the young soldiers in Afghanistan, the ones who looked to him for guidance and reassurance. 'It's not your fault, Callum. If they knew about you, you'd be dead already.'

Porter was sweating and his heart racing. He had hoped that the authorities would realise someone had murdered Justin. He hoped he could go back home to the states and rebuild his life. He wasn't a naturally courageous man. He was quiet, timid, an introvert. The man sitting in front of him, on the other hand, looked the opposite. 'What do you...they...I mean...'

McGill had to secure the information he was looking for and get out as soon as possible. 'The call to the consulate mentioned a notebook.'

Porter nodded. 'Justin gave me a book. He told me that if anything happened to him, I had to keep the book safe, and watch my back. I thought he was being over dramatic.'

'I'll need to see the book, is it here?'

'Yes, I'll get it.'

Porter went into his bedroom and slid the wardrobe away from the wall. Taped to the back was a small, brown, paper parcel. He pulled it off and took it through to the living room. He held the parcel in both hands, reluctant to let it go. 'I promised to keep this safe.'

'You can trust me, son. It'll be safer with us.' McGill held out his hand.

Porter knew that he couldn't protect the book and the information inside, he knew that McGill was right. He handed the parcel over and stepped back, sitting down on the couch.

McGill tore open the brown paper parcel and revealed a small notebook. The front cover was plain and a little dogeared with J Wyatt written in the top left corner. McGill opened it up and flicked through it, page after page of handwritten notes and drawings, names, dates and places filled the book. McGill recognised some of the names but most of the information meant nothing to him, it would be something for the geeks back home to have a look at and de-cypher. He put the notebook into a plastic zip lock bag and tucked it into the inside pocket of his jacket. 'What were you planning to do with the book, Callum?'

Porter shrugged his shoulders. 'I don't know, maybe post it to the Embassy in Berne but I didn't know who to trust. There are some high-ranking officials mentioned in there.'

'You've read it?'

Porter shook his head. 'No. Justin told me about some of

the people who are in it. I'm not sure I believed him, to be honest. What if he was right and they are involved? If his notes fell into their hands, no one would know about them. He would have died for nothing.'

McGill patted his pocket. 'You don't have to worry about it now, Callum. All you need to think about is staying safe.'

'I should call my dad. Tell him what's happened. He can help, he's a...'

'US Senator. Yes, we know. I'll stay with you until you're out of harm's way. We don't want anything to happen to you over this.'

The conspiratorial atmosphere in the apartment was shattered by a loud knock. Porter jumped to his feet and stared at the door. Within seconds, McGill was standing next to him and whispering into his ear, 'Are you expecting anyone?'

Porter shook his head. McGill moved silently over to the hallway and pulled a silenced Glock from under his jacket. He signalled for Porter to open the door. The young man was unable to move, scared out of his mind. Another loud knock made him jump and McGill, once again, signalled for him to open the door. Porter, hand trembling, reached for the lock and turned it slowly.

The door was kicked open, violently, and a large man dressed all in black pushed his way into the apartment, forcing Porter backwards. 'Where is the book?'

The man didn't shout but spoke with quiet menace. He pulled out his own silenced semi-automatic and pointed it at Porter. 'I'm going to count to three. Tell me where the book is,' he lowered his weapon to point at Porter's legs. 'Or lose a kneecap.'

McGill had weighed the guy up quickly. If he had been a

real professional, he would have looked behind him by now to check for any threats. If he was police or security services, he would have identified himself and he wouldn't have been alone. There was no back up following him into the room, he had left himself wide open.

Porter was terrified. McGill didn't blame him; it can be very disconcerting having a gun pointed at you for the first time.

Porter's attacker started his count. '1...2...'

McGill raised his weapon and pointed it at the back of the big guy's head. '3.'

The man spun around, but it was already too late. Just as the realisation that he had fucked up showed in his eyes, McGill shot him in the forehead.

The big guy dropped to the floor like a column of water from an upturned bucket, straight down. There was no resistance in his legs to stop the fall. He was dead as soon as the bullet hit him.

McGill quickly checked outside in the corridor for any late arriving backup. The corridor was deserted. He stepped back inside the apartment and closed the door.

Porter was frozen to the spot. He hadn't moved at all. McGill grabbed his arm. 'Callum.' Porter didn't respond, he just stared at the dead body in front of him.

McGill grabbed both of Porter's shoulders and shook him. 'Callum. Snap out of it, or you'll end up the same way. We need to get away from here as quick as we can.'

Porter finally looked up at McGill. There was blood on his face and his skin was a pasty white. 'Who ...who was he.'

'I don't know but he wasn't here to invite you to a party. At least it confirms that Justin was onto something big. If you'd given that guy the book, he would have killed you. There's no doubt about that.'

Porter slowly shook his head, still rooted to the spot. 'I feel sick.'

McGill dragged him across the living room and pushed him into the bathroom. 'Do what you need to do Callum. Throw up, splash water on your face, whatever, but get on with it. Get your shit together. I'm leaving with or without you.'

Porter realised that McGill had just saved his life, but he wasn't used to such extremes of violence. He'd never seen a dead body before, never mind a man shot right in front of him. He looked down at his shirt. There was a fine spray of blood across the front of it. He closed his eyes. He could still picture the cloud of pink mist that had signalled the fatal shot. If he had been standing in the wrong place, the bullet could have hit him too. He shook the thought from his head. McGill was a professional, he knew exactly what he was doing.

Porter took two deep breaths. The feeling of nausea began to leave him. He splashed some water on his face and pulled off his t-shirt.

McGill checked through the pockets of the body. No ID or cash, just a car key and a photo of Porter with the address written on the back. Whoever had sent this guy had access to the same information that McGill did. When the bathroom door opened, he turned to check on Porter. 'You ok?'

'Yeah, I think so.'

'Good man. Now, do you have some kind of back pack?'

Porter pointed towards the bedroom. 'Yeah, in there.'

'Right, pack some clothes. Nothing fancy, just something to change into. Throw in any cash you've got, passport, that kind of thing. And hurry up.'

Porter pulled clothes out of draws and threw them into his

bag. T-shirts, socks, underwear, toothbrush. Did he need to take shampoo? Christ, he felt like he was packing for a holiday. He grabbed his wallet and shoved it into his jacket pocket along with his passport. He pulled on a clean t-shirt and was ready to go.

McGill opened the door an inch and looked along the corridor, it was empty. He opened the door fully and stepped out looking both ways, nothing. He looked back at Porter, who stood in the hallway. 'You ready?'

Porter nodded.

'Good. Follow me and stay close.'

Porter hurried after McGill, he knew that his best hope of survival was in this man's company. He also knew that the book was in McGill's pocket, so he didn't really need him. McGill could have just left him alone, in the apartment, with the corpse. He was helping him even though he didn't have to. That made Porter feel safer.

McGill led them along the corridor and through the door to the fire escape. After a quick check, they moved quickly down the stairs and out of the back door of the apartment block.

They stopped at the corner of the building as McGill retrieved his own small back pack, full of essentials, from behind a dumpster. He threw it on to his back and winked at Porter. 'Always travel light son, you never know what might happen.'

After one last check for any followers, they walked across the car park and out on to the street.

Porter kept his head down. He didn't want to make eye contact with any passers-by. He was sure they would know what had happened. Like he had a mark on him somewhere that let everyone know there was a dead man in his flat.

'Where do we go now? The consulate?'

McGill shook his head. 'We don't know who to trust, son. The guy in your flat had the same picture of you that I had. Someone had tipped him off, given him the information, probably blown my cover. Someone high up wants you dead and the notebook in their hands. We need to disappear.'

'How do we do that?'

'Just keep your head down and follow me.' McGill pulled up the hood on his jacket as the rain started to fall again. Porter pulled on a baseball cap and thrust his hands deep into his pockets as they headed back along the Rue Saint-Joseph, away from the apartment.

Acknowledgements

The publication of this book marks the realisation of a lifelong ambition. In common with all authors, I couldn't have achieved this on my own. I would like to thank the following people, without whom this book would not exist.

Ali, the inspiration for my main character. Matt Hilton, who published my first short story, read my first draft and made me believe I could do this. Jo Craven, my wonderful editor. Mike Craven, for the friendship and advice that helped turn my story into a novel. Graham Smith and all my friends at Crime & Publishment, you know who you are and you've all helped to get me here.

About The Author

L J Morris is an author with a love of books and storytelling that he developed as a child. After a career in the Royal Navy, which spanned most of the 80s and 90s, he settled back in the North of England, and soon realised that an unsuccessful attempt to write a serial killer novel at the age of 12 hadn't blunted his ambitions.

He started to write again and has enjoyed success with his short stories appearing in several anthologies. 'Blood on Their Hands' and 'Cold Redemption' were published in Volumes 1 & 2 of Best-selling author Matt Hilton's anthology series 'ACTION: Pulse Pounding Tales'.

Other anthologies he has appeared in include 'Happily Never After', 'Wish You Weren't Here', and 'Liminal Time, Liminal Space' where one reader described his tale 'True Colours' as *"Riveting and powerful"*

Although he still enjoys writing short stories, his dream has always been to write thriller novels and he has spent the last few years following that dream.

Printed in Poland
by Amazon Fulfillment
Poland Sp. z o.o., Wrocław

53760572R00169